# PRAISE FOR THE NORSE QUEEN

"A journey back into the heart and soul of ancient Viking realms. Queen Åsa of Tromøy, a true historical figure almost lost in the mists of time, returns to vivid life in *The Norse Queen*. Step inside a Scandinavian saga in all its richness. If you love *Beowulf* you will also love *The Norse Queen*."
--Margaret George, *New York Times* Bestselling Author

"*The Norse Queen* brims with action in a world both exhilarating and terrifying, peopled with sorceresses, warring jarls, and even shape-shifters. In its tale of one woman's steadfast courage in the face of tragedy, it gives life and breath to a long-forgotten 9th century queen."
--Patricia Bracewell, Author of *Shadow on the Crown* and *The Price of Blood*

"*The Norse Queen* is a well-written and exciting tale. Wittenberg's writing is nuanced, descriptive, and vivid. Her plotting and storytelling is also superb. I was happy to have been given the opportunity to read this wonderful tale, and I fully believe this

book has all the key ingredients of any good historical fiction and will delight fans for years to come."
--S.D. Reeves, Author of *The Melody of Three*

"Totally submersive reading...The author has done an amazing job with this story setting - weaving magic, believable character voices and insights into the way of viking life and culture. "
--Chimene's review--Goodreads

"...I would recommend this book to anyone who enjoys historical novels, but also to those who love books like the Harry Potter or Lord of the Rings series."
--Amazon Review

"When one is looking for a fresh, accurate and masterfully crafted story on Vikings this is the one. In-depth research couple with engaging characters, the story unfolds with a rich texture that drew me in and kept me in for the whole book. The touch of fantasy that develops is in keeping with the beliefs the Vikings held. I especially enjoyed this story."
--Emmet J. Hall, Author of *Runaway*

# BOOKS BY JOHANNA WITTENBERG

# THE
# FALCON
# QUEEN

## THE NORSEWOMEN BOOK 2

## JOHANNA WITTENBERG

*For my beloved husband, Brian, my faithful roadie.*

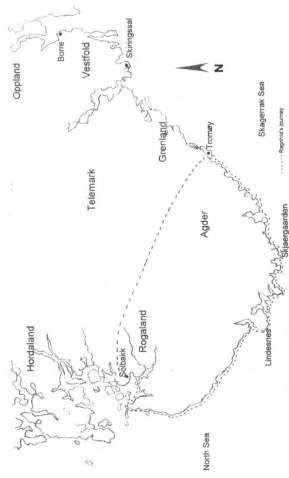

Oppland

Borre •

Vestfold

Skiringssal •

Hordaland

Telemark

Grenland

Tromøy

Solbakk

Rogaland

Agder

Skagerrak Sea

------ Ragnhild's journey

North Sea

Lindesnes

Skjaergaarden

Approximate locations of petty kingdoms in Asa's time

N

# CHAPTER 1

Tromøy, Agder, Norway
September, AD 820

The horns blared three times, the signal for attack by sea.

Heart thrashing, Åsa tumbled out of bed and ran for her weapons. Brenna hurried in and plucked Halfdan from his cradle, soothing the fourteen-month-old boy.

Heid struggled out of her own bed, seizing her iron distaff. In the brazier's dim light, the old sorceress' riot of frizzy hair glinted more silver than bronze and her hunched form cast weird shadows as she crabbed her way to the door.

Shivering in the chill, Åsa shoved her feet into soft leather boots. She pulled on wool breeks and tunic over her shift, then ducked into her brynja hanging from its hook. She shoved her arms into the sleeves and braced as the heavy chain mail shirt cascaded down her torso, then strapped on the halberd with her long and short swords across her back.

Beneath the blood throbbing in her ears came a sense of

relief. The moment she'd been dreading had arrived. Action was always better than lying awake, wondering when they would come.

Grabbing her shield and helmet, Åsa strode into the bower's main hall, Heid hobbling in her wake. The longfire had already been stirred to life, casting a flickering light on the women as they rose from their sleeping benches. Some struggled into leather armor, stuffing their braids up under helms. Heid's apprentices hefted their iron distaffs and rallied to their mistress.

It was no surprise that an attack came now, for all men had to get their harvest before winter. And now that work was done, it was the perfect time to go a-viking and raid the granaries of those who could not defend them.

Word must have gone out throughout the Skagerrak Sea that Tromøy was held by a woman.

Losing their winter stores meant certain death for the folk of Tromøy, so they would fight with their lives to keep their food. Better to die quickly on a sword than starve over a long winter.

Outside, Olvir had assembled the defense, their breath visible in the chill night air. They were a pitiful collection of warriors mostly past their prime, augmented by servants clutching spears. They shivered in the cold, damp night, snuffling and coughing.

On the trail, armor flashed in the torchlight, the clank of metal and thud of boots sounding as the enemy climbed the long hill from the beach. Åsa shuddered as she remembered the last time a raiding party had marched up that trail, bringing the destruction of her entire world.

She searched out Jarl Borg's tall figure, towering over the rest. The old warrior stood straight as his spear, though Åsa did not know how he managed. Her father's retainer had barely survived the vicious attack on Tromøy two years before that had left Åsa's father and brother dead. Somehow Jarl Borg had lived and healed after a fashion, and she was grateful that he had, for now they all relied on his experience in warfare.

Everyone capable of drawing a bow snatched one from the rack along with a quiver of arrows. Fingers on the string, Åsa waited for Jarl Borg's signal.

"Nock," he said quietly. "Draw." The bows creaked. With one eye, Åsa watched the old jarl's long fingers poised in the air.

"Loose." His long fingers dropped.

Åsa's arrow hissed through the air with twenty others. Distant cries confirmed that they had hit their marks, but in the pre-dawn light, the enemy kept coming. Åsa's stomach tightened.

"Shields," said Borg. Åsa took comfort in the old warrior's calm tone. He had survived a hundred shield walls. To him this was just one more. She set aside her bow and unslung the round shield of linden rimmed with iron. Taking hold of the grip, she raised the shield, overlapping it with Ulf's to her left. On her right, Olvir chocked his into place behind hers. Wood clacked on wood as the shield wall rattled down the ranks.

The attackers did not halt their march to return fire. Åsa drew Lightning, her short sword, better for the close work of the shield wall than her longsword, Gudrød's Bane.

Behind the shield wall, Heid's sorceresses raised a chant, and the raiders seemed to falter at the eerie sound. Their commander turned on them, bawling a threat, and they picked up their pace. In the growing light, Åsa counted at least thirty men. Her own force numbered just shy of fifty, but of them less than a dozen could be called seasoned warriors. Most of them were a little too seasoned.

The attackers closed the distance. None wore armor. Their shields were battered, some rimless with ragged edges. The rank and file carried spears. Few had swords, and of what quality, Åsa could not tell.

Desperate men.

Halting just out of spear range, the marauders screamed vivid threats designed to paralyze them with fear. Åsa hardened her face to hide the anxiety that seared her innards.

Tromøy's defenders held the high ground, forcing the attackers to advance uphill or stand there all day. A young warrior strode forward from the enemy ranks, shaking his spear.

"Come and fight me, you white-livered cowards!" he screamed. Ulf cut the youth's rant short by heaving a spear into his throat. The boy dropped to his knees, clawing at the shaft as blood gushed from the wound.

A tall, helmeted man stepped over the body. "Surrender and we will kill you quickly, with your swords in hand," he demanded. This generous offer ensured that Tromøy's warriors would die fighting and therefore be eligible to join Odin and Freyja in the halls of the slain.

"Throw down your arms and we will let you depart with your balls still swinging between your legs," countered Jarl Borg.

Tromøy's warriors jeered.

Despite the dawn chill, Åsa was beginning to sweat. How long before they discovered that her warriors were mostly untrained women and old men dressed up in armor and closed helmets?

"Send us your women," the enemy leader demanded. "We'll let you weaklings go free."

Åsa saw Jarl Borg's whiskers twitch beneath his helm. "Very well," he said, and gave the signal. Every warrior cocked their spear and waited.

Heid led her apprentices forward to gather behind the shield wall. Their iron distaffs held high, they keened a chant that raised the hair on Åsa's neck.

The attackers shifted nervously in their ranks as the chant rose to a howl. Sweat ran down Åsa's face. If this didn't work, they were finished.

"Charge!" shouted Jarl Borg. Åsa and the other warriors leveled their spears and stormed down on the enemy. Iron distaffs outthrust, Heid's acolytes strode behind them. Hair flying and eyes ablaze, they shrieked a spell that struck a chill even in Åsa's heart.

The raiders quailed, mouths agape. Faced with sorcery and spearheads, they turned tail and ran.

Roaring, the Tromøy folk pursued them down to the shore and fired arrows on the enemy as they dragged their boat into the sea. Two raiders fell into the boat as they boarded, arrows protruding from their backs. The survivors took to their oars with vigor and rowed away.

"Not much of a raid," said Olvir, accepting the horn. He drank and handed it back to Brenna, who carried it to Jarl Borg. The old jarl hunched over the tafl board across from Åsa. The gridded square of wood and the gaming pieces carved of polished antler was her father's set on which Åsa and her brother had learned the game of strategy. Åsa had recovered it from the loot at Borre.

Jarl Borg took the drinking horn, then moved a piece horizontally, the hammer on the anvil sandwiching one of Åsa's men and taking it. Tonight, Borg played offense, trying to surround Åsa's king while she moved him from the center to one of the corner safe zones.

"They wanted to see what we've got, and now they know." He spread a big hand. "Or they think they do."

"They don't realize that every third man was really a woman." Åsa slid a piece between his man and her king.

"Or that every second man was barely able to hold a spear."

"And they don't know how little we have worth taking, or they never would have come at all."

"More will come," said Jarl Borg. "But not this side of spring. I think our sorceresses have put the fear into them for now, and the winter storms on the Skagerrak will keep them home."

Åsa let out a long breath. Safe for the winter. Or safe from raiders, at least. Hrafn was out there with his outlaws. Whose side would the berserker chieftain choose this time? Then there was Hrolf, Olaf's half-brother, lurking in the hinterlands with what remained of his followers. Hrolf's shapeshifting powers hid him from her, but she couldn't shake the feeling that he was watching. Something deep inside her said he would find her—and at the worst possible time.

In the morning, she would stand for queen before the freemen of Agder. If they accepted her, the responsibility for defense of the region would fall on her shoulders.

*Am I ready?*

She hoped so, for she had no choice.

~

"ENOUGH." Åsa jerked her head away from Brenna's fussing hands and rose from the stool.

"This is important to them," Brenna murmured, nodding at the women who bustled about the bower's firelit recesses as they prepared their queen for her ordeal. Åsa stilled and eyed their gaunt figures. Some were newly liberated from slavery at Borre. Others had come out of hiding in Agder's hinterlands to rejoin their new queen. All had survived hardship and danger.

*This ceremony is as much for them as for me.*

They had dressed Åsa in her red gown of a finely woven wool diamond twill, and Brenna had braided her hair and wound it round her head in a coronet. Now Brenna settled a blue wool cloak on Åsa's shoulders and fastened it with a silver brooch. The serpentine beast gleamed in the lamplight, twining back on itself.

Brenna stepped back and looked to the other women, who nodded their approval.

Åsa started toward the door. Behind her came Heid, in full regalia, gems flashing on her iron distaff, followed by her nine apprentices. Tromøy's women fell in behind them. The entourage followed Åsa out of the bower and crossed the yard to where the men waited.

Knut, the famous skáld, had arrived the night before with his single apprentice, having made the long journey overland from the west coast. "Nothing could make me miss this," he said, embracing Åsa. "Your father would be so proud."

The old Tromøy folk who had been imprisoned with Åsa in Borre were assembled: Ulf, who had been her father's smith since before Åsa was born; Toki, Tromøy's steward; and a dozen other men whom Åsa had freed from Borre when she killed Gudrød. They had lost everything in Tromøy's destruction and had returned to rebuild their lives--if they survived the winter.

Beside them stood Olvir, once captain of Borre's guard. He and Åsa had become friends and sparring partners in Borre, and he'd opted to come with her when she returned to her father's kingdom.

Jarl Borg stood at the head of those few men who had survived Gudrød's raid on Tromøy. When Gudrød had given Hrolf charge of the island steading, they had fled from his cruelty. Three jarls who had sheltered them were also in attendance, accompanied by their húskarlar. A dozen bonders from outlying farmsteads had joined the men of Tromøy for this occasion, yet Åsa noted missing faces--many of Agder's freeholders had not come to swear to the new queen. Worry niggled at her. Did they lack faith in her despite the fact that she had avenged her father and vanquished the Danes?

Åsa drove the doubts from her mind. Tonight she would hold vigil on the burial mound she had raised to her father and brother. The mound was empty--their burnt bones lay mingled with the ashes of her father's hall under the floor of this new building.

It was well to have one's ancestors beneath one's feet.

Heid raised her distaff in blessing, and the warriors cheered as Åsa strode across the fields to the burial grounds. The new mound lay raw and bare beside her mother's hillock, long grown over with grass. Without hesitation, Åsa mounted the dirt flank and climbed to the top, where she turned and looked out over the steading. The great hall, its broad roof curved like a ship's hull, commanded the settlement. Beside it stood the low, oblong forms of the women's bower, the guesthouse, and the barracks. Smaller pit buildings dotted the packed earth of the yard, housing a smithy, storehouses, and thatched animal byres. Beyond the newly harvested fields, the wind raised waves upon the grasslands, forming a golden ocean that flowed down to the meet the sea that gleamed like beaten steel.

So familiar, yet so wrong. There stood her tree, where she had pondered life for hours. And there the hall where it had always been, but the bright wood and thatch of new construction made a jarring note among the weathered roofs of the outbuildings. Her father's sworn men gathered as they had in years past, but now they came to honor him in death. Her heart squeezed when she thought of all she had lost. Her whole family lay beneath the earth.

A tiny figure ran out of the bower on sturdy legs, Brenna hot on his heels. Halfdan. Her son, the last of her blood. A miniature container that held all her lost family—her father, her brother, her mother, and the long line of ancestors before them. He was the past and the future. She would raise him up to be a mighty king, the father of kings. Her line would survive, this she vowed.

Wrapped in her cloak, Åsa faced east and drew a deep breath. She sat and began to chant the vardlokkur, the song to call the spirits. Her tone was entreating, alluring. She called the land spirits to her and asked them to accept her in her father's stead. With every breath, she chanted the mysterious words in a language long forgotten, until her voice mingled with the wind.

As she sang, it seemed the wind rose up in her body and blew out of her mouth. The sun's last rays touched her hair, and the chill of evening swept over her body.

Her hands and feet became cold, and soon she could not feel them at all. The chill spread up her arms and legs, creeping toward her heart. Its beat slowed, struggling against the cold. She could not speak; she could not move. Breathing through the panic, she allowed the night to take her. Her fate rested with the spirits now, and she gave herself over to them completely.

For a while she floated in the stillness between life and death, no longer able to feel anything, even the cold. She knew that this was death, but she had no fear.

A faint vibration began in her heart. It deepened, flowing in waves outward to her extremities, consuming her. In the vibration, she could discern voices. Soft voices, chanting in a language she did not know.

THE SUN'S first rays warmed her face. She opened her eyes as the light flowed over the land. The night had passed in a flash. Åsa had been in the trance, unmoving, for hours, and now her body was all but immobilized.

She felt full somehow. The vibration, the chanting—it all had filled her.

In that moment, the knowledge of the land rose up within her like a flood tide. The spirits had accepted her, and she was bound to this island as never before. She rose and stumbled down off the mound on ungainly legs, across the fields to the steading.

Åsa entered the great hall alone. Her father's allies and warriors rose from their benches as she walked toward the high seat, each step like hefting iron ingots.

From that spot her father had presided over his warriors, but this was not her father's chair. Hrolf had built this seat on its charred remains after Gudrød had given Tromøy to him.

But she had killed Gudrød and taken back her father's kingdom from Hrolf. Today she claimed her inheritance.

As she approached the high seat, doubts crowded her mind. How could she keep Tromøy safe when her father had failed? Harald had been a seasoned warrior, wise and strong, yet Gudrød had murdered him in his own hall. She was little more than a girl, newly blooded in her first battle. Hrolf had slunk away, but he still lurked in the hinterlands.

She clamped her jaw and mounted the platform. She sat at the foot of the high seat as was the custom for an heir laying claim.

Heid entered, bearing the ale horn to her. Accepting the drink, Åsa thought of the kings to whom she had offered it in the past: to her father here, after her mother's death; to his murderer--her husband--in Borre's hall; to Olaf at Skiringssal. And now she took her place as claimant, being served in her turn.

She rose and hoisted the horn high in the air. "I am Åsa, daughter of King Harald Redbeard. I have avenged my father's murder and freed my people. I lay claim to my father's land and this steading on Tromøy." The host clashed their weapons on their shields in approval of her claim.

Åsa took a deep breath and spoke again. "In my father's place, I offer myself as Queen of Agder. I swear to protect the land and all folk who dwell here, or die trying." Her pledge made, she brought the horn to her lips and drank, the ale bitter on her tongue.

Knut stepped into the firelight and began the tale of Gudrød's attack on Tromøy. As the poet evoked the deadly duel between Gudrød and Harald, Åsa envisioned her father's shattered sword, the light dying in her brother's eyes, the hall in flames.

It had all been her fault. If she had not refused Gudrød, her father and brother would still be alive. She would be the queen of a man she hated, a price she would gladly pay to have them back.

Knut dramatized Gudrød's kidnap of Åsa, how he dragged her to Borre and forced her into marriage. He told of how she had endured rape, captivity, and childbirth, all the while gaining strength and skill in secret, until she killed Gudrød, taking her freedom and avenging her father and brother.

These actions supported her claim on her father's lands as well as her worthiness to rule in his stead.

As the old skáld finished his tale, the throng beat weapons on shields, signifying their acceptance of Åsa's leadership. She stepped down from the platform, holding the horn aloft in a fist clenched to keep it from trembling. She carried the horn sunwise around the longfire to consecrate the drink. Then she offered it to Jarl Borg, the senior warrior, who drank and passed the horn to Olvir. He drank and handed it off in turn, until all had drunk from the horn, legitimizing her claim and pledging their support to her oath.

Åsa turned to mount the platform and face the high seat. Gods and monsters leered down from their oaken posts. The big chair had been made for Hrolf, and she felt like a child before it. The ghost of her father rose once more as last she'd seen him on the high seat, his severed head and broken sword licked by flames. Forcing a breath against ribs tight as chain mail, she turned and sat. Her fingers gripped the carved oak armrests as she faced the uproar from her men beating their weapons on shields.

She was Queen of Agder.

Åsa drew Gudrød's Bane and lay it across her knees, ready for the men to swear to her. Jarl Borg was the first. The old warrior strode to the high seat, knelt, and laid his hand on the sword that had made Åsa a legend.

"I am Borg, son of Frode, son of Borg, son of Ivar, Jarl of Iveland. I have traveled far to the east, to the south, raiding and fighting for my king, Harald of Agder. I now swear my loyalty to his daughter, Åsa, rightful heir of Tromøy and acclaimed Queen of Agder. I vow to serve my queen until death releases me from this oath."

Åsa's heart drummed hard in her chest as she laid her hand on the old warrior's proud head. "I accept your oath, Jarl Borg. I promise to defend you and your family, to provide for you, to share with you all spoils of war and trade."

A cheer rose up as the old jarl got to his feet, still nimble as a lad.

One by one, the men of Agder approached the high seat and pledged their loyalty to their queen. Among them, Thorkel, who had brought her home with a broken arm when she was ten and never told her father that she had gotten it trying to ride Harald's stallion on her own. Ulf, her old friend and her father's before her, knelt and swore on the sword he had made for her; Yngvar, whom she remembered as the gangling lad whose legs had always tangled and tripped him up, grown into a sturdy warrior; Olvir, once her jailor, now swearing to serve her to the death.

Still, the men that lined up to swear to her were too few. So many had not answered her summons. She feared they had no faith in her, an unproven girl.

Agder was a vast region, and the far-flung steadings were scattered across the hinterlands. The settlements were linked by a system of signal fires, but rarely could a man respond in time to answer his neighbor's need. Her father had not even had time to light the fires during the raid that had killed him.

Tromøy had been left unprotected after her father's death. Those who had survived the raid and stayed had fallen victim to Hrolf. Many fled to the hinterlands, and now a few had found their way back to her, too few. Fewer mouths to feed for the winter, to be sure, but in the spring, not enough to defend the island steading from the Danes who would come roaring across the Skagerrak with their fleet of dragon ships. The Danes had lost men and ships in their failed attack on Borre two months before, but they had all winter to recover, to build more ships, and to train more men. While Åsa had won the battle, her losses had been heavy, and she had no reserves.

With no wealth to offer and barely enough food, Åsa had little hope of recruiting more warriors before spring. The best she could hope for was to survive the winter.

When the last oath had been sworn, Heid had made her rounds and refilled the ale horn, bringing it to Åsa once more. The next toasts were to Odin for victory in battle, to Frey for peace and good crops, and to Thor for protection. Åsa pledged with fervor. Then began the round of toasts in remembrance of the fallen.

There were many, and the drinking went on late into the night.

# CHAPTER 2

The feast lasted three days. When it was well over and the last visitors had departed for their own steadings to prepare for winter, the inhabitants of Tromøy spent half a day setting the hall and grounds to rights. That night it rained, as if to wash the steading.

The next morning the sun shone. Heid looked out the bower door and sniffed the air. "The weather is right for gathering mushrooms."

The women eagerly pulled their woolen jumpers over linen shifts, helping each other secure the straps with intricate bronze brooches shaped like turtle shells. They donned soft leather boots, tying leather laces around their ankles, and drew on hooded cloaks against the morning's chill. Åsa picked up Halfdan, and the other children gathered by the door as their mothers bundled them in woolen wraps. The women picked up rough-woven sacks and trooped out of the bower.

The mist was still thick upon the ground as they crossed the yard and entered the wood. Soon the sun would burn it off. Halfdan toddled among the other children, grinning hugely. Åsa cast a practiced eye over the undergrowth and very soon picked out the telltale shape and color. She knelt and carefully cut the mushroom with her knife, bagged it, and resumed her search. Once she spotted the first one, they seemed to be everywhere, and soon her sack was heavy. The sun had burned the mist away, and Åsa joined the others in the mid-morning light beside a waterfall where they drank their fill, glad to enjoy the last lovely day of autumn. While their children napped, the women fell to talking, their chatter blending with the running water. With Halfdan nestled beside her, Åsa closed her eyes, not trying to follow their conversation but letting the sound soothe her into a pleasant daydream.

"A ship!" Tromøy's lookout shouted in the distance.

Åsa jerked awake. She struggled to her feet, grabbed Halfdan, and ran for the hall. The women snatched up their children and mushroom bags and scrambled after her.

In the bower, Brenna took charge of Halfdan while Åsa shrugged into her brynja, strapped her swords onto her back, and grabbed her shield and helmet. She hurried to the great hall. In the dim light, she made out Jarl Borg and Olvir already donning armor. They spilled out the door, blinking in the sunlight, and strained to make out the new arrivals on the beach.

The ship was a small karvi with no more than thirty warriors —no more than the last raid. Åsa had butterflies in her stomach as she watched them march up the trail to the hall. What trouble would this visit bring?

"Danes," spat Jarl Borg, eyeing the banner. The old warlord's disdain settled Åsa's stomach. She waited impassively as the visitors labored up the hill. They had left their shields racked on the gunnels of their longship. None of them carried spears, and their swords were sheathed.

When the new arrivals reached hailing distance, they halted. Åsa stepped forward. "Who are you, and what brings you to my kingdom?" She managed to keep her voice from quavering.

A leather-clad warrior stepped forward and saluted, fist to his breast. His bare, muscled arms were loaded with silver rings, each representing a reward from a grateful king for victory in battle. An important man.

"I am called Gorm, lady. We come in peace, with greetings from Rorik, King of the Danes."

Åsa clamped down hard on the fear that rose in her throat, choking the bile back before she could speak. She was surprised at how smoothly her voice came out. "Welcome to you. Please refresh yourselves while I make arrangements for a meal."

"Thank you, lady. Please don't trouble yourselves on our account. We need but little."

This was a lie. Åsa knew the finest feast she could muster was expected, though that would be little enough.

While her húskarlar led the Danish contingent off to wash, Åsa set the folk to work, preparing what they could. They slaughtered a goat and put the meat to cook in a cauldron in the yard, and gathered cabbages and berries. Fortunately, they had baked a fresh batch of flatbread just the other day.

At last Åsa retired to change her gown. In the privacy of the bower room, Heid said, "He brings a marriage proposal from his master, of course."

Åsa's stomach knotted. She had been trying to avoid thinking about it, but of course she must face it.

"I know," she said. "I will refuse." If she were to marry anyone, it would be Olaf.

Heid fixed her with a harsh stare. "You can't refuse."

"What are you talking about? I'm not going to marry a Dane!"

"There are many strategic advantages to an alliance with them."

"They are the enemy!" Åsa rose and paced in agitation. "They just want to take over Tromøy."

"Yes, of course," Heid soothed. "A wise ruler keeps her friends close, and her enemies closer."

Åsa stared at her, aghast. "You can't be serious."

Heid narrowed her eyes. "No, of course not. But you aren't strong enough to fend them off. What is to keep this Dane from simply coming and taking you?"

As Gudrød had, attacking by night, killing her father and brother when they tried to stop him. Åsa felt the blood drain from her face. Heid didn't have to say it. If she accepted the proposal, she and her kingdom would be under the control of a Danish warlord. But if she refused, he would attack, and Tromøy was far from ready for that.

Yet Åsa couldn't just give in. "I beat them once."

"You had Borre's army, and Olaf brought Vestfold's fleet. Even then it was a miracle you survived. By comparison, Tromøy is nearly defenseless," Heid said.

"I'll put him off," Åsa said in a flash of inspiration.

"How?" asked Heid.

"I'll send him back with questions for his master. It is late in the season; by the time he returns, the storms will rise, and it will be too late to cross the Skagerrak again. It will give us until spring to get ready."

Heid nodded thoughtfully. "Yes, that might work."

It was the only option. This would take all her wits.

Åsa entered the hall and mounted the platform, turning to face the assembly before she sat. Heid did the honors, making a point of seating the Danish leader below Jarl Borg and serving the old warrior first. However, Gorm took the ale horn she offered with good grace.

The aroma of meat wafted in through the door, and in the firelit gloom, the carved and painted pillars came to life with scenes from legend. Shields lined the walls next to spears and axes, and if the number of warriors on the benches was a bit sparse, they all looked stout and healthy.

Once everyone had been served ale, Åsa cleared her throat and began the conversation. "How was your crossing, lord?"

"Cold and rough, my lady."

17

"I am glad to see you have not suffered for it." When Gorm did not elaborate, Åsa cast about for a new subject. "And how has your fishing been this season?"

"Scanty, lady. The cod are farther north this year." Gorm seemed a man of few words.

Åsa was at a loss as to how to draw him out, but she tried again. "It's been a wet season so far," she ventured.

"Yes, my lady, too wet for the barley." Gorm clamped his jaw shut and stared into the fire.

Åsa sipped her ale and stared at the flames herself. Gorm was obviously afraid of giving too much information to the enemy. Well, let him be silent. She would not allow this terse warrior to make her ill at ease in her own hall. She let the silence extend.

At last the meat was served. Everyone attacked their food with relief, and if the conversation was still strained, at least the sound of eating knives scraping trenchers filled the silence.

As soon as the boards were cleared, Åsa turned to her guest. "Now tell me, what is it your king wishes?" She strove to keep the impatience from her voice.

"My lady, he sends gifts." Gorm turned and nodded to the men behind him.

Two men carried forward an oaken chest bound with brass. Gorm fitted an iron key in the lock and raised the lid.

Inside, gold glinted on silk. Åsa could see the shine of silver and carnelian. Gorm held up drinking glasses of fine Frisian glass and a Tating ware pitcher, glass encased in silvery tin. Two more men rolled a wine barrel into the hall.

"Finest wine from Francia," Gorm said.

Åsa tried not to appear impressed. The Dane's port city, Haithabu, controlled the richest trade, with links to Francia, Ireland, and the eastern lands. By comparison, Tromøy was a backwater. Its main trade items were soapstone for cooking pots and whetstones. Yet she knew the Danes coveted her island for its location, controlling the shipping routes on the Skagerrak and north to Vestfold. If only she had more warriors, she could be a rich queen.

"Thank your king for his generous gifts."

Gorm stared at the floor for a moment, then raised his gaze to meet hers. She watched him take a deep breath. *Here it comes.* She froze her face into an impassive mask even as the sweat broke out beneath her gown.

"My lady, as you know, King Rorik is a strong man, vigorous and in the best of health."

Åsa nodded, waiting.

"But my lord has spent so much of his life fighting for the throne."

*And fighting us for our land.*

"He has had no time to think of marrying. Now the Danish kingdom is at peace. King Rorik and his brother Horik have allied with their uncle, Harald Klak, and the three rule together."

Åsa forced a smile, though her stomach roiled. "I thought there were four brothers?" she asked sweetly.

Gorm looked a little uncomfortable, but he soldiered on. "There are four sons of King Godfried, but two have been driven from the realm."

Åsa wasn't going to let that go by. "I would not have thought anything could divide those four."

Gorm closed his eyes for a moment, then he opened them and continued resolutely. "The younger two would not accept peace with their uncle, Harald Klak."

"But I thought none of the brothers would accept their uncle's rule." Åsa smiled again, showing her teeth.

Drops of sweat were beginning to form on Gorm's forehead. "That was true, lady. But the Franks have brokered a peace between them, and two of the brothers rule jointly with their uncle."

"I see." Åsa's tone was skeptical. "So Rorik and Horik betrayed their brothers to please the Frankish king. It sounds as if it is the Franks that rule the Danes."

Gorm cleared his throat but did not reply to her taunt. The sweat was pouring freely down his face now. He was a brave man. Åsa couldn't help feeling sorry for him, just a little. *But after all, he's a stinking Dane.*

She frowned. "Come, sir, tell me why you are here."

"My lady, King Rorik has sent me to ask you to become his wife."

Åsa throat was dry. As her panic rose, she schooled her expression into a blank stare, as if this were the last thing she expected.

"He asks you to be his queen," Gorm clarified.

Åsa found her voice at last. "This is quite a surprise, sir," she said. "I'm flattered, of course, but I must consider the proposal. I will speak with you in the morning."

"Very well, lady," said Gorm. He rose.

As Olvir led the Danes to the guestroom, Åsa let out a deep breath, eager to confer with Heid in private.

ÅSA AND HEID sat up late that night, rehearsing Åsa's words. She must send the envoy home with hope, but no promises.

In the morning, Åsa rose early and dressed with care. She was sitting on the high seat before the Danes emerged from the guesthouse. Her foot drummed beneath her gown. She stilled as Gorm entered the hall with his men, reining in her impatience while he made a suitable bow and took his seat.

She marshalled the questions she and Heid had come up with during the sleepless night. Furrowing her brow as if in deep thought, she said, "I'm flattered by King Rorik's proposal, of course. Tell me, if I accept your lord's generous offer, where will I reside, then?"

Gorm looked startled. "Er, King Rorik would want you by his side, of course."

"Oh, I see." Åsa mimed thought again. "And what would become of Tromøy?"

Gorm blinked. He seemed completely unprepared for this discussion. Perhaps it was because she was a woman. "Why...it would come under King Rorik's protection, of course."

"And how would Rorik provide that protection?"

"I...I don't know. But of course my king will have a good plan in mind."

Åsa nodded. "And what of my son, Halfdan?"

"Why..." Gorm's mouth formed words that did not come. "Why, he would also come under King Rorik's protection."

"I suppose," she ventured, "the king would want heirs of his own."

"Oh, of course he would, lady." Gorm frowned as if he sensed a trap but could not see how to avoid it.

Åsa pressed on. "If that were to come to pass, how could I be certain that Halfdan would inherit Tromøy?"

"King Rorik would see to it, I am sure."

"And he would guarantee my son's safety?"

"Of course, my lady. King Rorik is not given to murdering infants."

"That is not what I have heard, and my son will not remain an infant forever." Åsa narrowed her eyes. "But as I understand you, Rorik is only one third ruler of the Danes. He shares the throne with his brother Horik and his uncle, Harald Klak. How would his co-rulers feel about my son's status as Lord of Tromøy?"

"Er, well..." Gorm stammered.

Åsa allowed her voice to rise. "How do I know that Rorik could protect my son and enforce his claim if his co-rulers object?"

Gorm opened his mouth, then closed it again.

Åsa stared at the man as he struggled for words. *Now or never.*

She rose. "I thank your lord for the gifts, and I thank you for coming all this way. Please ask your king for the answers to my questions, and I will consider his offer."

Gorm paled. "My lady, King Rorik expects an answer now, before the storms make the Skagerrak impassible. If I return with questions, it will be spring before we can come back for your answer."

"I am sure your master will understand that as a mother, my concern is for my child's welfare. I cannot consent to the marriage until he has set my mind at ease." She turned to her men. "Now, I won't keep you. I know you must make haste to catch the tide. Olvir, show our visitors to their boats."

Gorm gaped at her as Olvir took a firm grip on his shoulder and levered him out of the room.

Fear gripped Åsa's stomach, but she kept a pleasant smile on her lips until the Danish contingent was out of sight.

"You handled it well," said Heid. "Now we have the winter to prepare."

"Even so, how can we prepare? We need more warriors, and I have no way to get them."

"Much can change in a season. Your fortunes could improve. Rorik's position may change by spring. The Danish throne is far from settled. What of Rorik's unhappy brothers, exiled in the hinterlands? I am certain they are plotting and gathering an army of their own. Their antics may discourage your suitor for a while."

"I hope you are right," said Åsa.

Åsa LAY in bed in her chamber off the bower hall, longing for sleep. There was much here that made it home, yet much had changed. Her mother's embroidered comforter covered the down mattress, and on the wall hung a tapestry Åsa remembered from childhood. These textiles had been carefully stored by the women who survived Hrolf's rule in Tromøy. The familiar sights set off little sparks of happiness that were quickly dampened by memories of death and destruction. When Åsa closed her eyes she still saw the hall engulfed in flame.

Tonight she called her fylgja, Stormrider. When the peregrine falcon lit in the rafters with a flurry of wings, she willed her spirit up into the bird's body as she had a hundred times before. She felt the falcon's great heartbeat, the breath quicken, and the stretch of wings and talons. Her vision sharpened and broadened far beyond what a human could perceive. Colors appeared where none had been visible. Her mind linked with Stormrider's and she let the bird's consciousness dominate while her human mind receded into the background, still present but passive, observing.

Winging through the smoke hole, the falcon soared out over the forest, knowing where to find the upper wind current. She was searching for Hrolf. He was out there. Watching. Night after night she patrolled the water and the land, but even her fine-tuned intuition could not find him. It worried her that he could hide himself from her.

Tonight the sea was vacant, the moonlight dancing uninterrupted on its surface. The falcon gave in to the northerly pull and turned toward Skiringssal, her journey up the coast hastened by desire. Distance was no obstacle to her will in spirit form. Tonight her need was urgent and the roofline of the Shining Hall came into sight almost as soon as she thought of it.

Soaring past the silver-gilt dragonheads that jutted from the roof, the falcon glided through the smoke hole to land on a rafter, cocking her head to eye the sleeping form below. In the brazier's glow, a golden head glinted on the pillow. Warmth flooded her, then she lay beside him, her shape human but shimmering, translucent. She inhaled his scent of new-mown hay and her entire being tingled. In this form she was pure emotion, unshielded by her physical body.

Olaf's arms went around her. "It's been so long," he murmured into her hair. He pulled her close and his heat flowed into her like sun-warmed honey. She placed her hand on his heart and let herself merge with him. Intense bliss flooded her and their merged spirits took on a glow, filling the room with light. There was no more thought, only feeling. Only joy.

The union may have lasted hours or minutes, there was no way to know. All she knew was that their spirits began to lose contact. She separated herself with a sense of loss and lay beside him, savoring the fading echoes of bliss.

Eventually she was able to speak. "I was accepted as Queen of Agder."

"Congratulations," said Olaf. She could not make out his face in the dark, but his voice sounded sincere. "I am happy for you. It's what you have wanted."

She steeled herself and said what she must. "The Danes came with an offer of marriage."

His breath caught and his arm tensed, as if he could hold her spirit. "And what was your answer?"

"I sent the envoy home with more questions. It will put them off until spring at least."

"Did you not tell him about me?"

She stared into the darkness. "Olaf, I dare not anger the Danes. After the last battle, we are yet too few to stand against them."

"The war beacons will bring me if you are attacked."

"Even with a fair wind, Skiringssal is a full day's sail from Tromøy. Even together we cannot match their strength. And Hrolf—he is still out there. I can feel him. He wants Tromøy back. And he means you harm."

"I miss you," he said, drawing her toward him. The force of his grip told her of his need. "I need you beside me. I need you here where I can keep you safe."

Åsa slipped from his grasp and sat up. "We don't have the luxury of what we need. Not now."

In the dark, Olaf's voice sounded distant. "Alfgeir has taken back the Vingulmark."

Åsa drew in a sharp breath as she felt his distress course through her. Half of Vingulmark had been Olaf's mother's dowry. It should have gone to her son, but her father, Alfgeir, had taken it back on Gudrød's death. It was an insult to Olaf, a threat even. What more would Alfgeir take from his grandson?

"I'm sorry."

He shook his head. "I have not the men to regain it. I fear that trying to hold Borre, Skiringssal, and Tromøy, we will end by losing everything. Our enemies are on all sides, and we are so few. We can only hold out so long."

"Tromøy is mine," she said. "Mine by right of inheritance, just as Borre and Skiringssal are yours. And I will hold Tromøy for my son." *Your son,* she thought but did not say.

The thought of Halfdan propelled her upward, into the falcon's body.

"Don't go," Olaf said.

But the falcon was already out of the smoke hole, lofting into the night air.

# CHAPTER 3

Mountains of Agder
November, AD 820

Ragnhild's skis hissed over the snow crust. Her bow and quiver was slung across her back atop her shield, and a stolen sword hung from her belt. Over her wool tunic she wore a leather jerkin studded with metal rings, each of which she had painstakingly sewn onto the leather the previous winter. She had tucked her wool leggings into tall leather boots, lashed with leather straps to the raised footbed of her skis. The skis were carved from pine, grooved on the bottom and rockered on both ends so she could easily reverse them. Her hair was stuffed up under a knitted cap with a long tail that wrapped around her throat and covered her mouth to warm the frigid air she sucked in gulps. She gripped her spear with wool mittens sewn with leather strips on the palms.

She stopped to catch her breath, snatching off the wool cap to let the steam rise off her sweaty head. She pulled the water skin from inside her jerkin, where her body heat kept it from freezing, and drank. Fishing around in the leather pouch that hung from her belt, she found a piece of reindeer jerky and put it in her mouth, sucking until it was soft enough to chew, letting the salty juice run down her throat. Her stomach growled. She had eaten nothing since leaving her father's hall the night before.

The sun was high overhead, glinting on the snow crust. She pulled the stocking cap down over her head again before the sweat froze. Already, a rime of frost coated the cap's tail where it covered her mouth. She had to keep moving.

Crossing the high mountain pass, she rejoiced under the vivid blue sky. Her problems lay in the valley far behind. She was on top of world, and she was free.

It was stubbornness that kept her going, she thought wryly. The same stubbornness her father possessed had driven her from his hall. He should have known better than to try to force her into marriage, but once their two wills were locked, it was war. She had gone to bed in a huff, rising in the night and taking to the hills.

On the other side of the mountain range lay an island where a woman ruled. Ragnhild had heard her father and his men talking about this queen derisively, saying she needed a strong man to set her right. But their talk lit a tiny fire in Ragnhild's breast that had led her out into the night, giving her the courage to cross the mountains alone.

By now her father would have dispatched warriors. From her vantage point high above, Ragnhild spotted three figures on skis in the distance, cutting swiftly across the snowfields. They were two or three hours behind her and wouldn't catch up to her before dark, but they could track her. She had to rest eventually, and the only shelter would be one of the saeters scattered throughout the mountains that formed the spine of the northland. The huts were summer dairies for the maids who tended the herds in the mountain pastures, and they were left open in the winter to shelter travelers such as herself, usually stocked with wood and maybe a little food.

It was near dark when she spied the roof-shaped mound of snow belonging to the hut she remembered. Without light, her pursuers would not be able to track her here.

The saeter's entrance was buried under deep snow, and Ragnhild had to use her ski to dig down to it. The door was frozen shut, and she hurled herself against it three times before it gave, tumbling her into the chill dark, where she bashed her shin against the central firepit. She snatched off her mittens and fumbled the firesteel and wisp of dry rushes from her pouch. With numb fingers, she struck the steel over and over until the precious spark fell on the tinder. Cupping her hand around the tiny flare, she breathed on it carefully. The flame bloomed, casting a wavering light through the room.

The hut was damp and chill as the inside of a barrow. Ragnhild shivered as much at the thought of draugr and other evil things that might lurk in the shadows as from the cold.

In the flickering light, she climbed onto the firepit's stone rim and poked her spear butt into the smoke hole until it contacted the cap. She pushed it through the thick snow layer and flipped it aside, letting the faint stars peer down at her. Ragnhild found kindling and leaned a few sticks over her rushlight, grateful that the wood was dry. It caught quickly, and scant smoke rose straight up, drawn through the smokehole where it obscured the stars.

Gradually, her shaking subsided. She drank from her water-skin and chewed more dried meat. The day's work had built an appetite in her. She could eat a whole moose raw. As the room warmed, a familiar stink arose. Ragnhild's nose led her to a high shelf, on which lay a grass-wrapped package of gammelost. She eagerly peeled back the wrapping, and the pungent odor of the aged cheese set her stomach to growling. She nibbled the potent stuff with care. Too much would make her give back all she had eaten.

Strength surged back into her limbs. She stoked the fire and burrowed into the dusty pile of sheepskins, falling instantly asleep.

Cold roused her in the middle of the night. She staggered out from under the skins to lay on more wood, but not enough to burn past sunrise, when her pursuers would spot the column of smoke from miles away. She burrowed into the skins and slept again.

A FINGER of sunlight reached through the smokehole to touch her face. Rising, she gulped some water and nibbled a little more gammelost before carefully rewrapping the redolent cheese in its grass covering and returning it to the shelf.

Shouldering her pack, she took up her skis and spear and ventured outside, where she kicked the snow back over the doorway and replaced the smokehole cover.

The sky was clear. No possibility of snow to cover her tracks. She would have to stay ahead of them.

Ragnhild skied fast across a broad snowfield, staving off a gnawing hunger with plans. She should reach the eastern shore soon, then head south along the coast to find the queen's island settlement. There she would offer her services as a warrior to the queen, who would take her in and feed her. She could almost smell meat cooking. She skied faster.

A shadow fell across the snow. Looking up, she spotted a white gyrfalcon winging across the plateau. She halted and watched as the big bird flew over her, then put her head down and resumed skiing.

Late in the afternoon, a dark shape emerged on the northern horizon. At first it appeared to be a stand of trees moving with the wind, yet the air was still. The shape resolved itself into a huddle of figures, moving in her direction.

Ragnhild could not count them at this distance, but there were far more than three. Too many to be her father's men.

Fear jolted through her. She scanned the snowfield for cover, but the broad plain stretched white in every direction, and she stood out like a beacon on it.

Ragnhild calmed her breathing and forced herself to think. How could she improve her situation? There were not many options. All she could do was change direction. Perhaps they were not pursuing her and had some other mission. She angled toward the south so that she was skiing at right angles from her original course.

By late afternoon, they were definitely closing on her. Looking back, she fought off despair. If she could just maintain a reasonable distance between them until dark, she could dig a snow shelter that might hide her in the night, in hopes that they would miss her in the dark.

She kept skiing hard, forcing herself to count to two hundred before she looked back over her shoulder. When she did, her heart sank. They were still gaining on her. If they caught her, she would draw her sword and die fighting. That would be the last choice the situation allowed her.

She was not out of choices yet.

At last the sun set, and the man pack was still distant enough that her plan might work. Ragnhild skied on a little farther in the dark. Then she stopped, undid the straps on her skis, and pivoted on them so she faced back the way she had come. Strapping her boots back to the skis, she backtracked on her own trail as far as she dared without getting too close to the hunters.

She stopped, unstrapped her skis again, and took a long step off them to the side, perpendicular from her track. She leaned over and picked the skis up and took a few more long steps through the snow, pausing to smooth over her tracks with the edge of a ski. She hoped, in the dimming light, this ruse would keep her pursuers from spotting her new trail.

She donned her skis once again and set off on a course away from her trail, praying to the ski goddess, Skadi, to help put enough distance behind her before her pursuers discovered that her trail petered out.

Skiing through the dark, Ragnhild's nervous energy carried her a long way. The sky was clear, and the stars glittered like icy jewels. It seemed to her exhausted mind that the gods must surely be with her, leading her to her destiny.

Her face hit the ice crust hard. Scrambling in the snow, she realized she had dozed while skiing. It was time to take shelter.

Backtracking again, a shorter distance this time, Ragnhild doffed her skis and took another giant step, then plowed through the snow until she found a tall pine where the snow had piled up, forming a sizeable drift far enough off the track not to be spotted.

She paused and quieted her breathing, listening. Sound would carry a long way over the vast snowfield, but the night was silent.

Satisfied, she used her ski to dig deep into the crusted snow, hollowing out a space big enough to crawl into. She laid her shield down in her snow burrow and scrambled in, scraping snow over the opening with her ski, careful to leave a tiny opening at the base for air intake. She poked her spear into the cave roof, making a small air hole directly above her head. She hoped the dawn light coming in the hole would wake her so she could get away before full daylight.

She settled in. The snow cave was fairly snug, her body heating the small space. The shield kept her bottom dry, and the quiver she leaned against protected her back from the snow. In the utter darkness, her mittened hand fumbled at her water skin. She drank a little, and nibbled a piece of dried frozen cod. She hated not being able to see her pursuers. Even now they could be outside her cave, ready to burst in on her. Taking a firm grip on her panic, she pushed away every thought of discovery and capture and began to recite the alphabet of twenty-four runes, picturing them in her mind as she mentally spoke the name. Eventually a trancelike sleep came over her.

The sound of skiers swishing past startled her awake. Swallowing the panic that rose in her throat, Ragnhild held her breath and listened. No daylight pierced the air hole. She prayed that it was still too dark for them to spot her burrow in the shadow of the pine.

The swish of skis did not slow. As their noise receded, Ragnhild allowed herself to breathe again but forced herself to stay in the burrow while she recited the runes and their meanings to herself backward and forward twice. Only then did she let panic drive her out of the snow pit. She burst into the open, then stopped and listened, straining to see in the dark.

A sliver of a moon sliced the sky. Strapping on her skis, Ragnhild quickly backtracked to find her old trail. When she crossed the perpendicular tracks, she pivoted and set out in her original direction.

As the sun flared on the horizon, she was heading east again, breaking new ground. Looking over her shoulder, she saw no sign of pursuit. A small surge of elation shot through her. It appeared that she had sufficiently perplexed her hunters, or at least delayed them.

She skied on across the endless snowfield.

At midday, a shadow fell over her. A gyrfalcon again. Was it the same one she had seen yesterday?

A while later she stopped to drink. Looking back, her heart stuttered in her chest.

Her pursuers had found her, and they were closing in fast.

# CHAPTER 4

As Åsa patrolled the snowfields in Stormrider's body, she spotted a lone figure skiing against the white backdrop. In the distance, a war band pursued on skis. She flew close enough to count nine of them before veering out of range. If it was Hrolf, he might recognize her for more than just a wild falcon and bring her down with an arrow. Åsa flew across the plain for a closer look at their prey.

The lone figure wore a leather jerkin studded with metal rings. A sword and shield were slung over the skier's back, a bow hung from the shoulder and a quiver from the belt. A knitted stocking cap was pulled down low on the brow, but the eyes flicked up to meet hers.

A girl.

The falcon shot up into the air and hovered, watching the war band close in. The girl halted, drew her bow, and began firing arrows at her attackers, but they sheltered beneath their shields and kept coming.

Over the western horizon, a new trio of warriors skied in fast. They joined the girl's lone figure, shooting arrows at the war band.

The attackers fended off the hail of arrows beneath their shields as they closed on their quarry. The falcon hovered above, helpless. She must not reveal herself. She risked a closer pass to see if she could identify Hrolf, but their shields hid the attackers' identities.

Out of arrows now, the girl and her defenders threw aside their bows and drew swords. Without hesitation the girl launched herself at the warband, hacking her way with skill and strength, flanked by the other three.

The four defenders fought ferociously, holding the attackers at bay until one of them closed on the girl. She chopped with her sword, lacerating his arm, but he kept coming, drawing the other three. Another attacker managed to lunge in from the side and grab the girl in a bear hug, his knife at her throat.

"Lay down your weapons."

Glowering, the defenders laid their swords in the snow. Their captors swarmed over them, collecting the weapons. One wrested the girl's sword from her grip. The attackers bound their prisoners' hands with hide ropes and set out on skis, forcing their captives to ski along behind them.

The falcon winged after them, staying high enough to escape notice. The war band dragged their captives across the plateau to a hidden valley where a wisp of smoke rose among the trees. Her excitement flared. This could be Hrolf's lair. She flew down and perched in a tree, counting five men outside a rude shelter. Each of them appeared to be physically impaired, limping or moving slowly. Hrolf was nowhere to be seen, yet who else could own this remote camp?

The sun was already setting in the short winter day. Åsa lofted into the sky and set off for Tromøy, marking the location in her mind with the falcon's acute sense of direction. She soared across the water, circling her island homestead, and flew down to the bower's roof. She hopped in through the gable end and perched on the rafter, gazing down at her human form, inert on the bed. The human form drew Åsa, and she released her hold on Stormrider. There was a moment of panic while she hung disembodied in the air, then the body's reassuring pull brought her in. Åsa lay still, concentrating on the rhythm of her breath while strength flowed to her limbs. Flexing her fingers and toes, she forced open her eyes and struggled up from the bed, staggering to the door and shouting for Olvir.

The captain of her húskarlar came running.

Åsa supported herself on the doorframe while she spoke urgently. "I think I've found Hrolf's lair and what remains of his followers on the mainland. There are nine warriors and five others who do not appear to be fighting men."

"My lady, I will light the war beacons." Olvir did not question her vision, knowing Heid had trained her in the sorceress's ways.

"We cannot wait for help to arrive; there is no time. They have prisoners, one of them a girl. We will have to do it without him. Twenty warriors will be enough to take on the nine I saw. Ready the boats and prepare for battle. We leave at first light. I will guide you to the lair. I pray to Thor that we arrive before they harm her."

"At once, lady."

KNEES BENT, back straining, Ragnhild fought to keep her skis under her as her captors hauled her along by the rope that bound her hands. If she fell, the bastards would just drag her through the snow as they were doing to Einar. He had gone down, whether from wounds or exhaustion, she couldn't tell. She risked a glance at him as their captors towed him along on his belly. His jaw was clenched in his white face, but she couldn't see any blood or obvious wounds. Thorgeir and Svein were still on their feet, although Thorgeir hunched over, his trail spotted with blood. Possibly a gut wound. She wished they would stop soon so she could examine him.

They were dragged into a pine grove where the ground became uneven. Einar gave a bleat of pain as he hit a stump. Their captors didn't slow until a hovel appeared, hunkered among the firs. A lame man split wood beside the door. He set aside his axe and grinned as they approached.

The crippled man pulled aside the hide that covered the hut's entrance. Inside, the filthy lair stank of rancid grease. A fire burned sullenly in the hearth, surrounded by benches piled with rank furs. Through the haze Ragnhild made out a tall figure seated in a rude chair, elevated slightly above the benches. She almost laughed to see a high seat in this hovel.

Then a shiver went through her. On the back of the chair perched the white gyrfalcon.

Their captors dragged them before this makeshift high seat, shoving them onto their knees. A groan escaped Einar, but he managed to stay upright. Thorgeir straightened, and Ragnhild caught her breath at the sight of his red-soaked tunic.

One of the kidnappers yanked off Ragnhild's cap. They gasped when her thick brown braid flopped out. The man on the high seat stared at her, his blue eyes searing into hers, a smile forming at his lips. His hands were massive, his hair long and blond, and his handsome features sculpted.

"My lady, welcome. I am Hrolf Gudrødson. I rule here." He pondered her awhile, still smiling. "I wonder why a girl would be crossing my lands alone, with three men pursuing her. Who are you?"

*Don't answer him.* Ragnhild clamped her jaw and stared sullenly ahead.

Hrolf's grin widened, baring his white teeth. "She is very nice looking," he said to Einar. "As you can see, there are no women here. Wouldn't she be a welcome distraction on a long winter's night?"

Out of the corner of her eye, Ragnhild saw Einar's face go from white to purple. She would have grinned at his outrage, but the situation was too dire. Even if they survived and managed to escape, her father would have Einar and his men flayed alive for letting her fall into this man's hands. She wished Father hadn't sent Einar after her. But of course he would. Einar had always been her man, loyal as a dog. Guilt seared into Ragnhild's chest. She had gotten them into this mess, now she must get them out.

Somehow.

"She is the daughter of King Solvi," said Einar. "Her father sent us to bring her back."

Ragnhild winced. *Here it comes.*

Their captor regarded them for a long moment. "I suppose her father would pay a fair ransom for her."

*Not happily,* Ragnhild thought.

"That he would." Einar was sagging. *How badly was he wounded?* Ragnhild tried to sneak a look at him without seeming too concerned.

Hrolf smiled. "If I were to hold a wedding feast with her, would that make me Solvi's heir?"

Ragnhild choked at the image of her father's eyes bulging.

Einar's voice was steady despite his high color. "She has two elder brothers. The ransom would be the better bargain. Solvi will pay what you ask—if she is untouched."

"And I suppose you want me to send you back as emissary?" Hrolf said.

Einar scowled at the implication that he was a coward. "I will not return without her."

"Well, then, you are of no use to me," said Hrolf. "I can't imagine why I would keep the three of you alive. Food is scarce this time of year, and the gods are always looking for a sacrifice."

Einar stared ahead stoically.

*Damn him. Why couldn't he use his mind? I must get loose.*

Ragnhild realized there might be a chance. Her own hands

were bound now, but if she pretended to be willing, or at least harmless, perhaps he would untie her and she could get at the knife strapped inside her boot. She wanted to signal Einar, but in these close quarters, she could not risk a direct glance at him. His eyes were showing white now. She had to do something fast, before the idiot made things worse.

"Don't send me back there," she blurted.

Hrolf shot her a surprised look. "And why not, girl?" he demanded.

Why not? Well, the truth, then.

"My father has pledged me in marriage against my will," she said.

Now it was Einar who winced.

Hrolf looked interested. "And who does he want you to marry that you are so opposed?"

"He wants me to marry an Irish king. I would have to cross the sea to live in their cursed country. And they would force me to forsake the old gods and worship their White Christ."

Hrolf's eyes widened. "And why would your father want that?"

"For silver," Ragnhild muttered, looking at the floor. "This Irish king is rich, and he offered to pay my father my weight in it."

"Well, then your father would be prepared to pay me quite a bit to get you back," said Hrolf.

Horror crept up Ragnhild's neck. "You can't do that. My father would sell me like a slave to that Christian. I'll eat his white liver before I will submit to him," she raged.

Hrolf looked at her pensively. "I think I understand you," he said. "But you're a healthy girl. That's quite a lot of silver. Give me one good reason not to sell you back to your father."

Ragnhild stared into the dark corner of the hovel desperately.

"I'll give you a reason," a voice croaked from the shadows. An old man hobbled forward. He was dressed in filthy skins, and his left eyelid had been crudely sewn shut.

"What reason would that be?" asked Hrolf.

"The witch will want her," the old man replied, his voice cracking.

"Heid?"

"Yes, Heid. And she will give more than that greedy king ever will."

"What will she give us?"

"She will give us *him*."

Hrolf's eyes seemed to glow like coals in his head. "Olaf," he whispered. Behind him, the white gyrfalcon roused.

A shudder passed through Ragnhild. Whoever Olaf was, she felt sorry for him. And for herself as well.

# CHAPTER 5

Tromøy

Before dawn, Tromøy's residents were up and preparing for the attack. They loaded two hand-drawn sledges with tents and supplies, and Heid's sledge was outfitted with furs and provisions for the journey. The party set off on skis for the ferry landing. Åsa led the way, Stormrider riding on her shoulder and Olvir at her side. Heid rode in her carved and painted sledge, pulled by her apprentices, while warriors towed the two working sledges.

At the landing, they boarded the flat, raft-like ferry that waited to take them across to the mainland. The warriors poled the craft across the narrow expanse of water.

The war party set out across the gleaming plateau under the winter sun. It was impossible to move secretly against the blank landscape of snow, and before long, a bird of prey's shadow fell across them. Åsa felt a tingle of recognition as she watched the big gyrfalcon circle once before heading back in the direction of the outlaw lair.

"It's Hrolf," she said quietly to Heid, looking up at the retreating raptor.

The sorceress nodded. "They'll be ready for us."

Already the short day was darkening. Åsa called a halt. "Make camp here. We attack at dawn."

A fire was built, and Heid and Åsa took their places with the apprentices. Heid led them in a vardlokkur, a song in an ancient tongue that called the land spirits to support them. The warriors gathered around the fire to pass the ceremonial horn of mead. Everyone partook of the drink, but they all remained carefully sober, and the evening ended early.

Åsa left the fire and entered her tent, where Stormrider waited on her perch. Åsa lay in her sheepskin sleeping bag and closed her eyes, breathing deeply and rhythmically as she prepared to enter the falcon's body.

The tent flap jerked open and Heid stormed in. She glowered at Stormrider. The falcon roused at the disturbance but stayed on her perch.

"You're overdoing it," the sorceress admonished. "You are exhausting yourself. What will happen if your spirit loses its way and you are unable to reenter your body? What will become of Halfdan?"

"I must see what we face when we attack," Åsa said without opening her eyes. "This will be the last time for a week, I promise." The familiar vibration already traveled up her limbs. In a moment she rose into Stormrider, leaving her human form in the sheepskin. She felt the falcon give way to her as she took control of the bird's body and launched into the air, flying out through the tent flap into the night.

Snow blanketed the vast plateau, gleaming under the moonlight. Soaring over the white terrain, she let the falcon's memory guide her to the outlaw lair on the side of a pine-covered hill, where firelight shimmered through the branches. Lighting in a treetop, she watched the men gathered around the bonfire, sharpening axes and spears.

So, they had decided to stay and fight rather than flee their cozy nest for the harsh plateau.

Three prisoners stood bound and noosed beneath a huge ash tree. Movement drew the falcon's eye to a tall man hefting a bear skin. He pulled the bear head over his own, fangs gleaming in the firelight. He draped the arms over his shoulders, the claws dark against his sleeves, and let the pelt cascade down his back like a cape.

Hrolf.

The drums thrummed as he hefted his spear and stepped, barefoot, onto a bed of raked coals and began an eerie dance. Others followed him, wearing the skins of boar and wolf, dancing across the coals. As they worked into a frenzy, their cries chilled her heart. She could feel the power rising from the fire.

Suddenly Hrolf threw his head back and looked up from under the bear's head, his stare like a spear thrown at her heart. She launched from the tree and winged back to camp.

RAGNHILD THRASHED IN HER BONDS. The beasts had come and dragged Einar, Thorgeir, and Svein away for sacrifice. She had to get loose. She would rescue them somehow.

"That will do you no good, child," came a cracked voice from the dark reaches of the room.

Ragnhild's heart flopped in her chest like a salmon on a hook.

A bent form shuffled into the firelight. The one-eyed man, Hrafn. A blade flashed, and Ragnhild's heart stuttered. "The ropes are good walrus hide," he explained. "You need a knife to cut the bonds."

The blade sliced through the leather ropes, and they fell to the floor. The old man grinned and put the knife in her hand. She almost dropped it in surprise, but her fingers closed instinctively on the hilt.

"Go," he whispered, melting back into the shadows.

Ragnhild did not wait to ask why he'd cut her loose. She crept to the door and peered out. Dark creatures cavorted around a bonfire, shrieking an eerie chant. They danced upright as men, yet their heads were wild animals—boars and bears and wolves. She spotted Einar, Thorgeir, and Svein bound and noosed under the branches of a massive tree. Ragnhild kept to the shadows, waiting for her chance.

∾

As soon as she reentered human form, Åsa forced her eyes open. Heid sat beside her.

Åsa forced out the words. "They are berserk and ulfhed."

"Yes, I know. Iron will not bite them, nor fire burn them," said Heid calmly, offering a steaming cup. "Drink this. You must be rested tomorrow."

Åsa pushed the brew aside and struggled out of her sheepskin. "They are preparing to sacrifice their prisoners tonight. We must go now." She staggered to the door, shouting, "Olvir! Muster the men. Hurry, they won't be expecting us to attack at night."

She pulled on her clothes and dragged her brynja from the war chest. Heid grudgingly helped her heft the mail shirt over her head and handed her both swords. Åsa slung their straps over her back, snatched up her spear and shield, and ran out to the yard where Olvir was gathering the húskarlar.

Åsa had to speak to the warriors, tell them what they faced without infecting them with the terror that seized her.

She felt Heid's gnarled, bony hand grip her shoulder. She

turned to meet the völva's sword-gray gaze and calm swept over her.

"We will be with you," Heid reminded her. "Our charms will weaken them."

Åsa nodded and turned to her warriors.

"These are no ordinary warriors we face tonight," she said. "They wear wolf and bear skins. They walk on fire. It may be that our swords and spears will not kill them."

She watched the fear flicker across the men's faces. She raised her voice. "We have killed their kind before, and we'll kill them tonight. The ulfhed and berserk may resist our weapons, but Heid and her sorceresses are with us. We shall prevail."

A cheer rose up among the warriors. The war party set out across the snowfield. Pale winter moonlight glinted off helms and speartips. Skis and sledge runners hissed on the deep snow.

As they neared the pine grove, Åsa slowed, treading more carefully. When the fire's glow flickered through the trees, she held up her hand to halt her warriors. They silently removed their skis, drew their weapons, and peered among the trees. The firelight revealed three captives trussed beneath the massive branches.

They were not swinging yet. Åsa's heart lifted.

A feral howl rose from the grove as the outlaws cavorted around the fire, their bear and wolf heads silhouetted against the flames. Åsa sensed her húskarlar falter.

She growled a challenge, echoed by Olvir. The air stirred, and she felt the men rally behind her.

She raised her spear and charged.

With a shout, they fell upon the beast-clad outlaws. War cries rang out, punctuated with shrieks. Heid gathered her women and they raised a chant to counter the berserkers' magic.

The berserkers fought like the wild animals they embodied. Åsa's húskarlar outnumbered them and were better armed and better trained, yet she saw her men pressed hard by the outlaws, who seemed oblivious to their wounds. Åsa rammed her spear into a wolf-headed man's chest, but he dodged sideways and the point glanced off his bare chest. He was on her before she could recover, wolf claws scraping her arms. His hot breath seared her face and he gripped her with a wiry strength. As her arm weakened under the pressure of his hold, she saw herself reflected in his glassy eyes and her courage faltered. As triumph came over his face, Åsa felt his hold lighten just a bit. She kneed him in the gut. As he reared back in pain, she jerked her shield up and rammed it under his jaw with all her strength. His head snapped back and he went down like a felled tree.

The women's chants competed with the berserkers' eerie shrieks. Åsa's húskarlar fought the beasts, horror on their faces. One of her men went down under an outlaw clad in a boar's skin. Åsa lunged over a tangle of bodies to get to him, meeting Olvir in the fray. Together they jabbed their spears into the boar man until he fell back from his prey. The beast pivoted and charged Åsa and Olvir. Despite the dozen stab wounds that covered his body, the boar was not bleeding. Åsa knew her spear had pierced deep into his body. He should be bleeding profusely and on the verge of collapse. Fear gushed into her veins like poison.

From the periphery of her vision, she saw a slender figure dart from the hut. The girl. She raced to the three captives, jerked the nooses off them, and slashed their bonds. They grabbed up weapons from the dead and joined the fray.

Åsa's strength flowed back into her limbs. She drew her sword and fought with renewed fury. The same wave of courage seemed to sweep over the húskarlar, and they surged over the enemy. The women's chants rose above the berserker's shrieks. As the spells gained volume, blades began to bite.

Hacking at the enemy, Åsa caught glimpses of the girl, fighting in a blur of speed. Where she struck the snow ran red, but none could land a blow on her. Her men flanked her, fighting grimly, never allowing an opening.

Inevitably the húskarlar's superior numbers decimated the outlaw ranks. Their bodies littered the red snow, and the stink of blood and bowels filled the air.

Åsa whirled once, then lowered her sword and scanned the scene. The outlaws lay in their animal skins, bleeding in the snow. Some of her own húskarlar bled too, but all remained on their feet.

A dark shape shot up from the battle scene and winged toward the distant mountains.

Hrolf. Åsa fumbled for her bow.

"Let him go," Heid said. "His body will be in the hut."

Åsa and Heid turned to the outlaw's lair, pushing aside the reindeer hide that covered the low door. It was dark inside the windowless hovel, and Heid struck a light that sputtered in the stinking air. Bones littered the floor, and greasy animal skins covered the rough benches lining the walls around the cold long-fire. Bird claws and bear teeth festooned the rafters.

Heid hissed. Something skittered, quick in the shadows. Åsa grabbed the wraithlike form and yanked him into the light.

"You!" cried Heid.

The one-eyed man grinned at them.

Åsa dragged the old man by his bony arm. It felt hollow as a bird's bone. As they emerged from the hovel's darkness, she saw that Hrafn had aged in the months since he had fought the Danes by her side. He seemed to have shrunk.

"Well, young queen, you have me now," he cackled. "What will you do with old Hrafn?"

"Where is Hrolf's body?"

"I don't know, my lady. He did not confide in me."

"He's lying," said Heid.

"Well, you tell us where it is, then," said Hrafn with a taunting grin.

Heid's eyes seemed to look inward for a moment. "It is well hidden by spells," she spat. "But you are no doubt the one who has hidden it. Tell us or I will make you regret it."

The old man smirked. "And how would you cause me regret? If not for me, you would still be the helpless prisoner of the haugbui."

Åsa shuddered, remembering how Heid and Ulf had been held in thrall by the old king of the grave mound. They had lain as if dead for days, and Åsa had sought out Hrafn to free them.

Heid bristled. "I was far from helpless. I had already freed myself and would have saved the smith when you interfered."

"If I hadn't interfered you would be lying there still. Your threats are empty, old witch, and you know it. There is nothing you can do to me."

"And what should I do with you, old man?" Åsa asked, hefting her sword.

Hrafn turned his eye on her. "Do not forget that I came to your aid when you needed me. If I had not, you might be slave to a Dane now."

"I have not forgotten. But that only evened the score between us," Åsa said. "You have taken up with Hrolf, and that makes you my enemy. We were allies once. Why have you joined him?"

Hrafn's voice creaked like a rusty hinge. "I have not joined him. It is true that I made him what he is and taught him the ways of power. I would have made him king, if he had only listened. But he has betrayed me. He keeps me prisoner here. Take me with you, and I will make it worth your while."

Heid pressed her lips together. "Bring the old goat back to Tromøy. I'll find a way to make him talk. Odin might appreciate his company."

"Odin has already enjoyed my company." Hrafn cackled and held out his skinny arms, allowing them to bind his hands.

"Bring Olvir to me," said Åsa. When Olvir ducked into the hut, she handed the old sorcerer over to him. "Guard him well.

Keep him apart from the others. Do not trust him, and don't let him speak to anyone."

Heid and her apprentices ransacked the hut for Hrolf's body in vain. They searched the grounds around the hut by torchlight, but the battle-ravaged snow gave no clues.

"I must fly out and find him," said Åsa.

"You must not leave your body again so soon," said Heid. "I will search for him. By night my owl's eyes are sharper than your falcon's."

Åsa reluctantly retired to the hovel and sat by while Heid lay down on the bench. She settled in to keep watch while the apprentices chanted their mistress into the trance.

In a flurry of wings, an enormous owl lofted in through the eaves and perched on the rafters. Heid's body went so still, it was hard to tell that she still breathed. The owl flew out of the hut.

Åsa waited with the women by the sorceress's inert body for a long time. Pale light filtered through the gable ends by the time the owl swooped in to light on the rafters. With a gasp, Heid sat up, supported by her women.

The old sorceress shook her head. "I could not find any sign of Hrolf. It's as if his body vanished into the air."

"That's impossible," said Åsa.

"Yet the magic that hides him eludes even my owl's sight," said Heid.

"We cannot waste any more time searching here. It's time we set off for home," Åsa said. "Set fire to the hovel. Hrolf is still out there. We need to deprive him of shelter. He won't last long without a place of refuge." She surveyed the bloody yard, littered with outlaw corpses but none of her people. "Divide up their weapons among the warriors," she said to Olvir.

His face furrowed with concern. "Lady, the men fear these dead may walk."

"And well they might, for there is dark magic at work," said Heid. "Cut off their heads. Burn the bodies with the hovel."

Olvir looked relieved. "And these?" He nodded to the three strangers who formed a protective knot around the girl.

Åsa squinted at the pale winter sun. "We need to get home before dark. Keep them under guard until I can question them."

The hovel caught fire quickly, sending a greasy black cloud into the winter sky.

They donned their skis, letting the prisoners put on theirs as well before binding them and dragging them back to camp. It was full light by the time they arrived, and the tents came down swiftly. They loaded the sledges and made for the ferry.

Though the prisoners slowed them down, by the time they reached the landing and loaded the raft, they still had good daylight left. Åsa breathed a sigh of relief when they had safely crossed the icy water and the sun still hung in the sky.

They made their weary way across the island. As they crested the last hill, Åsa welcomed the sight of columns of chimney smoke and Tromøy's roofs.

# CHAPTER 6

Snow began to swirl as the war party arrived at Tromøy's hall. They hung their shields on the wall, unstrapped their swords, and settled onto the benches around the longfire, glad to be warm and indoors.

Åsa took her place on the high seat, holding herself tall despite her exhaustion. Heid was right, she had been overdoing it. She took a deep breath and nodded to the warriors by the door.

"Bring in the girl."

Olvir led the girl to the high seat. She had been relieved of her weapons, but she still wore her ring-sewn leather jerkin and wool leggings. Her hat was gone, revealing a ratty brown braid and a face rosy with health, gray eyes rimmed with dark lashes, and fine dark brows.

Åsa met the girl's eyes and saw them widen in surprise. Smiling, she leaned forward. "Welcome. Are you surprised to see a woman on the high seat?"

To her credit, the girl did not blurt an answer.

"Who are you? From where do you hail?" Åsa asked gently.

At last the girl found her tongue. "My lady, I am Ragnhild, daughter of King Solvi of Rogaland. I must see to my men." Her eyes darted around the hall, searching.

It was Åsa's turn to stare. "Welcome, Lady Ragnhild. Do not fear for your men. They are being tended by the völva Heid and her apprentices."

Ragnhild seemed to relax at this news. Åsa could see that the girl was beyond exhausted. She must keep the interview short.

"What brings you to Agder, Lady Ragnhild?"

The girl dropped to her knees. "My queen, it is you I seek. I wish to swear to you."

Åsa's eyebrows lifted as the room hummed with chatter. "You wish to swear an oath to me?"

Ragnhild looked up at her with shining eyes. "Yes, lady. I have wished to serve you since I first heard your name. I want to be a shield-maiden in the service of a great queen."

Åsa cleared her throat. There was more to this story than the dreams of a starry-eyed girl. "But you have run away from your home. Why is that?"

Ragnhild hesitated. "I had a disagreement with my father."

"And what reason would a young girl have to disagree with her father?" Åsa kept her voice stern, hiding the smile within. She knew from personal experience how many reasons a girl could find to go against her father.

The color rose in Ragnhild's face. "He has promised me to an Irish king, but I will kill myself before I submit to that man."

"That seems like a rather extreme reaction." Åsa did not say that she had once felt the same way about her own husband.

"My father has promised me in exchange for silver. He is selling me like a slave," Ragnhild raged. "I don't want to live far from home, among people who worship the White Christ and forsake the true gods."

Åsa regarded the girl, whose eyes blazed and chest heaved

with passion. "Well, I can understand your objections. So to escape this fate, you crossed the mountains alone at night on skis?"

"Yes, lady."

"And the men who fought beside you, they are your men?"

Ragnhild hung her head. "My father's men," she said. "Sent to bring me back."

"And you refuse to return with them?"

"I will never go back." Despite her defiant words, the girl swayed on her feet.

Åsa did wonder what kind of trouble she was getting herself into, but she'd found a kindred spirit in this runaway. "Very well. I will not turn you out into the snow. I will accept your oath." Åsa took up Gudrød's Bane and laid it across her knees.

Ragnhild placed her hands on the blade and raised her eyes to Åsa's. "I, Ragnhild Solvisdottir of Rogaland, swear to serve you, Åsa Queen, to defend you with my dying breath, if you will only let me stay here."

*You are the bravest of girls.* A wave of emotion swept over Åsa, a feeling of kinship she'd never experienced. "I thank you, Lady Ragnhild. I gladly accept your oath. Please rise."

Ragnhild stood, her eyes glistening. Åsa rose as well, her drinking horn held high in salute. "This girl has a heart as strong as the greatest warrior. She has shown skill in battle and undaunted courage. She is now one of us."

The warriors cheered their approval, banging their ale cups on the boards.

"Sit, lady." Åsa gestured to the guest seat across the longfire. "Eat, drink, rest. None can take you against your will. Your father's men are my prisoners."

Ragnhild started up in alarm. "They are not to be harmed."

Åsa realized there was a strong bond between these men and this girl. "I promise no harm will come to them. They are under guard in my guest house, but well cared for."

Ragnhild sank into the bench with a sigh. The porridge and ale set before her riveted her attention. She sat up and attacked the food. But after she had eaten no more than a few spoonfuls, her eyes blinked, more and more slowly, until they seemed to be stuck together.

"Bring the girl to the women's bower," Åsa said to the women. "I will question the other prisoners tomorrow." Åsa rose and nearly stumbled as she stepped down from the high seat. She was beyond weary. She needed to see her son, then sleep.

The women surrounded Ragnhild and followed Åsa and Heid, half-carrying the girl across the yard to the women's bower, where they made room for her on the sleeping benches. Ragnhild's eyes never opened, and she was wholly asleep by the time the furs were tucked around her.

Åsa followed Heid through the door of the private chamber they shared. The flickering light of the brazier fell on Halfdan in his cradle suspended from the rafters.

The sorceress closed the door and hung her jeweled cloak on the hook, then hobbled to her own bed across the room.

With hands made clumsy by exhaustion, Åsa pulled off her woolen tunic and breeks. Shivering in the brazier's meager heat, she unlaced her leather ankle boots and got into the big bed. Burrowing gratefully under the down comforter, she snuggled into the warmth. Through half-lidded eyes, she watched Heid sink onto her own bed and lay down with a groan of relief. Then Åsa's eyes closed and she slept.

ÅSA STAYED in the bower after she woke, playing with Halfdan and telling the women the strange tale of the battle while Heid's apprentices reenacted their spellcraft.

The girl Ragnhild slept through the morning and was still asleep in the afternoon when Åsa departed for the hall.

"Do not disturb her," she said to the women. "She has been through much and needs her rest."

Åsa took her place on the high seat, Heid beside her. Olvir brought the three captive warriors before her. Their bonds had been removed, replaced by splints and clean bandages. In spite of their wounds, these men looked as if they had rested well.

"What brings you to my lands?" she asked. "Armed warriors-- it could be construed as aggression on the part of your lord. Are you spies?"

She watched the three men shift uneasily.

"No, lady," said one. "We are not spies."

"Well, if you are not spies, why are you here? Why do you pursue the Lady Ragnhild?"

The spokesman stepped forward. "Lady, I am called Einar. Lady Ragnhild is the daughter of Solvi, King of Rogaland. He sent us after her to bring her home. We cannot return without her. Our king would put us to death. You must let us take her back."

Åsa rose, looking down on them from the high seat. "I need do no such thing. The Lady Ragnhild has sworn to serve me, and I have promised in return that I will not give her over to her father. You may not take her as long as I am queen here."

She stretched out her arms to draw power from the air. Her eyes flared and her voice came out like thunder. "You are trespassers on my land. I have every right to put you to death. Jól is nigh. The gods would look kindly upon a human sacrifice in the first year of my reign."

Their eyes showed white, but the men remained silent. They had courage.

She softened her voice. "Yet, even though you were outnumbered by the outlaws, you defended your lady with your lives. I give you another option. Stay here. Swear to me. Do that, and I give you your lives."

Einar said, "Lady, you would make oathbreakers of us."

"Oathbreakers or corpses, I give you the choice. Yet I ask you, how best can you serve your lady? By taking her prisoner, dragging her back to her father against her will?" Åsa's voice rose as she remembered Olaf's betrayal, binding her and taking her back to Gudrød. "Or by protecting her here, where she chooses to be?"

The three prisoners exchanged looks in the unspoken discussion of those who have fought beside each other for so long they need no words.

Einar nodded and stepped forward. "Lady, protecting Lady Ragnhild is our foremost concern, even beyond our duty to our king. Therefore, we accept your offer, even though it will make us outlaws in our own land. We will swear to be loyal to you and to her while we live."

"We of Tromøy are brave, but few," Åsa said. "I have little to give you but food and shelter. Our enemies outnumber us. If you are willing to accept these odds, I welcome you among my húskarlar."

The three nodded their assent. Once again, Åsa laid her sword across her knees. Each of them stepped forward in turn, laying his hand on the blade as he swore his oath.

The Tromøy warriors cheered and made room for the newcomers on the benches. Åsa ordered them served with ale and meat.

At last Åsa turned to Hrafn. The sorcerer had already managed to insinuate himself among the húskarlar, where he drank and ate with abandon, grinning as if he were a victor himself instead of a prisoner on thin ice.

"What have you to say to me, old man?" she demanded.

Hrafn put down his cup and smiled at her. He rose and bowed with a flourish that belied the rags he wore. "Lady, I too offer you my service."

"I have Heid, the greatest sorceress in the land. What need have I of the likes of you?"

Hrafn's one eye gleamed in the firelight. "I am skilled in the ways of sorcery. There are many things I know that Heid does not. The old witch would like you to believe that she speaks with the gods, but they tell me otherwise."

"Liar!" Heid spat, rising from her seat of honor. She shook her distaff, but the old man only grinned at her. She glowered while Hrafn turned smug.

"I think that the völva is not accustomed to facing anyone who is not afraid of her," Jarl Borg observed quietly, moustache twitching.

"I've never seen anyone get her out of her seat like that. Thor help the old man," whispered Åsa.

But soon the völva resumed her chair and her ire was forgotten as the ale gave the assembly new strength. The hour was ripe for making extravagant oaths.

Einar rose unsteadily. In spite of the bloody bandage on his shoulder, he raised his cup and said, "I swear that I will best Olvir at wrestling, or break my back trying!"

Olvir stood, raising his cup high. "I accept the challenge."

The two men drained their cups and plunked them on the board. Wiping their beards with the backs of their hands, they advanced on each other. The húskarlar scooted back on their benches, cheering. Åsa leaned forward eagerly in her high seat as the two men grappled each other by the leggings in the traditional glima wrestling stance. They began to circle, now and then giving a sharp jerk to the other's legging, hoping to yank the other's feet out from under him. Åsa wondered how long they would stay upright in their drunken and exhausted state.

Einar succeeded in jerking Olvir's leg up and simultaneously kicked the other out from under him. Olvir went down, but he kept a firm grip on Einar and brought him down too. They thrashed in the straw, each trying to gain his feet first and win the match. But it soon became apparent that neither man possessed the coordination to rise. The ale went round and the merriment increased. Finally, amid great cheering, the two men managed to struggle to their feet by leaning on each other, only to collapse again in laughter. Arm in arm, they returned to their seats and took up their ale cups once again.

# CHAPTER 7

Ragnhild opened her eyes in darkness, not sure where she was. She lay on a fur-covered bench alongside a banked longfire. She sensed that she was alone. Her bonds were gone.

Then she remembered and smiled. She was in the women's bower of Tromøy. Queen Åsa had accepted her.

She lay a few moments relishing her victory. Then the worries flooded in.

Her father would come after her. He'd be wanting the Irish treasure. He wouldn't give that up, and certainly he would not allow himself to be bested by a woman. Ragnhild shivered at the thought of what her father and his men would do to Åsa for taking her in, and to Einar, Thorgeir, and Svein for failing to bring her back.

She wouldn't let that happen. Ragnhild threw aside the furs. She pulled on her wool breeks and stockings, stepped into her leather boots, and buckled her belt over the linen tunic she had slept in. She sheathed her eating knife but left her sword hanging on the wall.

Ragnhild stepped into the winter night. The crisp air promised more snow. She strode to the hall and pulled open the carved oak outer door. In the entryway she paused, listening to the sounds of revelry, before stepping into the hall.

Åsa was in the high seat, Heid beside her. The húskarlar sat on the benches around the crackling longfire, drinking together. Einar looked up as she entered. He moved over and Ragnhild sat between him and Thorgeir. She must establish her place among them right away. Even though she had slept in the women's bower, she would eat with the warriors.

A man scurried over with a wooden cup of ale for her, which she accepted with a nod. She sipped sparingly, letting her stomach accustom itself to nourishment after days of near starvation.

She braved a glance at Åsa and noted with relief the queen's approving smile. In the firelight, Ragnhild realized that Åsa was barely older than herself. For a moment she gazed at the queen in admiration, then she remembered what she must do.

Ragnhild got to her feet, and the small talk ceased.

"Lady, may I speak?"

"Of course." Åsa beckoned her forward.

"I fear I bring danger to your doorstep."

"How so? We have vanquished the outlaws."

"My father." Ragnhild hung her head. "He will come for me. The Irish king promised him my weight in silver. He will not let that go."

"I see," said Åsa.

"I am sorry, lady. I fear I must leave. I would not bring his wrath down on you to whom I owe so much."

"And where would you go?"

Ragnhild had not thought that far ahead. "If you will ferry me across to the mainland, I will leave on my skis." And go where? Back to her father? Never. She'd live in the forest before she'd go back to him.

Åsa gave her a stern look. "May I remind you of the oath you have made to me? I have no intention of releasing you from it."

Ragnhild's mouth dropped open.

The queen's laugh rang out, merry as sleighbells. "You have proven your courage and your skill with weapons. And you bring me three seasoned warriors. I have need of every sword."

Dread settled heavy in Ragnhild's stomach. "But my father has many warriors. I warn you, he is merciless."

"Let me worry about your father. Remember, he does not know where you are, and since Thorgeir, Einar, and Svein have agreed to join us, he has no way of finding out. Besides, he is far from my only problem." The queen stood and spread her arms. "Tromøy is in a precarious position, surrounded by enemies who would take this place and make us slaves. Your father is only one of many. We on Tromøy prefer to resist, to the death if need be. We will meet each challenge with courage and never surrender. But it will take every one of us. We all must fight. We all *will* fight."

The high ceiling of the hall resounded with the cheers of the húskarlar. Something stirred in Ragnhild's chest, wild and powerful.

Åsa's gaze swept the hall, her eyes ablaze. She fixed Ragnhild with a penetrating stare. "I expect you to fulfill your duties as warrior. I must train all my women to fight. You can help me."

Ragnhild's heart expanded and she had to squeeze out the words. "Yes, lady."

Åsa kept her to her pledge. The next day, the women lined up beside the men in the practice yard, bounded by hazel posts. Snowflakes fluttered in the chill breeze, lighting on their hair. They wore padded battle jackets and carried shields and spear poles tipped with leather instead of steel.

Ragnhild took her place beside Einar. She faced him and assumed the familiar fighting stance. Einar had trained her since she was a child.

All was silent for a moment, then Ragnhild shattered the icy air with a cry, thrusting her pole at Einar. He jerked his shield up to deflect the blow and drove his own pole at her chest. She caught the thrust on her shield, and they returned to the starting position. They demonstrated this move five times.

"Now, pair off, each woman with a man. You are going to have to fight men, so let's start off that way," Ragnhild said. "The men are bigger than you, but that is not the only advantage to be had. You can be quicker; you can get under their guard. You must constantly be looking for an opening and take it without hesitation."

Ragnhild watched the women attack their opponents with ferocity. They were not without fighting experience, and they made a fair showing. As children, girls fought in mock battles and played at wrestling along with the boys. They had no fear of men. What they needed was experience and finesse. She and Einar would refine their technique.

Åsa appeared on the practice field, wearing leather armor and bearing her shield. She stepped inside the hazel boundary, plucked a practice spear from the barrel, and clashed it on her shield.

"Who will challenge me?" she shouted.

"I will!" Ragnhild stepped forward, hefting her spear.

The two women circled each other, gazes locked over their shields. Åsa feinted but Ragnhild didn't take the bait. They continued to circle. Ragnhild hurled her spear, and Åsa brought up her shield to catch it. The blunt tip clattered off Åsa's shield. Åsa set aside her spear and took up a wooden sword as Ragnhild did the same.

Ragnhild rushed Åsa, who fended her off coolly. Ragnhild attacked again, and Åsa blocked her a second time. Ragnhild realized she was underestimating the queen. She had never fought a female warrior before. She must change her thinking or risk losing the match.

They were close in age and size. Åsa was agile and well trained, and she certainly didn't lack courage. So far, the queen had remained cool. Was there some way Ragnhild could rile her? Throw her off balance?

With a man she would use taunts, but Ragnhild could not bring herself to insult the queen. She didn't want to find any weakness in this woman who was her savior. Yet she had the will to win. How?

If she was underestimating Åsa, could she get the queen to make the same mistake?

Swinging her blade wildly, Ragnhild launched herself into an off-balance charge. She hoped to lure Åsa into an attack. But the wily queen dodged the charge, and Ragnhild saw her lips twitch into a smile for an instant before they resolved back to a grim line.

Åsa lunged, and Ragnhild parried. The queen continued to press her hard, but Ragnhild fended her off. The exchange continued for some time, with neither gaining the upper hand.

Ragnhild was beginning to tire when Åsa held up her hand. "I can see that you will wear me out long before you fall. Let us rest for today."

Gratefully, Ragnhild sheathed her sword and returned to the benches.

# CHAPTER 8

Solbakk, Rogaland
November, AD 820

From the high seat, King Solvi glowered down at his eldest son.

"Where is my daughter?" His voice thundered in the rafters of Solbakk's great hall.

Harald steeled himself in the face of his father's wrath. "Einar, Thorgeir, and Svein have not returned. Nor have we had word of Ragnhild."

"Have you sent more men after them?"

"Not yet, Father. I still expect them to return."

"They should be back by now," Solvi growled.

Harald swallowed and looked his father in the eye. "You know how cunning Ragnhild can be. Those three are our best trackers, but she could have eluded them. They may still be on her trail. I think we should give them more time."

Solvi glared. "You boys should have gone after her yourselves."

Harald pursed his lips. Beside him, his younger brother, Orlyg, hung his head.

"I have faith in Einar and the others. I still think they will return."

"They'd better. I'm holding you two responsible. The Irish king is growing impatient. He may rescind his offer if he has to wait much longer. I want my silver!"

"Yes, Father." Harald and Orlyg bowed their heads and backed away from the high seat.

~

Tromøy

ÅSA WOKE in her room off the bower and watched Halfdan in his cradle, his eyes tracking the shadows that flickered across the high ceiling. When he saw her, his face broke into an enchanting smile, and he reached his arms out to her.

"Are you my good boy?" she said. He gurgled in delight.

Åsa got out of bed and picked the little boy up. She carried him to her seat by the brazier, where Heid, who never slept much, already sipped from a cup of aromatic herbs. The old sorceress's face was etched with pain. At the sight of Halfdan, the tension receded from her features and she smiled at him, waggling her fingers.

The door opened and Brenna bustled in from the main room. "He'll need a change and breakfast," she said briskly, taking Halfdan from Åsa's arms.

The boy wriggled from Brenna's grasp and ran ahead to the bower door, where he was greeted with coos and clucks from the women.

Åsa dressed and followed Brenna and Halfdan into the bower

hall, where the women gathered around the longfire for break-fast. Åsa took her seat and accepted the porridge and small beer offered her. In the mornings she did not need to eat with the warriors. She luxuriated in the simple pleasure of breakfasting with the women.

Olvir had presented Halfdan with a wooden sword, and the boy was never without it. He waved it at Ragnhild until his victim leaped up and charged him. Shrieking with joy, he ran to Åsa, who tried to tickle him. He eluded her and flung himself in Brenna's lap. The fóstra hefted him into a sitting position and fed him porridge from her bowl. After a few bites, he squirmed down from her lap and began menacing the women again.

When Brenna had finished her breakfast, she rose and held out her hand. "Shall we go see what Olvir is doing?"

"Vir!" said Halfdan, taking his foster-mother's hand and hauling her toward the door. He had attached himself to Olvir. The húskarl captain seemed to like his little shadow, and Åsa considered fostering Halfdan with the warrior in a few years. She hoped by then she would have land and wealth to bestow on Olvir as befitted the foster father of a king's son. Jarl Borg, already a wealthy landowner, was the natural choice to foster Halfdan, but Åsa feared the old warrior would not live to see her son grow to a fostering age.

As soon as breakfast was cleared, the women took up their distaffs, now loaded with wool, and tucked them into their belts, chattering as they dropped their spindles.

As Heid entered the bower hall, they fell silent. The sorceress was elegantly dressed in a fine red gown, and her earlier haggard look had been replaced by a serene half smile. Heid took her place beside Åsa on the high seat and led the women in their morning chants to elicit the land spirits' protection. Åsa joined her voice with the others' as the vardlokkur rose, enticing and beautiful.

After the blessing had been sung, Åsa walked to the brew-house to meet Brenna, who had detached Halfdan from Olvir.

In the cool, dark brewhouse, the rich aroma of barley malt filled the air, with the cheery trickle of the brook that carried the brew water. Åsa took the brew stick from its hook and stirred the ale, closing her eyes and chanting the magical words to bring the brew to life.

She had brewed with her mother in this hut over the stream since she was a child, first toddling as Halfdan did now, banging the wooden ladle against the vat. She did not remember when her play had become help, or when her mother had stepped back into a supporting role. What she did now was instinct. She knew how long to soak the sacks of barley grains in the brook, how long to dry them on the stretched linen, and when they needed to be stirred, as if she could see the tiny white leaf growing secretly inside the grains. She knew how long to boil the mash and when it was cool enough to stir with the brew stick that would turn the mash to ale. It was all second nature, just as she knew when Halfdan would sleep and when he would grow irritable.

"It will be a good batch," said Brenna, sipping the ale from the wooden ladle. She handed the ladle to Åsa, who put it to her lips appraisingly.

It *was* fine ale. It would be ready for the first winter nights drinking feast since her father's death.

"I hope there will be enough of it," Brenna went on.

"I hope there will be enough folk to drink it," Åsa countered.

Brenna pressed her lips together. Åsa knew it was a worry. The harvest had been spoiled by rain, but Hrolf's hoarded granaries held enough to see the few people left on the island through the winter. There was a good herd of cattle in the byres and plenty of hardy sheep and goats roaming the fields where they would forage through the winter.

Åsa watched her son gallop a toy horse Olvir had carved for

him across the floor. His gray eyes glowed with mischief. His dark hair, inherited from his grandmother, fell across his cheek in a glossy sheaf like a crow's wing. Already they were calling him Halfdan the Black. Yet she also saw something of her father and her brother Gyrd in his determined march on his sturdy legs, the confidence with which he reached for things. Even at sixteen months, she could see his mind working in his lively eyes.

When she was with him, a sense of calm came over her. A certainty. She would protect him. She would raise him up to be a great king. This she knew.

Åsa picked up her son. The ale had turned out well. They would make it through the coming winter. And she had the long darkness to plan, to find a way to deal with the enemies who would come in spring.

IT WAS SLAUGHTER MONTH, the time when, based on the amount of fodder they had gleaned, the healthiest cattle were selected to winter over in the byres while the rest were butchered. Most of the meat was salted and smoked for the winter, but plenty was kept aside for the winter feast, simmered in iron cauldrons over outdoor fires. The feast included fresh bread, root vegetables, apples and dried berries, and the winter ale.

Folk from the hinterlands began to arrive. They overflowed the guest houses and barracks into skin tents, and an informal market sprang up in the snow-covered fields as they traded soapstone and smelted iron they had brought for barley, dried meat, and fish to see them through the winter. They also brought with them complaints against their neighbors and other cases to be settled at a public gathering, for this was the first assembly they had attended since King Harald's murder. During the year of terror when Tromøy had fallen under Hrolf's rule, the back-country folk had stayed hidden away.

Tonight Åsa would feast with her people. She scanned their ranks as they crowded in the door. Many of them had been present at her oathtaking, but she recognized a few faces that had been absent. Now they came for justice.

She took her seat as Heid brought the ale horn to her. Åsa blessed the ale and drank to the god Frey for peace and plenty, giving thanks for the harvest. Heid, followed by three acolytes bearing wooden buckets brimming with the winter ale, carried the horn around to the folk crowded inside the hall and those who gathered outside the door.

When all had partaken of the ale, the meal was served. Afterward, flyting contests of good-natured insults degenerated into wrestling matches.

Åsa retired early to her bower with Halfdan and Heid. Tomorrow would be her first day sitting in judgement. She had done so in Borre, but this was the first time she'd taken her father's place. She lay awake beneath the comforter, fretting. Could she measure up to Harald? The thought of sitting in his place, all eyes upon her, made her insides turned to water. Tromøy had no lawspeaker. Harald had always known the law better than anyone.

She could not avoid it. She must do her duty as best she could. Lying awake worrying would not help her. She owed her people a clear head.

Resolutely, she focused on Halfdan's even breathing. She matched his breath, imagining that her mind was as unburdened as her child's.

Sleep must have come, for the next thing she knew, Brenna was rousing her. She dressed in her best wool gown, topped with a thick cloak pinned with a silver brooch.

After breakfast, two men carried the high seat to the top of her father's mound. Åsa mounted the hill and assumed her place, bundled in furs against the light snowfall. From here she looked out over the steading and all the people gathered. She thought of her vigil here when she had become part of the land. The knowledge of the land rose up in her, she felt the spirits beside her, and she knew she could fill her father's place.

The first case was introduced. A woman stepped in front of the assembly and stated her name. "I declare myself divorced from this man, Anselm Björnson." She pointed to a man who stood in the front of the crowd. "I reclaim my dowry from him."

She gave no reason, for it was not considered the business of the assembly. Her desire to separate, declared before the people, was all that was required. Her husband stood silent. Åsa suspected the reason for his wife's dissatisfaction was a source of embarrassment to him and did not press matters.

Now that the divorce was official, the husband was required to return the woman's dowry before witnesses. He paid it out in silver with a dour look on his face, but still he said nothing. He obviously did not want to provoke his ex-wife to comment.

In the next case, two couples stepped forward and stated their names.

One of the men spoke. "My ox wandered onto my neighbor's property and trampled their son." His voice broke as the bereft mother stifled a sob.

Åsa's chest tightened, and a blade of fear pierced her. It could happen to any child, even one so protected as Halfdan. But she bit back her fear and hurried to set the weregild. This should not be drawn out any longer than necessary, for both parties were suffering.

"How old was the boy?" Åsa asked.

"My son had seven winters," the father said, his voice cracking as his wife muffled her sobs on his shoulder.

So hard to keep a child alive through seven winters, only to lose him this way. Åsa steadied her own voice. "A boy of seven is worth twenty ounces of silver." She turned to the ox's owner. "Can you pay?"

"I can." He weighed the hack-silver onto the scales, then turned to the bereft parents as his own wife wept. "He was a good boy. I wish I had killed that ox before it ever came near him."

The neighbors departed together in silence, heads bowed.

Two men came before the assembly, casting angry looks at each other.

"State your names and your business," Åsa said in a clear voice.

"My name is Alm Atlison, and this man has claimed part of my ancestral land."

The other man glowered at Alm. "My name is Bjarni Grimson, and the land he speaks of has been in my family for three generations."

Åsa sighed. Such disputes were common when fields were plowed or trees felled. "Can either of you prove your claim?"

"I have markers," said Alm.

"As do I," said Bjarni. Folk began to murmur. This meant that at some point both families had claimed the same land, unbeknownst to each other, perhaps for generations, until these two sons discovered the discrepancy.

"Do you have witnesses?" Åsa asked. The two men glared at each other but shook their heads. The voices in the crowd grew more excited. This was getting interesting.

"It seems that you both have claims to the same property. How do you propose to settle this?" she asked.

"We wish to resolve it by combat," said Alm.

A cheer broke out in the crowd.

"Are you both agreed to this solution?"

The two men nodded grimly.

"Very well. Take your places within the combat ground."

The assembly gathered around the arena, marked by hide

ropes stretched between hazel poles. Åsa had a bird's eye view of the combat from her seat atop the mound, and she would judge the match. The fight would be called on first blood or if one combatant went out of bounds.

Heid blessed the arena, and the adversaries stepped inside. They were two doughty farmers, both young and broad of shoulder. Their seconds stood outside the ring with their weapons, in this case axes, and the three shields allowed each man.

The two men accepted their axes and first shields from their seconds as bets were taken. They turned to face each other.

"Are you ready?" Åsa demanded.

"We are," the opponents said in unison.

"Let combat begin!"

The onlookers cheered while the two men advanced on each other, axes raised. They hacked at each other, taking the blows on their shields until Alm's shield hung in shreds. Bjarni waited while he took his second shield. Alm stormed back into combat with such fury that he forced his opponent off balance. To keep to his feet, Bjarni planted one foot outside the rawhide ropes, going out of bounds, thereby forfeiting the match. The crowd cheered and groaned, depending on how they'd bet.

Åsa declared Alm the winner. Boundaries would be rectified before witnesses. The crowd cheered and silver changed hands.

By then the day was done and it was time for more feasting. Åsa descended from the mound, her feet numb from the cold. She took the proffered seat before the fire gratefully, accepting a cup of mead.

"You are wise, like your father," said the farmer next to her.

The mead slid down her throat and settled warm inside her chest.

Agder Forest

A ONE-EYED WOLF made his way through the forest, birds and squirrels scattering before him. Under the full moon's light, bare tree branches cast a skein of blue shadows across the snow.

The wolf arrived at the rotted stump of a huge ash tree and flung himself gratefully to the ground, where he lay panting.

Presently, a cry split the air and a winged shadow crossed the snow. A white gyrfalcon lit on the stump.

The two creatures remained motionless as the air shimmered. Their hugr flowed out to manifest in the forms of two men, wavering and translucent.

"Glad to see you survived," said Hrafn. "When the old witch couldn't find your body, I had my doubts."

Hrolf's visage wavered as he chuckled. "When I saw which way the battle was going, I hid my hamr in a place no one would ever find."

"Clever of you." Hrafn cocked an eyebrow. Behind him, the old wolf dozed. One ear twitched at the sound of the sorcerer's voice. "Why could the owl not track you?"

Hrolf grinned. "Because I left no trail."

Hrafn's eyes widened. "I'm impressed! You have become a greater student than I had hoped."

"I've done all right," said Hrolf dismissively. He gazed at the gyrfalcon as it preened itself. "Now, about the girl. She said her father would pay well to get her back."

"Find him, and we will have wealth to share."

"You are prepared to do your part, old man?" Though Hrolf's voice was thin, the doubt in it came through.

"I have my plans." Hrafn rubbed ethereal hands in glee.

Hrolf's stare bored into the old man. "I want Åsa and Tromøy."

Hrafn flashed him a mocking smile. "And your brother?"

"If I take Åsa, that should lure him down from Vestfold."

Hrolf's voice strengthened, gaining nearly its full volume. From its perch, the falcon's head swiveled toward the sound. "Then I will kill him."

"What of Åsa's son?" Hrafn asked. "He is Gudrød's legitimate son. His claim to both Tromøy and Vestfold is far greater than yours."

Hrolf shrugged. "Infants die all the time."

"They do, indeed." In his nest in the snow, the old wolf woke and shook himself. It was time to go. "We will meet again when the moon is next full."

"Very well. Until then." The men's shapes wavered and flowed into the waiting wolf and gyrfalcon.

# CHAPTER 9

Tromøy
December, AD 820

As Jól drew near, Åsa decided to take advantage of a break in the weather to journey to Skiringssal's winter market and trade some of the extra soapstone pots and smelted iron from the hinterlands for other things Tromøy needed. Even better, she relished the thought of seeing Olaf in person. She left Jarl Borg in charge. On impulse she invited Ragnhild, thinking the girl would enjoy a visit to the trading port.

At dawn the stablemen loaded working sledges with trade goods. Åsa and Heid's sleighs were outfitted with furs and provisions for the day-long journey. The horses were hitched up, shod with crampons to help them grip the snow, and the party set off for the ferry landing. Åsa and Heid drove their sleighs, escorted by Olvir and a small party of mounted men. Halfdan, bundled in furs, rode between Åsa and Brenna. His eyes sparkled, taking in every sight. Scorning the sleighs,

Ragnhild rode with the warriors, surrounded by her sworn men.

At the landing, they coaxed the horses onto the flat raft that waited to ferry them across to the mainland. The warriors urged their mounts onto the planks, setting an example for those hitched to the sleighs. Åsa's well-trained horses mounted the boarding plank without hesitation and pulled her sledge aboard, while Heid's horses balked until Olvir led her.

Finally, all the horses and sledges were loaded, and the warriors poled the boat across the narrow waterway to the mainland. The horses were eager to step foot on land, and when the ferry neared shore, they had to be held firmly to prevent them from bolting before the raft was made fast to the dock.

Once everyone had safely disembarked, the expedition set off north along the coast to Skiringssal. Settled in for the long ride, Åsa gave the reins to Brenna and burrowed into the furs to doze. Heid was right, she had not recovered sufficiently from all her night forays. The sledge's steady motion and the silvery jingle of the sleighbells lulled her to sleep. She slept through most of the journey, waking refreshed as twilight fell to see the settlement spreading out before her.

Skiringssal had grown since Olaf had taken it over the previous year. Smoke rose from two new guest houses built beside the great hall, and merchants' booths crowded the board-walk along the water's edge. Traders had arrived by sledge and ski from all directions for a lively winter market.

Åsa climbed out of the sledge, picked up Halfdan and carried him along the boardwalk. He squealed at the sight of booths brimming with colorful goods never seen in Tromøy. Åsa eyed the lengths of fine-spun wool and linen, dyed blue with woad and red with madder. Comb makers fashioned fine-toothed combs from reindeer antlers, and traders from the far north displayed thick winter furs and walrus tusks. A jeweler stocked beads of glass and amber next to a metalworker who offered mold-made dress brooches, trefoil cloak pins, and copper or silver charms of Valkyries and Thor's hammers.

The evening darkened quickly, and torchlight glimmered on the hillside as the welcoming party rode down from the great hall. Åsa's heart beat faster when she spotted Olaf's tall figure mounted on a gray horse. She watched him approach, his hair glinting in the torchlight. He wore a fine red wool cloak trimmed with winter ermine.

He smiled down at her from the saddle. "Welcome, lady. Please join me at the Shining Hall. Ale is freshly brewed, meat is cooking. I have plenty of room in my guesthouses for your party." His gaze made Åsa shiver in anticipation.

He broke into a smile when he saw Halfdan peek out from her skirts. "Ho, little brother. See what I have for you." He presented the boy with a tiny wooden shield, which Halfdan immediately seized. Producing his practice sword, he clashed the weapons together in affirmation.

Olaf laughed. "I see he is a warrior already."

*Can't you see he is your son?*

*Tell him. He deserves to know the truth. But would he use that knowledge to take over Tromøy? Would he try to take control? How can I trust him?*

*No, best to wait.*

As always, the legal implications crowded her mind. Halfdan, as Olaf's half-brother and second son of King Gudrød, was entitled to half of Gudrød's holdings. That right would be threatened if he was declared Olaf's bastard.

Olaf broke into her thoughts. "You must all be tired from your journey. Please refresh yourselves in the guest house, then join me for a feast."

Her gaze followed him as he turned his mount and headed back up the hill.

Åsa returned to her sledge and drove up the long trail to the Shining Hall. With its high roofs, every corner guarded by carved, silver-gilt dragon heads, it was Olaf's pride. The Danes had ousted his grandfather from this hall long ago and developed the trading port. Olaf had fought beside his father, Gudrød, to win Skiringssal back, and had inherited it on Gudrød's death, along with the hall at Borre.

Åsa scooped Halfdan from the sledge and followed Brenna to the guesthouse. She played with her son for a while before Ragnhild took over, entertaining the little boy by galloping a carved wooden horse across the floor.

Brenna had laid out the red gown for this evening. Åsa stripped off her traveling clothes and pulled on a linen shift, letting the light fabric float down her body. Brenna lifted the wool gown over Åsa's head and tugged the form-fitting bodice down over her breasts and hips, letting the skirt flare. Then she spun Åsa around to pull the laces tight.

Åsa sat patiently as Brenna combed out her long red-gold hair and caught it in a knot at the back of her head. Åsa donned calfskin ankle boots and pulled a finely woven wool shawl over her shoulders. She stepped out into the chill night and crossed the yard to the great hall.

Inside, the fire crackled, scenting the air with pine smoke. Whale oil lamps lit the great room and a low murmur of conversation rose from the benches. Heads turned as Åsa entered. She smiled and greeted those she knew as she joined Olaf in the high seat.

The elderly widow who kept house offered Olaf the ale horn with little grace. He took the horn and drank, then passed it to Åsa. She imbibed and handed it back to the widow, who lumbered off to the other guests. The old woman did her best, but Olaf needed a wife who would greet the guests with pride and honor his great hall with the proper rituals.

A prick of guilt speared Åsa. She should be that wife. Olaf had asked her many times. But it was not possible for her to abandon

Tromøy to live in Skiringssal. She shook off her doubts and got down to business.

"I have news," she said. "We discovered Hrolf's lair. His outlaws captured some travelers, and I came to know of it. I found where they were hidden." No one asked how Åsa came by her knowledge. Everyone knew the queen had special powers. "We hunted down the outlaws and killed them in their lair. Hrafn is my prisoner."

"And my brother?"

"I am sorry. Hrolf escaped. We searched, but could not find him. He is hiding somewhere. Hrafn swears he does not know where, and if he does, so far Heid has not been able to induce him to tell us. But we did rescue the travelers, and now I have four new warriors of great skill. One of them is training our women to fight. Lady Ragnhild, come forward."

Ragnhild stepped into the firelight. Brenna had dressed her in a pleated linen shift and a wool gown Åsa had given her. The blue wool was becoming on the brown-haired girl, making her look soft and pretty.

Olaf's eyes widened at the sight of her. "This little girl is a ferocious warrior?"

Ragnhild glared at him. "I could make you regret those words."

Åsa intervened. "King Olaf, allow me to present Lady Ragnhild, daughter of King Solvi of Rogaland. She may look like a gentle maiden now, but she arrived armed like a warrior, and that she is. She fought with the best of us, single-handedly freeing her men from Hrolf."

Olaf looked at the girl with new respect. "I beg your pardon, lady."

Ragnhild returned his gaze haughtily.

"She brings with her three sworn men," Åsa continued. "Allow me to present Einar, captain of Lady Ragnhild's guard, and the warriors Thorgeir and Svein."

The newcomers stepped forward and saluted Olaf.

Olaf smiled. "Welcome to my hall, all of you. Please feast and drink with us."

The ale made the rounds and the horn came back to Olaf. Servants distributed wooden cups to the guests and the drinking began in earnest.

Åsa turned to Olaf. "I am sorry that we failed to capture Hrolf."

His eyes gleamed and he bared his teeth in an uncharacteristically wolfish grin.

"I would have been disappointed if you had," he said. "Hrolf is mine." He rose from his high seat and lifted his horn, calling out to the company. "I congratulate the brave warriors of Tromøy for cleaning out that nest of outlaws."

The company raised their cups and drank to that. Olaf raised his horn once more. "I swear before the gods that I will kill Hrolf this year or die trying."

The warriors beat their wooden cups on the trestles in approval.

Olaf resumed his seat and leaned close to Åsa. "Meanwhile, we can spend some time together," he whispered in her ear.

Åsa smiled, feeling her color rise in anticipation. As the evening wore on and folk stumbled off to the guest houses, Åsa and Olaf slipped away to his bed chamber.

He pulled her close and ran his hands down her back, sending tingles up her spine.

"It's been too long," he breathed. She didn't answer, but drew his face to hers and kissed him, long and slow, tasting the ale and salt on his tongue. His familiar scent of sweat and leather lit the flame of her desire. He maneuvered her to the bed and brought her down with him. They burrowed under the eiderdown comforter, shivering, and snuggled close. Olaf reached over, pulling her into his heat.

After an hour of slow lovemaking, they lay in his bed, limbs entangled, bodies pressed together. His heart beat against her ribs.

"Marry me," he whispered into her hair. "Be my family. We can divide our time between the three kingdoms."

Her heart leaped, then fell back hard. Her hands began to tremble and her heart thumped erratically. She fought the urge to run.

As her husband, Olaf would have a right to Tromøy while he lived, and he would be King of Agder by virtue of marriage to its elected queen.

Panic rose in her at the thought of giving rights to Tromøy to any man, even Olaf. He had betrayed her once, leaving her at his father's mercy. True, he had been younger then and still under Gudrød's thumb. They had not yet grown as close then as they were now. But the memory loomed in her mind. Bile rose in her throat. She took a deep breath, trying to regain control as she cast about for an excuse.

"You know I cannot. I have put the Danes off for now. If I married you, they would attack."

"We fought them off before, together," he said.

"Yes, but we lost many men in that battle, and we have not recovered. We are too weak to meet the Danes. And Hrolf is still out there. We must wait. Come," she said, distracting him with a kiss. "We have so little time together. Please don't waste it."

Olaf sighed heavily. He gathered her into his arms and stroked her hair.

She kissed him again and laid her hand on his chest. Her trembling ceased as she caressed him, and she felt his muscles ease beneath her fingers. Her own heart slowed, her breathing calmed. For tonight, she and her people were safe in Olaf's keeping, and she could let down her guard for once. She shook her head to chase the conflicting thoughts away and let his kisses blur her worries. Their warm bodies seemed to melt together until she could not tell where she ended and he began.

They went as one into their dreams.

In the morning she roused his passion before he could make conversation. No sooner had they finished than the door burst open and Brenna came in, plopping Halfdan down on the bed. The little boy squealed with delight and hid his face in the comforter, peeking out at them and laughing. They roughhoused until Halfdan's laughter degenerated to a whine.

"He's hungry," said Åsa. They rose and dressed to join the others in the hall for morning porridge.

After breakfast, Åsa led her party down the trail to the market, where they unloaded the sledges and displayed the unworked soapstone and whetstones, bog iron, a selection of Ulf's finely made tools, and some weaving from Tromøy's women. Åsa bartered for furs and ivory from the far north, new antler combs with attached cases, glass and amber beads, and a piece of weaving in a pattern she had not seen before. The day passed in a daze, her heart simmering to be with Olaf once again.

Once they had traded all their goods, they trooped back to the hill, where another feast awaited.

When Åsa was seated and the ale horn had been passed, Olaf brought out a small oaken chest bound with brass. He fitted a small brass key in the lock and opened the lid to display cumin and mustard seeds, half a dozen walnuts, and an intricately crafted silver brooch, all nesting on a bed of silk.

Åsa felt tears spring in her eyes and for a moment she wondered what it would be like if she were Olaf's wife. After she had killed Gudrød, Olaf had put his own feelings aside and supported her claim to vengeance. But what feelings did he harbor deep within? Once she gave her power to him, would he use it against her?

There was no clear answer.

She put those thoughts from her mind, laughing at the stories and weeping at the songs as if she were a girl again, safe in her father's hall. As she shared a cup of mead with Olaf, her eyes kept straying to his lips, remembering them brushing her throat, nuzzling her ear.

Finally, as the merriment slowed and the last guest tottered off to the guest house, Åsa and Olaf stole into his chamber once more. Their clothes were on the floor before the door swung closed. Giggling, they dove under the down comforter and found each other with lips and hands. This time, Olaf made no mention of marriage.

In the morning, they rose early and strapped on wide hunting skis, with rough fur sewn to the bottom for traction. They set out before breakfast. The sun shone fiercely between the trees, casting deep blue shadows over snow that glittered with frost diamonds. The scent of pine needles stung her nose, and the cold air chapped her cheeks.

Skiing beside Olaf, a bubble of joy rose in Åsa. *Why not accept him? Why not tell him the truth about Halfdan? Wouldn't that make things right?* But in her heart she knew their kingdoms were too weak, their hold too tenuous for her to leave Tromøy without a strong ruler in residence.

And she still had not forgotten his betrayal. He'd done so much to make amends, but as hard as she tried to let it go, she could not trust him completely.

Silent on their skis, they sneaked up on some fine partridges. They raised their bows, their arrows snicked through the air, and each struck a bird. Before the rest of the flock had noticed anything was amiss, they each shot one more bird. After that, the birds scattered and they went forward to bag their prey.

As blue shadows lengthened on the snow, they made their way to the hall. They stopped in the kitchens to hand off their game birds to the cooks.

After another night of feasting, Olaf led her to his bed. She was acutely aware that this was their last night together—for who knew how long? Tomorrow she would take up the burden of queen again, but tonight she clung to him urgently, surrendering herself to pleasure.

The next morning Åsa woke early, her mind abuzz with arguments once more. Olaf was sleeping soundly. She slipped out of bed, dressed quietly, and made her way down to the shore. Her people were already busy loading the sleighs for the long journey home.

When they were nearly ready to leave, a shout drew their attention to Olaf, pulling a laden sledge down the trail from the hall. He arrived with a broad grin.

"You almost left without these," he said, throwing back the cover of an oaken chest. Inside, six iron ingots gleamed dully, each the size to make a sword. "They're for Ulf."

Åsa stared at the ingots. "Wootz steel," she breathed. The steel to make the best swords in the world, swords that held an edge, were strong, and never broke.

Olaf nodded, beaming with pride. "Björn brought them up the Itil River from Bolghar." Björn was a sea trader from Birka, who had purchased Olaf from Hrolf's henchmen in a slave market. Björn had taken Olaf on a trading expedition to the eastern lands, following the Itil River to the great Bolghar fur market. After Olaf saved Björn's life, the trader had freed him and given him a stake of furs to trade. In Bolghar, Olaf had traded with the caravans for the wootz steel, a mysterious product of the eastern lands, its manufacture a closely guarded secret. Its forging was also a secret, one that Ulf had learned a lifetime ago, when he'd been enslaved by a swordmaker in the Caliphate. Here in the North, Ulf alone knew how to forge wootz steel, but even he didn't know the secret of manufacturing the steel itself.

Each ingot was as rare as gold, and as valuable. Olvir loaded them onto Åsa's sledge, and she covered them with a tarp and made it fast. They set off down the coastal trail, Olaf skiing beside Åsa's sledge for awhile. When at last he turned back, she watched him go with stinging eyes.

Heid drew her sledge alongside Åsa's.

"You can't marry him. Neither one of you is strong enough. The Danes would slaughter you both."

"I know," said Åsa, fighting the tightness in her chest.

"And even if that were not the case, you should think carefully about giving your power to a man."

Heid shook the reins and pulled ahead, leaving Åsa to ponder her words.

Skiringssal

A WEEK PASSED, and another visitor arrived in Skiringssal. With a broad smile on his face, Olaf greeted the sledge driven by the skáld Knut.

"Greetings, Knut," he said.

"Greetings to you, King Olaf." The old skáld stepped nimbly out of the sledge and clapped his former student in an embrace. "You've fulfilled all the promise I saw in you as a lad."

Olaf's smile broadened at his tutor's words. After the death of Olaf's mother, Knut had been the lonely boy's only friend in Gudrød's rough and tumble household.

"Come to the hall, I have refreshments awaiting you." Olaf led his old friend up the trail.

Knut looked appreciatively at the Shining Hall's high roofs, the carved dragons glittering in the sun. "It is a wonder."

Olaf beamed at the compliment as he conducted the skáld through the massive oaken doors to the high seat, where Knut sat looking at the tapestries and finely carved pillars as they waited for the ale horn to arrive. The wait drew out, and Olaf's smile began to sag a bit on his handsome face.

At length, the old widow who served Olaf trudged in with the silver-chased horn.

"Drink, Olaf King," she mumbled, sloshing the contents as she handed it up to her lord.

Ignoring the woman's clumsiness, Olaf took the horn from her and drank, then offered it to his guest.

"How are things with you, lad?" Knut accepted the horn and lifted it to his lips, eyeing his protégé over the rim. "You have peace and prosperity, yet something is amiss."

Olaf didn't answer, just stared at the fire.

"So, tell me, what could possibly ail you? You're young, handsome, and wealthy. What more can you want?" The old man scrutinized his host, then smiled. "It's a woman, isn't it?"

Olaf shook his head ruefully. "You always could read my face like a line of runes. Åsa refuses to marry me."

Knut blew out a gust of air. "After what she's been through at the hands of men, I can't blame her." His stare pierced Olaf. "And you betrayed her when she had need of you."

Olaf stared at his hands, color rising in his face. "I was young then, and under my father's sway. I'm a different man now. I've sworn a thousand times that I would never betray her again."

"Yet I can understand why she doesn't trust you." The skáld eased his accusatory stare a fraction. "Does she have other reasons?"

"She holds the Danes at bay with the prospect of marriage to one of the brother-kings. She claims that Tromøy and even Vestfold would fall prey to them if she married me."

Knut nodded. "She is right. This possibility of marriage is the only leverage she has over them to buy time while you and she gain strength." The skáld stared into the firelight, considering. After a long pause, he took a breath. "What if you chose another wife?"

Olaf stiffened. "I don't want anyone else. I only want her. You know I am the right man for her, and uniting our kingdoms is the best course of action. I have tried every way of persuading her."

"Åsa needs breathing space, room to maneuver. Your constant pressure does neither of you any good. Yet you need a wife, and Skiringssal needs a queen. There are any number of young women of suitable birth who would gladly marry the King of Vestfold."

"I'd lose Åsa forever. I couldn't survive that."

"You say that now, but you are young. You would survive, and you'd forget in time."

"I don't want to forget."

Knut sighed and quaffed his ale. "Unhappiness seems to be the choice of the young."

# CHAPTER 10

Tromøy
December, AD 820

Asa held council in the hall with the experienced warriors of her hird, making plans to defend against the attacks that were sure to come in spring.

"If only there were a way to stop the ships from entering the harbor," said Einar.

"What if we made a barrier?" said Åsa.

"There are trading ports with stakes under the water, blocking their harbors," offered Olvir.

"It would take us years to sink that many stakes," objected Einar. "We don't have the manpower to accomplish such a thing before spring."

"What about a log boom—lashed with ropes, strung across the narrowest part of our harbor?" said Åsa. "We could manage that."

"The attackers will be able to cut the ropes," said Olvir.

"True," she replied, thinking, "but it will hold them in arrow range while they do. If we had archers stationed on shore by the boom, they could pick off the enemy, whittling down their numbers and buying us more time to assemble our forces."

"That might just work," said Jarl Borg, settling the discussion.

In the morning, Åsa deployed men to fell the trees they needed. Ulf forged sturdy ring bolts so that the logs could be lashed together. Once assembled, the log boom lay on the shore, ready to be deployed at a moment's notice.

Snow fell, gradually covering the logs with a white blanket.

Jól came and went, and the weaving season began. The looms were brought in and nailed to the bower walls, and soon the air reverberated with women's voices raised in chants as they wove the magical patterns. Though Åsa insisted the women spend time training at arms, the necessity of producing cloth took precedence.

Ragnhild refused to take any part in it, and Åsa let her have her way, remembering how she herself had once hated weaving before the enchantment of the loom came upon her.

Each morning, regardless of the weather, the girl strapped on her skis and set out with her bow. While many hunters came back empty-handed, Ragnhild kept the hall supplied with hare, grouse, ducks, and the occasional red deer. The meat was welcome this time of year, when the stores were running low and hunger was a familiar companion.

The winter storms had moderated and a stretch of fair, sunny days descended over the island. The women's chatter and the smoky, stifling bower began to close in on Åsa. She envied Ragnhild's freedom. One morning she strapped on her skis, offered her leather-clad shoulder to Stormrider, and escaped to the crisp air of the silent woods. Her dog, Flekk, romped at her side.

She sighted Ragnhild and put on a burst of speed to catch up. The shield-maiden whirled as she approached, startled.

Åsa took a deep breath of the crisp winter air. "I used to hate wasting the winter days in the bower. And my mother always let me go." Her throat tightened at the memory, stopping the words.

"Mine too," said Ragnhild. Then she fell mute too. Åsa wondered about Ragnhild's mother but decided not to intrude on the girl's thoughts. They skied on in companionable silence.

Åsa began to spot familiar landmarks. "Follow me." Ragnhild fell in behind her as she laced her way through the trees.

The winter sunlight glinted on iced branches, weaving delicate blue shadows across the snow. It had been a long time, but the forest had not changed. Each tree stood just where it belonged. Squirrels scampered through the branches as their forefathers had, pausing to look at Åsa as if in recognition.

"This is where I hunted with my brother," she said, and again her throat tightened. She could say no more and moved on.

"I used to hunt with my brothers too," said Ragnhild.

The snowbound forest's hush seemed to discourage speech. As they skied on, the trees gradually thinned, until they broke into an open field of brilliant white.

Åsa saw the hare's ear twitch an instant before it melted invisibly back into the snow. Stormrider roused, then launched herself into the broad blue sky, tugging at Åsa's spirit to follow. The falcon hovered an instant, locating her prey, then folded her wings and plummeted from the sky, striking what looked like a snowdrift until a spot of red bloomed. The two women hissed forward on their skis. Åsa pulled a piece of quail breast from her satchel. She laid it on her glove and lured the falcon from the kill. As Stormrider feasted on the meat, Åsa carefully lifted the falcon to its place on her shoulder while Ragnhild bagged the hare.

The shield-maiden glanced up at the sky, which had turned leaden while they hunted. "Smells like snow."

Åsa sniffed the air and nodded. "We'd best be getting back."

Soft flakes were drifting down as they arrived at the hall, doffing their furs and skis in the entryway before entering the main room. The warriors were gathered on their benches around the longfire, mending harnesses and sharpening blades while they joked. They all looked up when Åsa and Ragnhild burst in and rose as one to hail their queen.

Åsa smiled as she took her high seat, Stormrider lofting to her perch on the chair's carved post while Ragnhild joined the warriors on the benches. They admired the hare she pulled from her leather bag. Ragnhild took out her knife and began to skin it.

Åsa called for ale. Brenna brought in Halfdan, and Åsa took him on her lap. The fire's crackle and the men's low voices gave the hall a soothing air, taking her back to the days of her father's rule. She could almost see his red beard from the corner of her eye. If she squinted, a fair head among the húskarlar might be Gyrd's.

She let the illusion linger while she sipped her ale, the memory of evenings like this with her father and brother warming her through the winter's bitter chill.

By morning the weather had cleared again, and the new snow sparkled under a vivid blue sky. Åsa, Stormrider ever present on her shoulder, brought her skis into the yard where Ragnhild waited with the game sledge.

"I hope you don't mind some extra company," Åsa said.

Ragnhild gave her a quizzical look.

"He might slow us down," Åsa warned.

Brenna burst out of the bower leading Halfdan, so swaddled in furs he looked more like a bear cub than a boy. When he saw Åsa he broke into a grin and ran into her open arms. She swooped him up and strapped him onto the sledge. The little boy's eyes sparkled out from the furs as he peered about in wonder. Ragnhild gripped the lead rope and set off on her skis, singing a hunting song. Halfdan shrieked with delight.

They found the branch-marked trail under the new snow. Åsa skied alongside Ragnhild, taking hold of the rope to help drag the sledge through the heavier drifts. A vision came of her own mother pulling her on this same sledge, singing the same song. Tears rose in her eyes, but the winter air dried them before they could fall.

When they reached the meadow, Åsa unstrapped Halfdan from the sledge and let him trot circles in the snow, burbling to himself a wordless rendition of Ragnhild's song. Åsa released Stormrider. Halfdan halted in his ring and stared as the falcon launched from her fist in a flurry.

Flekk flushed a flock of grouse, and Stormrider, circling high above, folded her wings and dove. Halfdan watched the falcon with rapt attention, head forward, arms tight to his sides. As Stormrider struck her prey, the boy let out a shrill of triumph.

Halfdan trailed after Åsa as she retrieved the falcon from her kill, rewarding Stormrider with choice tidbits of quail. *Soon my son will be ready for a falcon of his own. A young king in the making.*

Hunting was good that day, and they returned to the hall with a hare and a brace of quail in addition to the grouse. As Åsa sat down to pluck her field-dressed quarry, Heid stormed up to her.

"That old goat! I can't stand another day of him." The völva gestured toward Hrafn, who sat muttering in his corner. The old sorcerer never ventured out in the cold or even moved from his spot. Åsa thought the will had gone out of him.

"Would you have me turn him out in the middle of winter?"

Heid scowled but said nothing. Even the worst guest was kept on through the winter.

"Surely you can put up with a harmless old man until spring," Åsa reasoned.

"Old he may be, but he's far from harmless," the sorceress grumbled.

"What harm has he done? All he seems to do is sit by the fire all day, muttering."

Heid glared at the old sorcerer. "He's turned your head, for starters."

"Don't be silly. I pay no attention to him."

"That's what he'd like you to believe. But he has insidious ways. He has infiltrated your mind far more than you realize."

"And how do you know this?" Åsa turned on the sorceress. "Do you have firsthand experience of infiltrating minds?"

Heid made no reply to this. She stomped off, muttering under her breath.

~

ULF'S old wounds pained him in the cold, keeping him by his forge. He was still able to swing a hammer, although he let Bram take over the everyday work more and more.

Before him lay the six precious ingots of wootz steel that Åsa had brought. These would be forged by him alone. He had learned the secret of forging this steel long ago, on a journey to the East with Åsa's father. Ulf had been captured in battle and enslaved to a Persian swordsmith. The Persian had no fear of his slaves learning his secret methods, for he invariably worked them into their graves. But Harald had rescued Ulf, though the smith's injuries had left him crippled and unable to fight. When Ulf returned home, he used the skills he had learned from his Persian master to become the greatest blacksmith in the North.

Ulf picked up his tongs, gripped one of the precious ingots, and thrust it into the fire. His apprentice Bram trod the foot bellows ceaselessly, keeping his eye on his master for signals to tell him when to increase his efforts and when to slack to keep the furnace at just the right temperature. A new boy named Odd ran back and forth, feeding the fire with charcoal, while Ulf kept a close watch as the metal glowed dully, the red brightening into orange. He would never forget how to forge wootz. His cruel master had beaten the knowledge into him indelibly.

Ulf pulled the ingot from the furnace and laid it on the anvil. He gingerly hammered the precious metal just a few light blows before returning it to the furnace to heat again. Judging the temperature of the steel by its color, he quickly pulled it out and forged the metal a little more until it cooled. Patiently he drew the egg-shaped ingot out, flattening and lengthening it, folding it back on itself time and again to form the watered silk pattern as the Persian had taught him. Back and forth for two days, the crucible steel made countless trips from furnace to anvil as Ulf coaxed the lump of metal into the shape of a sword.

After days of forging, the sword had been drawn out to its full length and shape. Ulf chiseled runes into the steel and inlaid them with iron, which he heat-set in the furnace.

He began the laborious work of grinding off the excess metal to give the sword its final polish, then etched it in vinegar to reveal the watered silk pattern.

When the blade shone and the patterned steel undulated in the firelight, Ulf fitted the tang with a flat metal guard and a three-lobed pommel bound with silver wire, then riveted on a grip of oak, carving it with protective runes.

Ulf hefted the finished sword, blade gleaming in the forge's light. It was as fine a sword as Gudrød's Bane. He sent Bram running to fetch Åsa.

Her hurried steps sounded, and she ducked through the low doorway of the smithy. Ulf stood by the forge, holding the sword out to her hilt first.

When she saw him, she slowed her pace and approached. Gaze fixed on the blade, she put her hand on the pommel. Ulf released it into her grip and stepped back.

Eyes sparkling, she swept it whistling through the air. "It is so much lighter than a pattern-welded sword," she said. "The balance is perfect. It will be a much better weapon for a shield-maiden to wield." Ulf bowed his head at her praise.

She smiled at him. "Did you ever think we would see this day?" Tears glittered in her eyes, and Ulf felt a sympathetic moisture rise in his own eyes. "Back in your own smithy on Tromøy at last."

"Lady, I had faith in you."

"How could you believe in me? I was a young fool."

"You were Redbeard's daughter."

"And I was the death of him." The tears were flowing freely now.

"Hush," Ulf said softly, pulling her into his arms as he had when she was a child. He stroked her hair and let her cry.

When her weeping stilled, Ulf put his hand under her chin and raised her face to his. "He does not blame you. It was his fate, his and your brother's. You could not have prevented his death, and you did not cause it."

"But if I had agreed to the marriage...become a peace-weaver instead of a defiant brat..."

"Nay, your sacrifice would not have brought peace. Old Gudrød was looking for a reason to take his helping of cold revenge on your father for winning your mother from him years ago. And he wanted your father's lands. He would have murdered Redbeard one way or another, and Gyrd too since he was next in line."

With relief, he watched her features calm. He prayed that she believed it, for he believed it fervently. Redbeard would never have wanted her to feel responsible.

ÅSA BROUGHT the sword to the practice field and called Ragnhild.

"Try it," Åsa said, placing it in her hands.

Ragnhild slashed the sword through the air, and her eyes widened. "It's so light! And I have never felt such balance in a blade."

"There are very few like it," said Åsa. "It is yours."

Ragnhild turned to her with eyes full of wonder. "Why me, lady?"

Åsa smiled. "I believe that none could use it better. You are my smallest warrior, but also my fiercest. This blade will level the field when you fight men who are bigger than you. What will you call it?"

Ragnhild considered the shining blade. "A sword like this must have a special name. I don't want to give it a name of death and terror." She thought for a moment, then said, "I will call it Lady's Servant."

A clever name. It honored Åsa, but at the same time dedicated the sword to the goddess Freyja, whose name meant *lady.*

Åsa hid her pleasure with a stern look. "A good name. Use it well. I expect great things of you."

The girl turned to her, eyes glowing. "I hope that I can live up to your expectations, lady. I would gladly give my life for you."

*Do I really deserve this girl's devotion?* "Let's hope it never comes to that," Åsa said gruffly.

She left Ragnhild staring at the play of light and shadow on the blade.

# CHAPTER 11

Hrafn sat in his corner near the longfire, cackling as he chewed his meat. The once terrifying berserker seemed to have degenerated into a harmless old man, and Åsa was strangely saddened to see him lose that spark.

Heid bent grudgingly to fill his ale cup. "I don't know why our lady feeds you, you worthless old fool."

Åsa smiled into her cup. The sorceress was accustomed to being feared by all and she didn't like sharing her turf with Hrafn.

"Our lady couldn't get along without me," Hrafn answered, grinning his gap-toothed grin.

"Bah," said Heid. "What do you do for her that I can't do a hundred times better?"

"I'm a man," Hrafn leered.

Åsa choked on her ale.

"That's like calling an earthworm a dragon!" Heid returned.

The warriors looked up from their cups, eager to hear a flyting match between the two sorcerers.

Hrafn rose from his nest of reeking furs and struck a pose, a parody of a warrior. "You and I are both getting older, but you must admit that when we were younger, you longed for me."

Heid snorted ale through her nose. "It was you who longed for me, like every man in those days."

"Or so you thought. You wonder why I never sought you out. You believed you were Freyja's gift to man. Yet those who took you did it out of pity."

A groan from the húskarlar told Åsa that Hrafn had scored.

"If you had sought me, I would have sent you packing."

"You could never have resisted me, no woman could in those days. I had the charm of Frey."

"You had the charm of Loki."

Hrafn smiled. "Loki is the most charming of gods."

"The charm of Loki when he took the form of a pregnant mare," Heid finished in triumph. The raucous laughter in the hall declared her winner of this match with her clever reference to the well-known tale of Loki's shame. Hrafn's pale skin reddened and his single eye glowered. There was no worse slur to manhood than accusing him of giving birth.

The húskarlar demanded that Knut tell the story. The old skáld, recently arrived from Skiringssal, rose from his place of honor. He stepped into the firelight and began the popular tale.

"When the gods were building their halls, a builder came to them and offered to erect a palisade around Asgaard that would withstand the giants. But his price for this wall was the sun, the moon, and the goddess Freyja to wife.

"The gods wanted the palisade, but they had no intention of paying the price. They countered by stipulating that the builder must complete the work by the end of winter, with the help of no man. The builder agreed to their terms, but asked to use his stallion, Svadilfari, to help him. As Loki pointed out, there was no restriction on horses, and so the gods allowed the request."

Everyone groaned at this, knowing it was a mistake and what would come of it.

"The horse proved to be remarkably strong, and the palisade went up quickly. Three days before the end of winter, it looked as if the builder would complete his task and the gods would have to pay his price. They were furious, and they agreed that it was Loki's fault. They threatened the trickster god with a horrible death if he could not prevent the builder's success.

"The night before the deadline, a mare in heat ran out of the woods. Svadilfari immediately gave chase. The two horses ran through the forest all night, and in the morning the palisade was unfinished. The gods then discovered that the builder was a giant in disguise, and they summoned Thor to smash their enemy with his magical hammer, Mjölnir."

The húskarlar cheered at this. Thor was their favorite god, and they loved it when he smashed things.

"Svadilfari must have caught the mare at some point during that night, because several months later, Loki the shapeshifter gave birth to Sleipnir, the eight-legged horse that became Odin's steed."

Even though they knew the story well, the húskarlar roared with laughter when the shapeshifter Loki was caught in his own ruse. Heid looked smug. But Åsa noticed Hrafn staring at the sorceress with his single eye in a way that sent a chill down her spine. She would not like to be the target of the old sorcerer's ill will. But then, she wouldn't like to rouse Heid's anger either.

TWO MORNINGS LATER, Åsa woke to see Heid's face looking swollen and red.

"What's wrong?" Åsa squinted at her in the firelight. "You look like you rubbed your face with poison oak. But where would you find that in the dead of winter?"

The sorceress's hands flew to her red cheeks, touching the

rash. She seized her pillow. It crackled with dry leaves, and she found a hole where the leaves had been shoved in.

"It *is* poison oak. There's only one place this could have come from." Heid stomped over to the shelf where she kept her supply of dried herbs and took down a wooden box. She opened the lid and turned the box upside down. "Empty."

Åsa's eyes widened. "Someone came in here and raided your stores? Who would dare to do such a thing?"

"Only one I can think of." Heid shook the pillow wrathfully. "This will have to be burned." She stormed out of the bower, across the yard, and into the hall. Åsa trailed her, guts in a knot.

Hrafn sat in his usual spot by the fire, alone. The húskarlar were out hunting, chopping wood, or tending the livestock in their byres.

"Heid, you're red in the face. Did you do something to embarrass yourself?" he chortled.

"Not as red as the inside of your lungs are going to be," the völva retorted, throwing her pillow onto the fire. She turned on her heel and strode out as the toxic smoke filled the hall.

"You evil witch!" Hrafn cried as he scrambled up from his furs and scurried outside. He stood coughing and shivering in the snow. "I'll get revenge!" he choked, his voice like a rusty hinge.

Heid turned at the bower door and gave him a smile that would liquefy iron. "I wish you luck!"

Åsa didn't want to interfere, but now the hall was filled with poisonous smoke. She called a servant and said, "Keep the doors open, and see that no one enters the hall until the fire has burned down and the smoke has cleared out."

"Lady, where am I supposed to go? You can't leave an old man shivering in the cold," Hrafn whined.

"You have only yourself to blame, Hrafn. You shouldn't anger the völva."

"Pah!" spat Hrafn. "The day I'm afraid of that old wench is the day I'll tie on my Hel-shoes and take the road to Nifleheim."

In spite of the fire in his single eye, the old man was shivering in his rags, and his lips were turning blue. From the look of him he might soon truly visit the goddess of death.

"Let's go to the smithy," Åsa said, "and see if Ulf will give you a place by the forge."

She took the old sorcerer's skinny arm and steered him to the smithy. It lay at the outer edges of the steading, far enough from the dwellings to keep the noise, smell, and fire hazard to a minimum.

Ulf was making a blade from one of the precious wootz ingots. Åsa watched a few minutes, fascinated as always, while he heated and forged the metal.

The smith looked up from his work and set down his hammer with a welcoming smile. "Greetings, my lady." He scrutinized Hrafn for a moment before giving him a nod. The old sorcerer sniffed.

"Hrafn has been smoked out of the hall, and I wondered if he could stay with you for a while?"

"Certainly, I can always use another pair of strong arms." Ulf grinned, regarding Hrafn's scrawny wrists. "Can you swing a hammer, man?"

"I'll swing more than a hammer," Hrafn muttered.

Ulf shot Åsa a wry look, and she shrugged helplessly. "It's a long story," she said.

Hrafn craned his neck to examine Ulf's runes carved on the sword pommel. "If you add the *Isa* rune, it will add up to nine," he observed.

Ulf leaned over to look at his bindrune. "Why, so it would." Ulf picked up the pommel and inscribed the rune for ice. "It still reads well," he said, holding up the new inscription.

Soon Hrafn and Ulf were deeply engrossed in an esoteric

discussion of the uses of bindrunes, and Åsa crept away with a smile.

~

AFTER THAT, Hrafn spent his days in the smithy. Åsa hoped this would bring some peace to the hall, but this was not to be.

"It's dangerous, letting him meddle with Ulf's work," said Heid.

"Ulf seems to enjoy the company."

"That's what worries me. Who knows what kind of mischief that old hack is up to?"

"Ulf is happy to have another runemaster to consult with."

Heid's eyes bulged. "I knew it!" she hissed and stormed off to the smithy. Åsa followed hastily, hoping to prevent too much damage.

Ulf and Hrafn were seated by the forge, heads together over a wooden sword grip that Hrafn was inscribing. Åsa couldn't hear what they were saying, but Heid stomped over and jerked the grip out of Hrafn's hand.

"Get out of here, you fiend!" she cried.

Ulf leaped up, shock on his features.

"You get out of here, you old busybody!" Hrafn said.

"You are meddling with the weaponry," Heid shouted. "You are fouling the runes."

Ulf started toward her, his face glowering red. "I think I know enough of runes that there is no danger of that."

"Don't trust him!" Heid cried. She held her ground for a moment, but in the face of Ulf's indignant onslaught, she backed out of the smithy.

Åsa turned to Ulf. "Sorry. I tried to stop her."

Ulf's color had started to fade. He took his seat by the forge and waved her away.

During the outburst, Hrafn had remained sitting by the forge, completely composed. Now he picked up the grip and turned back to carving as if nothing had happened.

Seeing the damage contained there, Åsa started after the sorceress. She caught up with her in the bower. "Why can't you just get along with him?"

Heid whirled on her. "He is dangerous. Don't you understand? He is manipulating you all, bending you to his will."

"You mean the way you did to me? To my father?" Åsa found she was shouting. "My father died. My brother died. And I killed Gudrød. Because of you! You wanted them dead, and you got what you wanted." Åsa was shaking with fury.

White-jawed, Heid bent to unlock a chest with an iron key that hung from her belt. Her hands trembled so much that she couldn't get the key into the lock. The sorceress stormed into the bower hall, bellowing for her apprentices. They leaped from their benches as Heid flung her keys at their feet.

"Pack my chests. Bring everything! We leave today."

Åsa followed as the völva strode out into the yard. "Ready my sledge," Heid growled at the stable hands. "Hitch up my horses."

Eyes wide, the stable lads scurried off to do the sorceress's bidding.

Åsa touched Heid's arm. "You don't have to leave."

Heid whirled on her. "Oh, that's where you're wrong. That old bastard has undermined me for the last time. I'll not stay where I'm not wanted, where my queen mistrusts my motives and insults me."

Her apprentices spilled out of the bower, lugging Heid's wooden chests. The stable lads hustled out of the stables leading the sorceress's fretting pair of matched white horses and hitched them to the völva's sledge.

Heid jerked her arm out of Åsa's grip and turned on the women as they scrambled to load the sledge. "Hurry up now, you stupid girls!"

She snatched up a bundle, threw it into her sledge, and

hoisted herself onto the seat, slapping away helping hands. Picking up the reins, she said, "You are on your own."

Åsa watched the völva set off in a swirl of snow, apprentices scrambling to don skis, gather their things, and follow.

A shadow of foreboding fell across her mind. Something was happening that she needed to understand. But something told her it was already too late.

~

Skiringssal

SLEIGHBELLS chimed as the völva's sledge pulled up before the Shining Hall. Olaf, alerted to her arrival by his lookouts, stood ready to greet her and her entourage.

Heid's apprentices clustered around the völva's sledge, digging her out from under layers of fur. They helped their mistress down and escorted her into the hall, where they settled her on the seat of honor with pillows and a lap robe.

The húskarlar gladly made room for the women along the benches, and old acquaintances were renewed while Olaf called for his finest mead.

Olaf took the drinking horn from the old widow and greeted Heid with the formal salutation. "Welcome, Wand Bearer." He drank and offered her the horn.

As the sorceress accepted the vessel, he noticed a tremor in her hand. When she had drunk, he asked, "To what do I owe the honor?"

Heid took another long sip of mead before she spoke. "That old wizard, Hrafn, is still at Tromøy."

This sounded like professional rivalry to Olaf. "What's wrong with that? He's just a harmless old man."

Sparks seemed to leap in the sorceress's eyes. "That's what

everyone calls him. Hrafn may be getting old, but he is far from harmless."

Olaf used his most soothing voice, hoping to calm her. "Why should Åsa fear him? He's come to her aid in the past."

"Yes, he has," Heid said grudgingly, "but that doesn't mean I trust him. First, he ingratiated himself with the húskarlar. Now he's wormed his way into the smithy, meddling with the weaponry."

"Meddling? How?"

The sorceress fixed him with a glare. "There is much a rune-master can do with weapons."

The first pang of worry pricked at Olaf. "And you left Åsa there with him?"

"I had little choice. The old man has driven me out."

*So it is rivalry,* Olaf thought with relief. And Heid had lost. He imagined her storming out into the cold, in the middle of winter, without a thought of shelter for herself or her women.

"I would welcome you and your ladies for the winter, of course," said Olaf.

"We shall be quite comfortable here," she said imperiously, quaffing her mead.

Tromøy

AFTER HEID'S DEPARTURE, peace settled over Tromøy. Hrafn continued to spend his time in the smithy, carving runes into the wooden hilts for the new swords Ulf forged from the wootz ingots. Ulf had given the rune carving entirely over to the old sorcerer. When Hrafn wasn't in the smithy, he was ingratiating himself with the warriors by telling tales of ancient battles and magic.

Åsa watched him with a pang of guilt, wondering if Heid's suspicions were only from jealousy. The old wizard had an easy charm that Heid did not possess. Where the men had always feared the völva, Hrafn gained their confidence, helping them with their problems and advising them.

Åsa found herself missing the völva. She laughed at Hrafn's jokes and enjoyed his stories, but there was something reassuring about the sorceress's manner that had gone with her when she left.

But Åsa had brought out things that could not be unsaid. Heid's manipulations had cost Åsa's father and brother their lives and led Åsa to kill Gudrød in revenge. Despite all the sorceress had done for her, Åsa could not forgive the death and destruction she had wrought.

It was good the witch was gone.

～

ULF WAS ROASTING a load of bog iron over an open charcoal fire, lecturing a rapt audience of Hrafn, Bram, and Odd.

"Before, I always forged bars of hard and soft metal together. But what if I melt them together in a crucible, mixing the hard and soft into one piece? If I am right this time, then I will be able to make swords for every warrior to equal those I made from the six ingots that Olaf gave me."

"That would give our lady a great advantage over her rivals," observed Hrafn.

Ulf nodded absently. "And King Olaf as well," he said. "If every warrior were armed with blades of wootz steel, they would be unbeatable."

When the iron cracked, Bram, newly muscled from months of heavy lifting, loaded it into a clay-lined smelting furnace charged with charcoal. Odd trod the foot bellows while the iron heated. The slag liquefied and ran out through the drain hole, leaving a lump of purified ore in the furnace.

After the ore had cooled, Bram tipped the gray lump onto the hard-packed earth of the smithy and beat off the remaining slag with a hammer. He raised his axe and split the iron. Ulf picked up one half, examined the quality of the metal, and nodded.

"The iron is pure."

"As pure as the wootz?" Hrafn asked.

"I hope so. I will only know when I forge it. Now we make it into steel."

Bram loaded the iron into a small ceramic crucible.

"Now," said Ulf, "we add a piece of harder, more brittle iron and heat the two kinds of metal until they are molten. If it works, we will have something like the wootz steel, hard and soft metal combined. It must heat over a low fire long enough for the two metals to liquefy and mix."

He banked the fire in the furnace, then returned the crucible and let it heat. They passed the time mending broken tools and weapons to keep their minds off what was forming in the crucible. After what seemed much longer than half a day, Ulf set aside the hay rake he was working on, picked up his tongs, and carefully lifted the crucible out of the furnace. He set it in a corner.

"When can we open it?" Bram's eyes gleamed with anticipation.

"It has to cool for at least three days." Ulf itched to crack it open too, but he knew that slow cooling was crucial. "If we open it and the molten metal cools too fast, it could crack. Then we would have to start all over again."

The workshop was oddly silent for the next three days while they went back to mending. Finally, the third day dawned. Ulf nodded to Bram, who grabbed his hammer. Hrafn had abandoned his carving to watch the boy smash his hammer down on the crucible. The clay vessel exploded, sending ceramic shards flying across the smithy.

Among the shards lay a lump of dull gray metal.

"It looks just like all the others," said Hrafn.

Bram shot him a deadly look. Ulf said nothing but picked up the ingot with his tongs. He examined it carefully before thrusting it into the furnace. "Now we will find out if I have succeeded in reproducing the wootz."

Back and forth from furnace to anvil, Ulf gradually forged the lump into a bar. Over the course of a week, Ulf drew the bar out until it was the length of a sword.

All the while, Hrafn watched from his seat by the forge.

Ulf formed the tang and shaped the blade, forging the fuller down the center. He returned it to the furnace for the final heating. When he pulled it from the fire, he held up a sword.

When the sword had cooled, he nodded to Bram, who eagerly took hold of the tang. He hacked the blade down hard on the anvil, over and over, making the smithy ring. When he was finished, he held it out to Ulf, who examined the blade minutely.

At last the smith smiled and clapped his assistant on the shoulder.

"It did not fracture on the anvil, and the blade is still sharp and smooth. I think we have succeeded at last."

Hrafn stared at the new blade, rubbing his chin.

# CHAPTER 12

Agder Forest
January, AD 821

The one-eyed wolf arrived at the ash tree's stump. The gyrfalcon swooped down silently and landed next to him. In a moment, their shimmering hugr formed into humans.

"I have located the girl's father," said Hrolf. "His hall is at Solbakk, in Rogaland."

Hrafn's seamed old face cracked into a grin. "Good, good, lad. So you are ready to bargain with him?"

Hrolf nodded. "He is greedy for the Irish treasure. I will get him to agree to my terms."

"And then once he trades the girl for the silver, we will relieve him of it." Hrafn rubbed his hands.

"Have you fulfilled your part, old man?"

"Tromøy has about seventy-five warriors, men and women. I have driven the old witch away. I've been waiting a long time to get the best of her." Hrafn's visage cackled. "Better yet, I have access to the smithy and have gained the smith's confidence. He has manufactured a special metal."

Hrolf's expression darkened. "Will this new metal cause me harm?"

Hrafn shook his head. "You are berserk. Without the witch and her charms, metal will not bite you. And I have taken precautions with the runes to make the new weapons fail."

"Good. With Solvi's warriors we should take Tromøy with ease."

"I would not underestimate Åsa," Hrafn warned. "She killed your father and led Borre's defense against the Danish fleet. And Olaf is her ally."

Hrolf smiled. "If we arrive by night and take them by surprise, we will overrun Tromøy before they can light the war beacons to summon aid. Even if they manage to get them lit, Olaf is a full day's sail away. We will take Tromøy, and when Olaf arrives, I will dispatch him. Then I will hold a wedding feast with Åsa, and declare myself King of Vestfold and Agder. Victory is certain."

"Victory is always the choice of Odin," Hrafn cautioned.

Hrolf glowered at his old mentor. "I leave it to you to gain his favor," he growled.

"Of course," Hrafn said hastily. "But you must remember that the Allfather is a trickster. Those he favors do not always gain victory in battle. Sometimes he chooses them for Valhöll."

"I expect to take my place among the Einherjar in good time," said Hrolf. "But not until I send my brother there before me and take his place as Lord of Vestfold."

Hrafn smiled at him uncertainly. "One more thing. Åsa plans to deploy a log boom across the harbor's entrance, with archers stationed on the shore to pick off invaders."

"Clever," Hrolf growled. "But now that we know about the plan, we'll be ready. Old man, make sure the gods favor us. And that the smith's weapons fail."

With that, his hugr dissolved into the gyrfalcon and took to the air.

Solbakk, Rogaland

KING SOLVI'S hall was larger than Tromøy's, a huge structure rivaling the great halls of Borre and Skiringssal. Hrolf stood before the high seat, his gaze darting about the shadows. The húskarlar who flanked the king bore the finest weaponry, their arms heavy with silver rings. Goldfoil glinted on the carved oaken pillars, and many shields hung on the walls. The benches were crowded with warriors and jarls.

Solvi glared down at him from the high seat. Hrolf took in the old king's fur-trimmed robe, the heavy gold buckle cinching his fine leather belt, the golden bands encircling his arms, and the thick gold torque about his neck. The mead cup before him on the board was of the finest Frankish glass.

"What brings you here?" Solvi demanded.

Hrolf met his glare and smiled. "I have seen your daughter."

Solvi leaned forward in his seat, the color rising in his face. "Where is the brat?"

"That will cost you." Hrolf kept his gaze engaged with his opponent's.

"Why would I pay you to tell me where that worthless girl is? All I want her for is to give her a good whipping."

"That's not what she told me. She said that an Irish king offered you her weight in silver."

King Solvi's eyes bulged in his red face.

Hrolf kept his voice smooth and reasonable. "It would seem

that a small reward should be forthcoming for such information."

"I am a poor man," Solvi declared. "We barely survive here."

The húskarlar who guarded Hrolf did not flinch at this statement. Hrolf looked pointedly at the king's golden torque. Then he smiled and bowed. "Well, then, I'll be on my way." He turned to leave.

Solvi was silent for so long, Hrolf began to think he was really going to let him go. A long journey for nothing. Still, it had been worth a try.

When Solvi finally spoke, it was like the creak of key in a rusty lock. "Wait. If you lead me to her, when the Irish king pays the bride price, I will give you a tenth part."

Hrolf halted but didn't turn around, not wanting the king to see his smile. "Half," he said. He firmed his expression into a scowl and turned to face the king. "Without me, you will have nothing at all."

Solvi's face went from red to purple. "A quarter."

Hrolf insolently mounted the platform and sat next to the king in the high seat. "I will guide your ships to her, and when we have taken her, I will take half of everything we capture, as well as a third of the bride price."

"Done." Solvi looked sour. "Where is she?"

"If I told you, lord, how would I be sure you would keep your end of the bargain?"

"You're clever. But the Irish king is a Christian," Solvi warned. "My daughter must be untouched when she is delivered to him. Christians are particular about such things."

"She was when I left her."

"How can you guarantee that she remains so?"

Hrolf grinned. "I have a man on the inside."

Solvi grinned back at him. "Then we will attack as soon as the winter storms clear. Meanwhile, please remain as my guest for the winter."

# CHAPTER 13

Tromøy
April, AD 821

The rigors of winter's final weeks passed. The folk of Tromøy put Starve Month behind them and welcomed Ostara, the Dawn Goddess, feasting on the first eggs of spring as day and night became equal in length and the fowl began laying again after the long winter darkness.

But as spring calmed the waters of the Skagerrak and warmed the land, foreboding grew in Åsa's heart. She put all Tromøy's inhabitants on the rigorous training schedule that had slackened during the winter months.

At night she often woke to find herself in Stormrider's body, patrolling the sea, half in dream and half awake. By day she was grim and silent, watching the southern horizon.

Ragnhild watched to the west.

It was Ragnhild's fear that came first, but it was Åsa who realized it. On a dark spring night, she drifted on the air currents in

Stormrider's body, more asleep than awake. The clouds parted on the sliver moon, and far below, oars flashed in the waves.

Her bird's heart beating fast, she swooped down for a closer look. Five dragons. She dared not get close enough to count the warriors, but their silhouettes crowded the ships. Fully manned, each ship could carry between thirty and forty warriors. The shields that lined the gunwales were painted with stripes of black and some dark color, maybe red, the same as Ragnhild's men bore on theirs.

King Solvi, come to claim his daughter.

As she hung on the breeze, a form flashed and threatened the stars. A white gyrfalcon. Recognition sent a spike of fear jolting down her spine.

Hrolf.

She wheeled and made for home before he could spot her.

Stormrider soared over Tromøy's settlement. She lit on the bower roof and hopped into the gable end, peering down on the body that lay prone on the bed. Åsa dove into her human form in a flurry, sending the bird out the smokehole. Driving her will into slack limbs, Åsa lurched out of bed.

Åsa staggered into the bower hall and found Ragnhild, sleeping among the women on the benches. She shook the girl awake.

"Your father is coming. He will land on our shores at dawn."

Ragnhild bolted up and grabbed her sword and spear as if she had been waiting for this. She pulled on her boots and threw a fur-lined cloak over her shoulders, then ducked out to wake the men. By then women were tumbling from their furs to light the oil lamps and coax the fire to life. The sustained drilling was apparent as they armed themselves quickly and in silence.

Åsa grabbed up her own weapons and led the women across the yard to the great hall where the men were assembling.

She assigned men to deploy the log boom across the narrowest part of Tromøy's harbor, and sent a dozen of her best archers to hide on the shore where they could pick the enemy off as they tried to break through the barrier. Then she sent a boy running to light the war beacons, summoning Olaf to their aid. Åsa whispered a prayer to the sea goddess, Ran, for a fair wind to bring him quickly. With a good breeze, his dragon ships could cover the distance in half a day. If Olaf's warriors had to row the entire way, it would take them a full day and night to get to Tromøy, and they would arrive exhausted. She was on her own.

Her warriors took up their positions outside the hall. Forty-three fighting men stood side by side with twenty armed women. Behind them a force of eighty elderly, lame, and children held spears, filling out the ranks.

They waited, silent through the last dark hour of the night.

As dawn lightened the sky, the enemy fleet ghosted into the bay on the morning breeze. Their striped sails filled the harbor, and the young warrior beside Åsa sucked in his breath.

"Steady," Jarl Borg said as the fleet neared the log boom.

The dragons' sails dropped in unison and oars ran out, stroking toward shore. There was a shout as they reached the barrier. Arrows flew from the trees, streaking toward the enemy.

But the enemy shields came up, faster than expected. There were a few screams as arrows found their marks, but far from the devastation Åsa had hoped to wreak.

The rising sun glinted off a blade that slashed into the water. Åsa's hopes plummeted as the log boom drifted apart. The oars flashed again and the dragons came on. She prayed the archers were already abandoning their ambush and heading back to the hall as planned.

The Tromøy forces watched in silence as the sleek hulls slid onto the beach and warriors vaulted over the sides, splashing ashore, spears and war axes bristling. The early light glinted on helms and shield bosses as they mustered on the beach.

Åsa shivered, remembering another pre-dawn attack two years before, the night Gudrød had killed her father and brother, burned the hall, and taken Åsa captive. Her heart stepped up its rhythm, her breathing shallowed, and fear burned through her veins.

"Let them come to us," Jarl Borg said. "They'll wear themselves out climbing the hill in their armor." His calm logic shook the panic from her mind. She squared her shoulders and watched.

The enemy horde flowed up the trail, sinuous as a serpent. Åsa felt the boy next to her shrink back involuntarily. She could smell his sweat. Bram, his name was. Ulf's lad, old enough to fight in the shield wall for the first time. She bumped her shoulder on his encouragingly.

"The Norns decide the hour of our death at the moment of our birth," she recited, loud enough for her warriors to hear. "We cannot change the time of our death, only the manner of it." They took up the chant with her. "Let us then die at our appointed time with honor, and speed to Asgaard to feast with the gods." She felt the lad beside her draw himself up and roll his shoulders back.

"Shield wall," Jarl Borg called in his strong, no-nonsense voice. The trained warriors clacked their shields into place, forming a protective wall in front of the common folk. Åsa prayed the archers had made it back.

The enemy closed in. As they came within earshot, their leader held up his gloved hand and the serpent clanked to a halt. He was a burly, grizzled warrior, his small eyes gleaming beneath an old-fashioned boar-crested helm. It stood out from the streamlined helms the other warriors wore. The boar singled him out as king, but it also made a statement. The crest was a hazard in battle, an easy handle for an opponent to grab. It warned that his battle skill was great enough to compensate.

Åsa swallowed and stepped forward, willing her words not to come out as a squeak.

"Who creeps onto my shore like a wolf in the night?" she

demanded. To her relief, her voice was steady, resounding in the air.

"I am Solvi, King of Rogaland," the boar-crested one announced, his voice like a blast from a war horn. "And who might you be, *lady?*"

Åsa bristled at his tone. "I am Åsa Haraldsdottir, Queen of Agder. You're standing on my land. What brings you to my kingdom, Solvi?" She left off the title of king, addressing him as an equal.

Solvi's step ate up the distance between them. He thundered, "I understand that you have my daughter. I have come to fetch her home."

Åsa resisted the urge to give ground before this blowhard. She must draw this conversation out as long as possible to give the archers time to assemble. "Your daughter has sworn to me," she replied sharply, stepping forward. A miscalculation, for now she had to look up to meet his eye.

"I would hear this from my daughter's lips."

Ragnhild stepped out from the shield wall to stand beside Åsa, glaring at her father. "It is true. I am sworn to serve Queen Åsa. I will not break my vow."

Solvi's face turned a deeper shade of red beneath his helm. "A daughter owes her duty to her father first. I promised you to the Irish king. You make a liar of me."

Ragnhild's face was as red as her father's, and her voice matched his tone. "You had no right to promise me without my consent. The followers of the White Christ treat their women no better than slaves. You would enslave your daughter for silver. I will die before I let you sell me as a peace cow."

"Enough of this. You are coming home with me." Solvi thumped the butt of his spear on the ground.

Tightlipped, Åsa and Ragnhild stepped back into the shield wall. Åsa hoped the archers were in place. The time for talk was done.

For a moment Solvi stood there, his jaw slack in surprise. His face deepened from red to purple. He held up his fist. "Charge!" he roared.

Screaming, his men ran forward, spears bristling between their shields.

"Tighten up!" shouted Jarl Borg. Shield locked to shield.

"Archers!" he cried. "Nock! Draw!" To Åsa's relief, the creak of bowstrings sounded in the trees. "Loose!" From the forest a thicket of arrows rose, silver in the dawn light. They arced through the sky, then drove toward the earth, thwacking into enemy shields. Some hit their marks, drawing screams and thuds as the warriors hit the ground.

As the enemy pressed forward, more arrows whickered out from the trees, catching the outer ranks on the side. Their war cries turned to screams as the sniper arrows thinned their flank. But Solvi's main force thundered up the hill, shrieking war cries.

Åsa stifled a shiver and gripped her spear.

"Steady," said Olvir. "Tight to your neighbor." The shield wall contracted yet again, bracing for impact.

With a roar the enemy crashed into their formation. Spears pierced linden shields, sending up a shower of splinters. Tromøy's shield wall held against the first onslaught, but now the enemy drew their swords, stabbing above and below the shields, seeking unprotected legs and heads, trying to break the formation. Face-to-face with the screaming enemy, Åsa could clearly see the murder in their eyes. She held her shield tight to Bram's beside her, now giving ground, now pushing back. She silently thanked Ulf for outfitting each warrior with helmets and metal strips sewn in their boots to protect their calves from enemy swords. And she had confidence in the swords Ulf had made from the six wootz ingots Olaf had sent. In addition to Ragnhild, Åsa had bestowed them on Olvir, Dag, and Ragnhild's three sworn men. Ulf had forged five more blades from his new crucible steel. Bram and Jarl Borg each wielded one of these, the others by her most promising warriors.

An axe hooked the top of Bram's shield. At Åsa's nod he let the enemy drag it down. She drove her spear into the attacker's unguarded throat, ripping the blade out as he fell. She stepped over his body, surging forward with her men.

Under the enemy's prying, the shield wall loosened and broke apart into a free-for-all. Åsa drew her longsword, Gudrød's Bane. Her heart pounded as she fended off an axe blow from a red-bearded enemy who roared his foul breath on her. She rammed her sword into the attacker. Her blade slipped past his shield, piercing his leather armor and sliding between his ribs. He screamed and stumbled. She jerked her sword free and turned to meet the next attack.

She guarded her strength carefully, praying they could hold out until Olaf arrived. She hoped he'd seen the signal fire in the night and set out hours before. Yet even with the breeze filling in, he could not arrive before late morning. How could they last that long?

Bram still fought beside her. She was impressed by his ferocity and how confident he was for an unblooded boy. He wielded Ulf's new crucible steel sword with good form.

She glimpsed Jarl Borg in the crowd, marking him by his height and his deliberate, unhurried fighting style. The tall old lord held three men at bay. Each blow was well considered, carrying the full force of his big frame, and each told on his opponents. Yet as she hacked her way toward him, an enemy blade clashed with Borg's sword--and it shattered in his hand. As shards shot out in the air, the old jarl did not miss a beat. He drove the stub of his blade into his opponent's throat, felling him. But at the same moment, an axe smashed into Borg's helmet from behind.

His proud old head went down. Åsa's heart seemed to

explode as she beat her way to him with frenzied blows, scattering his attackers.

Borg lay face down on the ground, his shield beneath him, still gripping his shattered sword. Åsa could see no blood, but he was still as death. She stood over him, choking on tears as she beat back the tide of enemies.

Men fell beneath her blade, but they kept coming. Was there no end to them? Her sword arm spasmed and her hand was slick with sweat and blood, numb where it gripped the weapon. She prayed she would not lose her hold. She dared not look down at Jarl Borg.

Sweat dripped into her eyes, and she swiped at them with the back of her hand. A sudden chill passed over her heart. Through stinging eyes she saw a tall warrior stalking toward her, sword glistening with gore.

Hrolf.

# CHAPTER 14

Skagerrak Sea

Olaf stood in *Sea Dragon's* stern, gripping the tiller as the oarsmen drove the ship across the flat sea. He muttered prayers to Ran, promising her a gold sacrifice to grant him speed.

Heid, patrolling Tromøy by night in her owl form, had seen the fleet that lay in a hidden bay, perfectly positioned to attack the island settlement. The blaze of the signal fire on the headland confirmed her suspicions. Olaf had launched Skiringssal's six dragon ships in the dark, with two hundred warriors, all he could muster on such short notice.

At his feet, the sorceress's body lay prone on the floorboards under a pile of furs. She was gone again in her owl form to watch developments.

All night he had driven the rowers down flat calm seas, praying he was not too late. With the sunrise he knew the attack must have begun. Now he raced the sun to get there in time.

He tried to imagine the course of the battle, the enemy arriving at first light and attacking the hall in the dawn. Tromøy's signal fires had been lit in the night, so they must have had warning and met the attack prepared. Åsa was ever watchful for the raids she knew would come, but never sure from what quarter. The Danes crossing the Skagerrak, or Eystein from the north? Or Hrolf from wherever he lurked. Olaf's stomach knotted. It made no sense, but he feared his bastard half-brother more than all the rest. If Hrolf had followers at all, they would be the dregs, barely warriors. Did he dread his half-brother more because of their history, or because Hrolf was pure evil? The thought of him taking control of Tromøy—of what he might do to Åsa—made Olaf clench his jaw.

Cat's paws dappled the water.

Ran had finally sent him a breeze, filling in from the north.

"Raise sail!" he roared.

~

Tromøy

RAGNHILD SPOTTED her father's boar-crested helm among the sea of unadorned helmets. She fought her way toward it through flashing blades and flying splinters, hacking at the very men who had trained her to fight. She pulled her sword blows to avoid injuring them, and as they recognized her, they gave way, opening the path to her father.

She closed the gap between them. His eyes flashed as recognition crossed his features. For a moment gladness flickered there, but when she blinked, his gaze had become a glare.

"So, girl, are you ready to come home and do your duty?"

Fury spiked in her. "I'll never submit to be sold as a peace cow!"

"You'll do as I say!" he roared, swinging his sword down hard. She caught the blow on her shield boss. Pain seared up her arm, numbing her shoulder. He bore down on her, and she found herself retreating before him, one step, then another. She could not help it. He was her father.

She had to stop her flight. Planting her feet, she clenched her jaw and forced her shield up, steeled the tremble out of her arm, and met a blow that made her stagger. But somehow, she held.

Surprise made him hesitate. She took the opening automatically, sweeping her blade low. He leaped back to save his calves. Now she was the one advancing, keeping her guard up, her sword moving, relentlessly seeking an opening. But he had taught her every trick she knew. She had to use her youth to wear him down.

She conserved her strength, not raising her sword too high, just keeping up a steady onslaught of blows, always from a new direction, forcing him to lift his shield over and over, never allowing him time to recover. His breath was ragged and a quiver ran up his arm. Ragnhild surged forward and he stumbled.

Jabbing and feinting, she pressed him until he stumbled again. Her blade slashed at his legs. This time he went down. Ragnhild stomped on his sword arm, forcing his hand to open. She kicked the sword away and lowered her blade to his throat.

"Why do you hate me?" she cried.

"I don't hate you, girl." His voice was faint, with no air behind it.

Ragnhild watched his blue eyes fade and the color leach from his face. His chest heaved with a shallow rasp of breath.

"You must hate me," she said. "You'd never sell your worst enemy to a Christian. Captive inside a hall of stone, stripped of all my freedoms. Staring out the window at a world that would never be mine. I would die in such a life." Tears prickled. "Better to kill me now than subject me to such torture."

Solvi's eyes glistened.

"If you hate it that much, girl, I'll not force you. I just want you to come home."

Relief flowed down her spine. Her throat closed and her sword arm wavered.

Her father leaped to his feet and smashed his shield into her hand, sending her weapon flying. He lunged for his own sword and brought it to her throat.

"Seize her," he commanded, and his men closed in.

FROM THE CORNER of her eye Åsa watched Hrolf hack his way toward her through the melee. She ignored the dread that coiled in her belly, concentrating on slash and drive, trying to conserve her strength. The onslaught was taking its toll, and she fought the urge to flee. She stood over Jarl Borg, who lay still as a corpse, but possibly alive. She would not leave him.

She raised her shield to block a sword blow. She forced her attacker's sword down with the metal boss and hacked Gudrød's Bane into his neck. Blood flowed and the air stank of fear and death.

Yanking her blade from the enemy's corpse, she felt the cold creep up the back of her neck and whirled to meet Hrolf's leer. The ice in his eyes sent a shiver up her spine. She firmed her legs against the tremble that started in her knees and faced him, reminding herself that she was a girl no longer, but a queen. She stood in her father's place now.

"So, little queen. We meet on the battlefield at last."

Åsa stared back at his mocking grin. "I killed your father," she said. "I'll kill you too."

"We shall see," he said, and swung.

She dodged, bringing her shield up. The rim was gone, but she caught Hrolf's blade on the metal boss, sending a jolt that numbed her left arm as she swung Gudrød's Bane with her right. Hrolf blocked with his more substantial shield, sending a second shock up her right arm that made her stagger. She jerked to a halt and whirled on him. He grinned, showing yellow horse teeth. She could see the grooves he had filed in them.

Suppressing a shudder, she charged. He leaped aside and pivoted into her, his sword edge slicing into her side. The chain mail stopped the blade, but the blow knocked the wind out of her. As she stumbled, he smashed his shield into her helmet and she went down, ears ringing.

She lay still for a moment, struggling to breathe in the stink of blood and shit. Beside her, Jarl Borg's face was white. The weight of her brynja pinned her to the ground, and Gudrød's Bane lay heavy in her hand.

Bram appeared, spattered with blood but still wielding his new sword with vigor.

"No, Bram," she called. He was far too young to fight Hrolf, even with his miraculous new sword.

The boy seemed not to hear her. He charged in and drove his sword at Hrolf with enough force to surely pierce chain mail. Hope surged in her as the blade hit Hrolf's armor.

The point drove in and the blade exploded. Åsa rolled to escape the flying steel.

Bram stared open-mouthed at the failed sword. Åsa shouted a warning, but he did not see the swordblow that smashed into his helm and felled him like a tree. By his staring eyes and the angle of his head, she knew Bram was on his way to Odin's hall.

Olvir charged. Hrolf laughed and swung his sword at Olvir, but the húskarl caught the blow on his shield.

"Surrender if you want her to live," said Hrolf.

"No!" she gasped, trying to thrash her way to her feet.

Hrolf stilled her with a swordpoint to her throat. "I will spare her if you throw down your weapon."

"Don't trust him!" she croaked.

But Olvir threw down his sword.

# CHAPTER 15

Tromøy's rocky headland reared from the sea. The sun was high, and Olaf prayed he was not too late.

His ships rounded the bluff and surged into the bay, where the crews dropped sail and rowed through the rocks and skerries.

Five dragon ships lay on the beach. Assuming the ships were fully manned, he still had an advantage. If the Tromøy warriors had taken a toll on the enemy, he might have a good advantage. Maybe enough to win.

With one final pull, Olaf's fleet slid up onto the beach. Barely pausing to catch breath, the húskarlar shipped oars and pulled on their brynja, buckling swordbelts and strapping on shields. They swarmed over the gunwales and splashed through the shallows.

The men assembled on the beach. It was full daylight now, and instead of the sounds of a raging battle, all was ominously quiet. He looked up at the silent hall and dread weighed heavy in his chest.

He exchanged glances with Kalv, the captain of his guard. The two rarely needed words. Olaf raised his sword, and Kalv brought his blade up in answer. The húskarlar pointed their spears and axes to the sky and fell in behind, striding up the hill. Olaf was impatient to reach the top but feared what he would find.

A vanguard of armed warriors emerged from the hall. With a flush of shock, Olaf recognized Hrolf at their head, wearing well-polished chain mail, carrying his helmet in the crook of his arm.

"Welcome, brother," Hrolf sneered. "You are late to my victory feast."

The blood heated Olaf's face, but he kept his expression impassive. He wanted to demand to see Åsa, but he knew if he showed interest, Hrolf would use that against him. He needed to get as much information as possible, so he remained silent, waiting.

"I have your woman inside," Hrolf said as if reading his thoughts. "She is untouched, as yet. What will you give me for her?"

Olaf bit back his answer.

Hrolf smiled, showing his teeth. "Lay down your arms, brother, and enter as my guest. We can negotiate in comfort."

Olaf was tempted. He needed to see Åsa, but he would never lay his arms down in Hrolf's presence. She was alive, unharmed, or so Hrolf said. His brother's word would have to do for now. Olaf held up his fist, signaling his húskarlar to back away.

"Afraid, brother?" Hrolf taunted after them. "You always were white of liver."

Olaf made camp at the base of the hill. He divided his men to watch the four quarters, barring any escape from the hall, and set a guard on the ships.

Heid had roused from her trance and now sat inside his tent, looking pale.

"You saw the battle?"

Heid nodded. "Hrolf is allied with the girl's father. They came by night with an overwhelming force. Åsa's húskarlar surrendered to save her life, and many of her people were still alive when she was taken. But we must get them out of there soon. The prisoners are all in danger. Hrolf will not harm Åsa. As a bastard, he needs the legitimacy of marriage. He will hold a wedding feast with her, establishing a valid claim to Agder."

Olaf's stomach roiled.

"But Åsa's son is in danger," Heid said. "Halfdan is the rightful heir not only to Agder, but as Gudrød's son, heir to Vestfold after you. The child stands squarely in Hrolf's way. He will certainly not let the boy live."

Olaf shook his head. "They arrived with five ships, maybe two hundred warriors. I need to know how many men he has left, how many of Tromøy's folk survived the battle, how many could fight. He claims Åsa is alive. I need to confirm that." He stared into the fire. "We can't storm the hall without risking the captives. We have them trapped for now, but if we starve them, the prisoners starve too."

The völva stared up at the stars. "I must go under the cloak again, to seek what answers I can find."

Olaf called for food and ale. When the old sorceress had eaten, she burrowed into the furs and was still. She must have entered a trance instantly. Olaf envied her as he lay awake, staring at the tent peak, worrying.

But Heid moaned and tossed fretfully. Olaf hoped the sorceress was having a vision from the gods.

Åsa lay in her bed in the women's bower, not daring to sleep in case Hrolf came. She didn't think he would. The prize here was marriage. He must hold a wedding feast with her, even by force, to establish a legitimate claim as King of Agder. But this did nothing to put her at ease.

Tromøy's men were imprisoned in the hall, while the women

had been separated and were held in the bower. Both buildings were heavily guarded, and Solvi's camp surrounded the steading.

The news of Olaf's arrival cheered her. She longed to see him, to feel his arms around her, but just knowing he was here comforted her. It had put the enemy on high alert, too busy to bother any of the women. She hoped the distraction would last until she came up with a plan. What plan? Her exhausted brain turned over hopeless ideas.

Ragnhild lay beside her. Åsa knew by her rigid shoulders that the girl was not asleep. Halfdan slept in his cradle. Thank goodness he was quiet. *Don't attract attention to yourself*, she willed.

As she stared into the gloom of the hall's rafters, a movement caught her eye. Up in the gable end, a gray shape perched. She strained her eyes to make it out. A bird. An owl? Could it be Heid?

The thought was comforting, and she finally slept.

# CHAPTER 16

Ragnhild lay under the furs, staring into the shimmering red coals of the brazier. Why had she trusted her father? She knew better. Why had she let her heart open to him? She was too weak to survive as a warrior. Maybe she would be better as a peace cow.

Åsa stirred beside her. "I am sorry, my queen," Ragnhild whispered. "I let you down."

Åsa turned toward her, eyes gleaming in the fire's glow. "There was nothing you could have done. We were outnumbered. Our defeat was inevitable. I should have surrendered sooner and saved more lives."

Ragnhild sat up. "You had to fight." *Don't give up.*

"I know." Åsa looked tired.

*Defeated,* Ragnhild thought with dread. Her chest felt hollow as she understood how much Åsa's decisions had cost her. "Your choices are not easy."

A faint smile flickered across Åsa's features, but sadness lingered in her eyes. "No, they are not."

Ragnhild shook her head, trying to throw off the dread. "Now what?"

Åsa shifted restlessly under the furs. "I don't know."

Ragnhild's chest tightened at the queen's defeated tone. "You can't mean to give in to Hrolf?"

"Never." Åsa's eyes glinted like polished steel.

"And I'll die before I marry the Irish king," Ragnhild vowed.

Åsa gripped her arm. "Don't do that."

"If there's no other way."

"There's always another way," said Åsa. "Give it time. Olaf is out there."

OLAF WOKE with the impression of huge wings beating the air. When he opened his eyes, Heid was sitting beside his cot, staring down at him.

He jolted up and seized her arm. "What have you seen?"

The völva shook him off with a frown. "She lives. Her son is alive, for now. Most of the Tromøy folk survived, though some are injured. The women are imprisoned in the bower, the men held under guard in the great hall."

"How can we free them?" Olaf buried his head in his hands. He wanted to weep.

Heid gripped his shoulder with a steel claw. "What is Hrolf's weakness?" Her voice held an intensity that made him look up at her.

He shook his head. His brother had always seemed invincible. "He doesn't have one. He's a powerful man."

"Yet you have defeated him," the sorceress asserted.

"Only because the Danes betrayed him."

"Think about that," said Heid. "His allies betrayed him. How can you bring that about in this situation? Hrolf is a ruthless man who cares only for himself. His allies and followers have no personal loyalty to him. He is in league with Solvi, who wants his daughter back, or at least he wants the silver and the Irish alliance his daughter will bring. What kind of wedge can you drive between them?"

Waves of despair washed over Olaf. "I don't know…"

~

ULF SAT in the corner of the hall with the other Tromøy warriors, glowering at Hrafn, who was bandaging a wound on the smith's arm.

"It will mend well enough," said the sorcerer, giving Ulf's shoulder a pat.

"You betrayed me."

Hrafn smiled. "I was surprised you fell for my rune meddling. I thought you were a deep-minded one. I didn't really think I'd get away with it."

"I'm the trusting kind," Ulf growled, feeling sick. Bram's death was his fault. And how many others?

"Sorry, my friend." Hrafn went to join his allies.

Solvi sat in the high seat, Hrolf beside him. Hrafn took a seat just below them, in a place of honor. Solvi's jarls and their sworn men flanked the longfire, toasting their victory with Tromøy's mead. The smell of cooking meat wafted into the hall from the yard, where a freshly slaughtered hog simmered in an iron cauldron suspended from a tripod over the fire. Ulf's stomach growled, but he knew he'd get none of the meat. He'd be lucky if they'd feed him a thin gruel.

"To victory," Hrolf said, raising his cup.

Solvi glared. "I could hardly call this a victory. Your brother's men have us surrounded. Our forces are evenly matched."

Hrolf and Hrafn exchanged a smile that stood Ulf's neck hairs on end.

"We have the high ground," Hrolf said. "Olaf must attack uphill. With even forces, we will defeat him." Ulf's heart sank.

"And how will you get him to attack?" Solvi snarled. "He can just starve us. My men will go through the supplies and livestock in a couple of weeks. Then what?"

"It won't take that long. Remember, we have what my brother holds dear. We have Åsa and her son, Olaf's brother and heir. If we starve, they will starve along with us. No, Olaf will attack long before that."

A sea of acid churned in Ulf's gut.

Åsa FOUND herself perched in the bower rafters. Once again she had entered Stormrider's body in her sleep. She hesitated, worried that Hrolf might sense her, yet the air around her held no presence. She hoped he was asleep. This might be her only chance to scout the area.

She hopped out through the gable end and flapped her wings up to the roof, where she surveyed the settlement. Smoke rose from the great hall, casting a film over the stars. Campfires flickered outside tents that surrounded the yard, interrupted by the dark forms of sentries as they patrolled the perimeter.

Far below on the beach, a second ring of campfires punctuated the darkness, kindling a pinpoint of hope. Olaf.

The thought of him drew the falcon like hunger. She took to the air and soared down toward the lights on the beach. Drawn to the one shining with lamplight, she landed on the peak. The tent flap opened, and Heid peered up at her.

"Well, are you going to come in?"

The sight of the völva filled Åsa with relief. Her spirit flowed out of Stormrider's body and into the tent, coalescing into a shimmering likeness of her human body.

Olaf looked up and caught his breath. The lines between his brows vanished as he smiled in relief. Åsa warmed, her essence drawn toward him.

Heid smiled. "How are you, child?"

"I am well enough," said Åsa. "Some of our folk were killed in the battle. Jarl Borg fell. I don't know if he lives or how our men fare. Hrolf is holding them in the great hall, while the women are imprisoned in the bower. Solvi's camp surrounds the steading, but I don't know how many men he has left."

Olaf said, "Judging by the number of ships he brought, we should outnumber them, but attacking uphill puts us at a disadvantage no matter what our numbers. And it puts you all at risk."

"Not if we fight back," Åsa said. "If Tromøy's survivors can rise up and fight as you attack, it will even the odds."

"What help can they be without weapons?" asked Olaf.

"They can hinder their captors and give you an advantage, however small." Åsa felt hope kindle for the first time. "I will tell the women and get word to the men. Give us time to get ready. Attack at dawn tomorrow."

"Agreed," said Olaf.

"Now you must get back," said Heid. "It's nearly light. Don't risk coming here again."

"I won't." Åsa turned her attention to the falcon's body and willed herself into it. With a last look at Heid and Olaf, the falcon took flight.

The dawn glow lightened the sky as she neared the settlement. It was too risky to try to enter the great hall. She would have to find another way to get word to the men. As she approached the bower roof, she caught movement from the corner of her eye. She was thinking Hrolf had found her when the arrow struck. She was knocked out of the air, spinning. Falling.

The one-eyed wolf loped out of the forest. The falcon fluttered on the ground, dark against the snow. The wolf approached cautiously and took the struggling bird in its mouth.

∽

THE FALCON WOKE in a willow cage, hanging from the rafters of the great hall. Her wing burned.

"The falcon is a fylgja." Hrafn's voice. The falcon's heart stumbled. Did the old sorcerer recognize her?

"Whose fylgja?" Hrolf peered into the cage. His glance struck an icy spike of fear in her. She winced, remembering the arrow strike, the wolf.

"I don't know," said Hrafn. The falcon's heart regained its beat. Was he telling the truth, or hiding his knowledge from the others?

"How can we find out?"

"The sentry who brought her down said she came from Olaf's camp. It might be a völva."

Hrolf's eyes gleamed. "It could be Heid?"

Hrafn nodded. "Or one of her apprentices. It seems unlikely that Heid would allow herself to fall into such a simple trap."

Hrolf leaned back, his eyes narrowed to slits. "If we don't know who she is, how can we use this to our advantage?"

Hrafn grinned. "Leave that to me."

"IT'S A WHITE SHIELD," the sentry reported.

Olaf squinted into the mist. He could make out a throng of warriors, one of them bearing a white shield mounted on a spear. "They want to talk."

Heid hoisted herself from her stool and picked up her iron wand. "Let's hear what they have to say."

Flanked by Olaf's húskarlar and Heid's apprentices, they made their way uphill toward the figures at the crest. As they came closer, Olaf recognized Hrolf. Beside him Hrafn carried a small cage made of willow switches. Olaf's blood chilled as he recognized the heap of gray-barred feathers that struggled within. He heard Heid's sharp breath, quickly suppressed.

Hrafn cackled when he recognized her. "So, it isn't you, old witch. Is this one of your girls?" He surveyed the women. "Who is missing?"

"He doesn't know my apprentices," Heid murmured to Olaf. She strode forward and peered into the cage. "I don't recognize this creature, old man. You have managed to capture a common falcon."

"Hrafn knows a fylgja when he sees one." He shook the cage, forcing a cry from the falcon.

"You are welcome to your delusions, old man," Heid said, ignoring the fluttering bird.

"You won't care if we kill the creature, then."

"Not a bit. Is that all you have to say?" Heid waited a moment, then shrugged and turned away. She came to Olaf's side and took his arm, digging her nails in hard. "Come, Olaf, they are wasting our time."

Olaf burned with the urge to seize the cage from the sorcerer, but he understood that caution was required and allowed Heid to usher him away.

"They're bluffing," Heid hissed when they were out of earshot. "Hrafn may or may not know who he's got, but he knows a fylgja has value only while she is alive. He'll take good care of her."

"You'd better be right, old woman."

"I am. She's wounded. Shot in the wing. That means Åsa's human body sustained the same injury. My fear is that they'll discover Åsa with an arm wound and they'll know who they've got. That will give them enough leverage to stop us." Heid sighed. "I need to get into the bower."

"You can't. It's too risky."

"The risk is greater if I don't."

"Hrafn will be expecting you."

"That's a chance I'll have to take."

⁓

BRENNA FINISHED BINDING the splint on Åsa's upper arm. The wound had appeared in the night. She was certain it had not been there before. Her mistress had remained inert through it all. She had not even groaned when Brenna cleaned the wound and set the broken bone. Now Brenna stuffed the blood-soaked tunic under the mattress, and dressed the unconscious woman in a clean garment.

She stared down at Åsa's still form. "Where are you?" she pleaded.

There was a flurry of wings in the gable. A gray owl glided down to the bed and landed on the down comforter with a soft thud.

Brenna gasped, laying her arm across Åsa protectively.

The owl coalesced into human shape. The vision further resolved into Heid's likeness.

"Where were you when we needed you?" Brenna hissed. "Our lady lies as if dead."

Heid's likeness shimmered, returning the fóstra's glare. "I have no time to chat. Listen to me. They have captured Åsa's fylgja. It is caged in the great hall. She is injured. They don't know who they've got, for sure. If they come, you must hide her injury from them."

Brenna nodded. "I understand."

Heid's tone intensified. "Olaf will attack tomorrow at dawn. You must get someone into the great hall and tell Tromøy's warriors to be ready to help."

Brenna stared at her. "How?"

"You must find a way. I can't stay!" Heid hissed. "Do not fail!" The human form dissolved and flowed into the owl, which spread its broad wings and lofted off the bed.

"But how?" Brenna whispered after the owl as she flitted out the gable end.

Brenna stared down at Åsa's form, still under the coverlet. An idea formed in her mind.

She hurried into the bower's main hall, where she found Ragnhild and shook the girl awake. In hushed tones she told of Heid's visit and the message for Tromøy's warriors.

"You must do it," Brenna said. "You can ask to see your father. That will get you into the hall."

"I don't want to see that old bastard ever again."

"You must. You are the only one who has a convincing reason. You have to swallow your pride. Beg him to set us free. Appear weak."

"I can't humble myself before him, not after he betrayed me!"

"You must warn our men to be ready when Olaf attacks."

"But what can a bunch of wounded prisoners do? They have no weapons."

"I have a plan which you must pass on to them." Brenna laid a hand on the girl's arm. "It's our only hope. If you succeed, you will be paying your father back in kind. By tomorrow morning the tables will be turned. Think of the look on his face when he realizes how you tricked him."

Brenna proceeded to tell Ragnhild the plan. A gleam appeared in the shield-maiden's eye, and Brenna let out a sigh of relief. "Can you do it?"

"I can."

RAGNHILD PEERED into the great hall's gloom. Tromøy's warriors crowded the benches along the walls, guarded by her father's húskarlar. Jarl Borg lay on one bench, his eyes closed. She strained to see the old warrior's chest move slightly with shallow breath. She sought out her sworn men. Einar, Svein, and Thorgeir sat with the other prisoners, alive but wounded—how badly, she couldn't tell. They still wore their chain mail, splotched with blood. Their wounds had not been cleaned or bandaged, but it appeared that her father had not punished them for their betrayal—yet.

Her father shared the high seat with Hrolf. Beside them hung a willow cage, suspended from the rafters by an iron chain. On the floor of the cage, a heap of barred feathers lay ominously still. Ragnhild forced herself to look at her father, who grinned down on her triumphantly.

"So, daughter, you have come to petition me?"

"Yes, Father." Ragnhild kept the fury from her voice. She kept her eyes downcast so he would not see the gleam of hate in them. "I beg you to set the Tromøy folk free."

"What have I to gain from doing such a thing?"

"I will submit to marriage with the Irish king." She choked on the words, even though they were a lie.

Hrolf leered down at her. "That gets your father what he wants, but what about me?"

"I don't know what I can do for you, lord," she said. Could he hear the spite in her voice?

"You will convince my brother to surrender Vestfold to me. Then we will set the captives free," said Hrolf.

"How can I make him do that?"

"That's up to you."

Ragnhild forced a scowl to hide her excitement. "Very well. I will try if you will allow me to go to their camp to negotiate. But first I must see that my men are well treated." She was already on her feet, making it harder for him to forbid it.

"See for yourself."

"I will need water and clean bandages," she said. She crossed to Einar. "How are you?" she asked, pulling back his bloodstained sleeve.

"We are well enough, my lady."

"Are you being fed?" Ragnhild accepted the water and clean

linen from a slave. She bent close to wash his wound. "Olaf attacks at dawn. Be ready," she breathed.

She raised her voice, turning to the slave. "These men do not have blankets. They must be kept warm. There are some in the storeroom; go get them."

The slave scurried to the storeroom and returned with a pile of wool coverlets.

She distributed the blankets among the captives, washing and bandaging wounds and breathing her message to each one. Most of the men had cuts and bruises, but six were too badly wounded to fight, with broken bones or deep lacerations. She did what she could for them.

One was a lad she remembered besting on the practice field. His face was twisted with pain. When she pulled up his bloody shirt, she had to stop herself from flinching at the gleam of intestines bulging from a broad gash in his stomach.

Ragnhild gently washed the wound and wound a linen bandage around his middle. She tucked a blanket around him. "What is your name?" she asked.

"Garth." His voice was barely a whisper, and she had to lean close to hear him.

"Well, Garth, you are a very brave man. I will tell of your deeds before the longfire this night."

For a moment, a smile chased the agony from Garth's face. Then his expression contorted again.

She put her lips to his forehead before moving on. She prayed the corpse goddess would come for him before the night was through.

Ulf, the smith, sat apart from the others. His wound looked well enough, but the smith was clearly miserable--as well he should be. Ragnhild's spike of anger subsided into pity. He'd been taken in by Hrafn with all the rest. She'd laughed at the old sorcerer's jokes herself, and been relieved at Heid's departure. The old witch was hard to like.

She bent her head to the smith's ear and whispered her message. His shoulders squared and his mouth firmed. Determination glowed in his eyes. That was the best she could do for him.

When Ragnhild had completed her rounds of the captives, she stopped to bid farewell to Einar. "Do you think your men have enough blankets now?" she asked him pointedly.

"Yes, lady." A light in Einar's eye told her he understood.

Solvi's warriors escorted Ragnhild down the hill, bearing a white shield mounted on a spear. By the time they reached the camp, Olaf was waiting for them. He looked tired, his handsome face drawn with worry.

Ragnhild stepped forward and mustered strength for her voice. "Olaf, if you surrender Vestfold to Hrolf, he and my father will have peace with you and let the Tromøy folk go free." She read the question in his eyes.

"I must consult with my hird before making such a decision," he said.

"Very well," she said, trying to send him a meaningful look. "My father gives you until dawn tomorrow to decide. The captives await your response."

His eyes seemed to clear, and she hoped he had gotten her message. She turned to go, surrounded by her escort.

# CHAPTER 17

In the hour before dawn, Olaf's men fanned out around the hillside and stole silently up the slope. They moved in pairs, weapons and armor muffled beneath their cloaks so no gleam of metal could betray them. Behind them Heid and her apprentices ringed the base of the hill.

The warriors worked in silent coordination, reaching the crest of the hill together. Olaf uttered a bird cry so authentic that only those waiting for the signal recognized it for what it was. Working in pairs, they crept up on the sentries. One man grappled the guard, silencing him with a hand over his mouth while his partner slashed his throat. The lookouts fell without a sound. When all the sentries were down, Olaf gave another bird call and his men attacked the hall. The guards outside fell to the same tactic as the sentries without a sound. When the last had fallen, Olaf uttered one more signal and they rushed the hall. He led a team of burly warriors to ram the oaken doors while others ran for the back exit.

The clamor roused the falcon in her cage. She jerked upright with a hoarse cry. Pain lanced through her wing, and she sank back down in a heap of feathers.

Solvi's warriors drew their swords and rushed to meet the attackers at the door.

Einar threw aside his coverlet and sprang up from his bench, shouting to rally the captives. They leaped up and threw their blankets over their captors, blinding them and fouling their weapons as the door burst open and Olaf's warriors stormed into the hall.

The Tromøy prisoners grappled their entangled captors, wrestling them to the ground while Olaf and his men dispatched them with axes and spears.

In the fury of battle, only the falcon saw Hrafn creep from the shadows. The old sorcerer lifted the willow cage from its hook and made for the back exit. The falcon flung herself against the willow bars, screeching, but she couldn't force her bird's body through the narrow openings and her cries were lost in the din of battle.

Hrafn stole through the back door into the dim light, stopping short when he saw some of Olaf's men. He drew back into the shadows.

The falcon cried again, but the warriors' attention was on the battle and they paid no attention to her as they rushed through the door to join the fight inside.

The falcon glimpsed a familiar form jostling against the tide of combatants.

Ulf.

The smith shoved his way toward them, his face contorted with fury. Hrafn glanced back at the movement and gaped.

"I've got you now, you treacherous troll!" Ulf snarled.

The old sorcerer dropped the cage and fled into the trees, Ulf in pursuit.

The falcon found herself abandoned. Cries of battle and the clash of weapons in the hall drowned out any hope of her being heard. She threw herself against the bars once more but succeeded only in knocking the cage over. She lay on her side in defeat, recovering her breath.

A low, dark shape slunk from the forest, nearly invisible in the shadows. The falcon froze, staring at the one-eyed wolf.

The wolf picked up the cage in his mouth and slipped away from the hall, while the falcon beat her wings against the bars, screeching frantically.

*Where was Ulf?*

As the wolf crept into the undergrowth, she looked back to see the smith emerge from the woods. Ulf stood in the clearing outside the hall, scanning the area.

The falcon stilled as the wolf carried her away. There was no point in fighting now. Best to save her strength and wait for the moment the cage door opened.

The raptor heard the faintest whisper of wings and her sharp vision caught movement in the sky. She looked up as a huge owl soared down on them.

The wolf bared his teeth, the cage still clamped between them. A low growl began deep in his throat. The owl dove, but the wolf dodged the attack, keeping a firm bite on the cage. The owl flapped powerful wings and lofted straight up in the air, then plunged into another attack. This time the owl snatched a tuft of hair from the wolf's neck, but the wolf kept his jaws clamped shut on his prize and dashed into the woods, the owl gliding in pursuit.

The wolf loped through the trees, dodging around trunks. The owl followed silently, folding her wings to glide between branches. The falcon called out to help the owl track them. The wolf found a thicket and burrowed deep into the undergrowth, creeping on his belly. The falcon let out a muffled, desperate cry as the wolf hunkered down in the middle of an impenetrable copse of thorn bushes.

A long time passed and the falcon fell silent, certain the owl had given up its search. The wolf apparently thought so too, for he picked up the willow cage once again and slithered out of the thicket on his belly. The forest was quiet and so dark that the falcon could see nothing, but she called out. The wolf stepped silently into the open.

With a whoosh of huge wings, a shadow swooped down on them.

The wolf stood at bay as the owl plunged feet first at his face, talons extended. The owl drove her claws directly into the wolf's single eye, forcing the lid open and gripping the eyeball. The bird gave a powerful flap and wrenched the eye from its socket, leaving it dangling by the nerve.

The wolf shrieked.

The owl dove again and snatched the cage from his jaws just as they snapped shut. Lofting into the air, the owl carried the caged falcon high above the trees while far below, the wolf yowled in agony.

Dangling in the cage, the falcon watched as they circled the bower roof. The owl folded her wings to soar in through the smoke hole, then opened them and glided down to the bed where Åsa's human body lay inert beneath the eiderdown. The owl dropped the cage on the bed and flew back into the rafters.

The human body, still and white on the bed, pulled at the falcon. She let herself flow in. Pain shot through Åsa's arms and legs as she drove her consciousness into them. She forced her fingers and toes to move, sending out pinpricks of pain.

She jolted upright to look into Brenna's anxious face.

"Get my armor," she croaked.

"Hush." Brenna tried to press her back to the pillow. "You are wounded. You must rest."

"It's not my sword arm!" Åsa jerked out of bed and dragged her brynja from its hook.

Shaking her head, Brenna hefted the mail shirt, and Åsa ducked her head in. Pain lanced through her as she forced her splinted arm into the heavy sleeve. Brenna caught her as she staggered.

"I'm fine!" She pushed Brenna aside and strode into the bower, where the women were already up and dressing. The guards had gone to join the fight, leaving the door open to the night.

"Olaf is attacking the hall," Åsa cried. "Arm yourselves!"

"We have no weapons," Ragnhild reminded her.

"Yes, we do," Åsa said. "We have our weaving tools. We've won battles with them before."

The women snatched up their wooden distaffs and sword-shaped weft-beaters and fell in behind Åsa. She led them out of the unguarded bower and across the yard.

The hall's great doors hung open and the battle had spilled out into the yard. Solvi's men poured out of the guest house and barracks to join the fight. The clash of metal and the shouts of men echoed through the steading. Firelight flashed on helm and blade. Wielding a heavy wooden weft-beater with both hands, Åsa stormed into the battle.

She scanned the crowd, searching for Olaf's helm. She glimpsed it for an instant in the sea of combatants, then turned to the enemy. Caught between Olaf's húskarlar and the captives, Solvi's warriors fought desperately. Åsa picked out the king's boar helm among them. He fought at bay, attacked from two sides, yet he held his own. If she could capture him, his men would be forced to surrender. She beat her way toward him and saw she was on a collision course with Ragnhild, fighting toward her father from the other end.

The girl felled a warrior with her distaff, then grabbed his axe and attacked the next foe. He went down. Solvi and his men were not immune to steel.

Åsa slowed her progress a little. The girl deserved to get to Solvi first, but Åsa would be there to back her up.

∼

THROUGH A RED HAZE Olaf spotted his brother across the hall, hacking with the vicious fighting style Olaf knew too well. Their eyes met for an instant, sending a jolt down Olaf's spine. Fixing his gaze on his brother's helm, he hewed his way through the brawl. He reached Hrolf just as his half-brother yanked his sword from a corpse.

Hrolf caught sight of him and bared his teeth. Men backed away, clearing the space between them.

A growl formed deep in Olaf's throat and came out as a roar.

Hrolf's sword came up and Olaf's rose to match it. Olaf closed the distance between them with one leap and swung.

His sword sliced Hrolf's neck with a force that should have taken his brother's head off, yet his blade did not bite into the flesh.

Hrolf grinned and slashed at Olaf's calves. The iron strips in Olaf's boots stopped the blade, but the blow swept him off balance. He threw himself forward into Hrolf, his weight bringing his half-brother down.

The two grappled on the rush-strewn floor. Hrolf dug an elbow into Olaf's eye socket, but Olaf jerked his head away before his brother could blind him. Hrolf scrambled on top, pinning him to the floor. Olaf thrashed violently and managed to throw his brother off. He staggered to his feet, but Hrolf yanked him back to the ground.

He landed hard on Hrolf's legs. A crack sounded. Hrolf's leg bent at a sickening angle. His eyes went wide as the blood leached from his face.

Hrolf struggled to rise like a hobbled calf, but Olaf knew he couldn't let his brother get to his feet again. A sudden jolt of loss flashed through his chest. He caught his breath and took hold of Hrolf's head. He looked down into Hrolf's fierce stare, blue with murder, then gave his brother's head a sharp wrench. Bone cracked as Hrolf's neck broke and his blue gaze iced over like a pond in winter.

*See you in Odin's hall, brother.*

From the high seat the white gyrfalcon flapped its wings and lofted into the rafters.

Olaf watched it fly out the gable end and knew that Hrolf was gone at last.

AXE SWINGING, Ragnhild closed in on her father. From the corner of her eye, she glimpsed Åsa converging on them.

The old king traded blows with Einar and Thorgeir, who had managed to acquire swords. Ragnhild reached Solvi as he parried a strike. His eyes flicked toward her and caught. Holding his stare, she swung her axe at his helm in a blow that rang on his boar's crest and sent him staggering. Einar took advantage of the opening to ram his sword into Solvi's midriff. The chain mail stopped the blade, but the blow knocked the wind from him. The old king crashed to the ground.

His eyes flickered open. Standing over him, Ragnhild read the defeat there. She almost pitied her father as his bannerman helped him struggle to his feet.

Åsa approached the old king, Olaf beside her. "You are outnumbered and defeated. Tell your men to throw down their weapons."

Solvi took his banner from the bearer's hands and leaned heavily on it for a moment. Slowly, he raised it for all his men to see, then waved it three times and cast it on the floor. The sign for surrender.

Gradually the bedlam subsided, the shouts and crash of steel quieting.

"Lay down your arms," Solvi commanded, throwing his sword to the ground.

The hall's floor resounded as his warriors followed their king's example.

"Gather their weapons," Åsa said to Olvir.

Åsa knew she should have them all killed, but Ragnhild's stricken face stopped her. Solvi had lost half his men or more. He was vastly outnumbered. But what would she do with them?

She would decide in the morning.

"You may tend to your wounded," Åsa said to Solvi. She turned to Olvir. "Put them in the guest house and the barracks under heavy guard."

Olvir herded Solvi and his remaining men off, dragging their wounded, leaving their dead behind.

Olaf and his men joined Tromøy's warriors in their search among the fallen for their own wounded. They carried them into the hall where Heid's apprentices tended their injuries. Jarl Borg's inert body was laid on a bench near the longfire, wrapped in furs. Åsa could not bring herself to give up on him.

Heid joined her at the old jarl's side.

"Thank you, Heid, for saving me from Hrafn," Åsa said, not looking up from the injured man.

The sorceress examined him. "You're welcome. I will always watch over you and your son." The völva knelt beside Borg, plucking a stray piece of down from the bedding. She held it beneath his nose.

Åsa held her breath. The tiny white strands seemed to move.

Heid thought so too. "He lives."

"What can be done for him?"

Heid shook her head. "He is with the gods now, and we must keep watch to see if they will send him back to us."

Åsa drew a deep breath. "Will you remain here at Tromøy?"

Though the völva did not look up from her patient, her expression seemed to soften. "We are needed here. We will stay."

Åsa hurried on to cover her relief. "What of Hrafn?"

The sorceress shrugged. "We haven't found his body. He must

have crawled off somewhere. He's blind. He won't last long in the forest."

"So you just left him for dead?"

"Would you take him in again, after all he's done?"

"He's a blind old man. What harm can he do?"

"Even blind, he's far from harmless," Heid said harshly "You should know that by now."

Åsa POSTED a double guard on Solvi's men for the night. She returned at last to the privacy of her bower room, where she shed her bloody clothes and washed away the battle grime in the water Brenna had heated over the brazier. She sat patiently while Brenna changed the dressing on her arm and helped her pull a clean linen shift over her head, topped by a woolen overdress and a thick shawl. She leaned back on the pillows, and Brenna brought Halfdan to her. She held her sleepy son and let peace descend on her for a few minutes.

She gave Halfdan back to Brenna and hoisted herself out of bed. Drawing her shawl tight around her, she made her way to the great hall.

After settling his men, Olaf joined her. He had cleaned up as well and changed his armor for soft wool breeks and tunic. His newly washed hair shone.

Åsa led Olaf to the partitioned room off the great hall that she never used. She eased her shift over her head, wincing, and slipped gratefully under the down comforter. Olaf shucked off tunic and breeks, his muscled body gleaming in the lamplight. He lifted the comforter, letting the chill air rush over her for an instant before his body slid in to blanket her. He gripped her waist, pulling her up against him so her breasts pressed into his chest, and she felt him hard against her belly. His lips brushed her throat, sending a tremor down her spine. Heat coursed through her limbs, banishing exhaustion, and she kissed him, running her fingertips lightly down the smooth muscles of his back. She heard his breath catch and he shivered. She moved her hands lower and around to his front, making him groan and pull her closer. They made love slowly, careful of each other's injuries.

Afterward they tumbled into sleep, limbs entangled. For once, Åsa remained firmly anchored in her human body.

~

RAGNHILD BURST INTO THE ROOM. "He's escaping!" she cried.

Åsa and Olaf sat up in bed.

"My father! He's getting away!"

Åsa and Olaf pulled on their clothes and rushed to the beach. In the distance, the moonlight glinted on two of Solvi's ships as they cleared the entrance. Olaf's men were launching ships to pursue them.

The shame-faced sentry greeted them. "My lady, they must have hidden weapons in the guesthouse and the barracks before Olaf's attack. They managed to break out and kill a dozen of my men. They launched the ships and got away before we knew it."

The news hit Åsa like a swordblow. She herself had once stolen a boat and escaped beneath a sentry's nose. She should have killed Solvi when she had the chance. She was too much a fool to be a queen.

"I should have known he would manage something like this," said Ragnhild. "I'm sorry, lady."

"They have too much of a head start. I doubt we'll catch them," said Olaf. Though his men had succeeded in launching the ships, the gap between them and Solvi was widening rapidly. Solvi's men were rowing for their lives.

"There's nothing to be done," said Åsa. "The old wolf has slunk away."

"But that old wolf may come back to bite," said Olaf.

"We will just have to be strong enough to meet him."

OLAF'S SHIPS returned without Solvi. Åsa ordered a quick meal of porridge and ale prepared and distributed before the folk of Tromøy tended to the dead.

The folk of Tromøy gathered the fallen and carried them to the burial mounds. Crows darkened the sky as they rose from the bodies, filling the air with their cries. Among the dead lay their weapons, which were collected and stored in the armory for distribution. Åsa and Ragnhild recovered their swords from the fallen enemy, as did Olvir, Einar, and many of the former captives.

The labor took most of the day. Olaf, coming late to the battle, had suffered minor casualties, losing thirty men. A dozen of Tromøy's warriors had also fallen. Åsa wandered among them, an ache in her chest as she recognized faces of those she had known, strangers now in death. Ulf stood bowed over Bram's body, and she joined him in silent mourning for the boy. Ragnhild gazed at Solvi's men mournfully. The enemy dead numbered more than one hundred, among them Hrolf. Åsa ordered his corpse beheaded so he could not rise again.

It was evening when they built a massive heap of logs before the mounds and piled on the bodies of friend and enemy alike. Olaf regarded Hrolf's head, storm clouds of emotion passing over his face. At last he nodded at Kalv, who helped him pick up the body and lay it on the pile. Olaf carefully handled his brother's head, setting it far from the body where it could do no harm, eyes staring northward.

Heid lit the kindling, stepping backward around the pile to baffle malevolent spirits while chanting a warding spell against the walking dead. As greasy smoke billowed from the pyre, her apprentices sang the vardlokkur to usher the spirits into the next world.

The fire burned all night. When the singing was done, Heid and her women went back to tend the wounded in the bower while Åsa and Olaf retired to the chamber off the great hall.

They made love more thoroughly this time. Despite the dull throbbing in her arm, a deep happiness suffused Åsa, something she had not felt since before her father and brother were killed.

It could not last.

"Come with me to Skiringssal." Olaf propped his head on his fist and fixed his soft hazel gaze on her.

She stared down at the comforter. *If only I were free to do what I want to do.* "I must stay and deal with the Danes."

"We can deal with them together."

She met his gaze, her eyes searching his, testing their depths. She remembered him dragging her, bound like a sacrifice, to his father. He had given her over to Gudrød when she had begged him to set her free. She had taken her own vengeance on Gudrød and gotten Tromøy back on her own, and now she would keep it.

"You know if I leave, they will overrun Tromøy. It will give them a toehold, a base to attack you in Vestfold. I must remain here and present a strong front."

Olaf flung himself down on the pillow with an exasperated sigh. "When will this end? I can't wait for you forever."

"Why can't you be happy with the way things are between us? Why must you own me?" she raged. "I'm an elected queen, not some peace cow."

The hurt on his face brought her up short. "I must marry," he said gently. "I need an heir. If you are unwilling, I must look elsewhere."

*You have an heir.* Fear welled up in her and strangled the words.

They turned their backs and spent an uneasy night. At some point Åsa must have slept, for she woke from troubled dreams.

She rose without waking Olaf, dressed, and went out to oversee breakfast. Olaf appeared among his men, avoiding her gaze.

After breakfast, Åsa and Olaf shared out the weapons and other booty among their hirds. In the afternoon, Åsa escorted Olaf and his warriors to the shore where their ships lay, Solvi's three abandoned ships beside them.

Olaf said, "I lack the crew to take the captured ships back to Skiringssal, so I leave them with you. I hate to leave you undefended."

Åsa met his gaze. "Don't worry about us. Solvi will be lucky to make it home with his wounded. He won't come back now."

"If the Danes come…"

"I'll have the signal fires rebuilt tomorrow."

"I'll be watching."

Olaf turned and went to his ship. Tears blurred Åsa's vision as he fell in with his húskarlar, dragging the ships off the beach. He scrambled over *Sea Dragon's* gunwales and turned to wave. He held her gaze while the rowers ran out their oars and dug the blades deep into the water, driving the dragons into the bay.

She watched until the fleet rounded the point, then turned and trudged up the hill.

Jarl Borg lay in the silent bower, unmoving and pale, yet his breath still stirred the down held to his nostrils. Åsa stayed by his bed through the night while Heid and her apprentices sang over him and burned herbs on the brazier, scenting the room.

By morning there was no change.

"He lives, for now," said Heid. She divided the women into shifts to keep the chanting constant over the unconscious man, and the bower scented with herbs at all times. She and Åsa took turns napping through the day so that they could keep watch throughout the night hours, when the soul was in the most danger of slipping away.

When there was no change the next morning, Heid said to Åsa, "We must make a sacrifice to the gods in exchange for his life, else he will waste away. The body can only last so long without nourishment."

"What would the gods require to return him to us?"

Heid stared into the fire, her eyes glazing into a trance. When her vision cleared, she said, "He has the heart of a wild boar. His line claims descent from Frey."

"Very well, a boar it is." Åsa marched into the hall where her warriors idled, still recovering from the battle. Though they were the victors, Solvi's escape and the loss of their comrades had left them silent and grim.

As she mounted the high seat, they looked up from their gaming pieces and whetstones.

"In the morning, we hunt the boar for the gods in exchange for Jarl Borg," she announced.

The faces of men who had a moment before been shadowed with defeat now lit up with purpose.

~

THE HUNTING PARTY set off the next morning right after porridge, led by eager dogs straining at their leashes. The warriors carried their boar spears, the beaters bearing sharpened sticks to flush the quarry from cover. Brenna had padded Åsa's arm with layers of linen, over which she wore a hard leather jacket. Heid sent her lead apprentice with the party, bearing a bronze bowl to catch the boar's blood.

The dogs caught a scent right away, leading the hunting party through the forest to a small cave in the toe of a hill.

At the entrance to the boar's lair, the dogs halted. Eyes ringed white, they sat back on their haunches and bayed. The warriors surrounded the cavern's maw, dropped to one knee, and grounded their spear butts firmly in the earth.

For a moment nothing happened while the dogs kept up their ruckus. Then the dark mouth of the cave exploded as the boar barreled out, charging into the baying pack. It hooked a howling dog with a gleaming tusk and tossed it aside, barks turning to yelps as the dog sprawled on the ground.

The boar stood at bay, red eyes glaring around the ring of spears. The tusks jerked convulsively, its shoulder muscles bunching under its thick dark hide as its hooves pawed the ground.

It lowered its head and charged straight at Åsa.

Her grip tightened on the spear shaft and she jammed the butt deeper into the ground. She met the red eyes and held the murderous stare. As the boar charged, she aimed the spear point slightly below the heart. The boar rammed the spear tip, the impact driving the point into the tough hide until it hit bone. Åsa twisted the spear until she felt the tip slide between the ribs. The enraged boar kept coming, hooves churning the ground, surging up the shaft to get at her. Its seething breath was hot on her face, its yellow tusks slashing at her eyes as it slammed into the spear's cross guard.

Bellowing, the boar bolted to the right, dragging her along as it struggled to shake off the spear. Her arm burned as she bore down on the shaft with all her weight while the spear savaged the boar's chest. The dogs were mauling the boar's rear quarters, and the warriors waded in, sinking their spears into the ridged spine. The boar went over, thrashing on its side, pulling dogs and men down with it. It kicked and tossed its head, then at last it lay still, sides heaving.

Åsa struggled to her knees, breathing hard as she drew her hunting knife. The apprentice brought the sacrificial bowl and held it while Åsa found the boar's pulsing throat artery. She drew her blade across it, releasing a gush of hot blood into the bowl. When the bowl brimmed over, the apprentice carried it to the hall. Åsa followed, leaving the warriors to butcher the carcass.

Heid was waiting, a sprinkler of fir twigs already in hand. Jarl Borg lay before the carved pillar depicting the god Frey. Heid took the steaming bowl and dipped the fir twigs into it. The women's voices rose in a vardlokkur as she spattered blood on the image until the wood was red. Then she turned to Jarl Borg's still form and sprinkled him with what remained in the bowl.

"Now we await the decision of the gods," said Heid.

They left the old warrior at the goddess's feet, wrapped in furs. Åsa and Heid kept watch beside him. All night he did not stir, his face still pale and cold as snow. Åsa fought the twin drag of sleep and despair.

Early next morning, Sigrid brought them a cup of warm ale. Åsa sipped gratefully with heavy eyes.

"Look!" said Heid. Åsa dropped her cup and stared at the old man. His eyelid twitched. It quivered.

Then Borg snorted. Åsa leapt to her feet as his eyes flew open.

"Ale," he rasped.

With shaking hands, Heid brought her cup to his lips, supporting his head as he sipped.

"Can you remember where you were?" she asked him. "Did Freyja take you, or Odin?"

The old warrior's voice was faint. "A great hall...many warriors. My father...my brothers." He smiled at Åsa as the ale brought color to his face. "I saw your father too." His voice grew stronger. "And Gyrd. It was for their sake that I returned. I promised to look after you a little while longer."

Åsa smiled back at her old friend, remembering her own visit to the afterlife, and how she had wanted to stay with her departed family. She had returned to the living for Halfdan's sake. "I'm glad they persuaded you. I need you."

That night they feasted on the boar's meat to honor the old warrior's return from the land of the gods.

# CHAPTER 18

Tromøy
May, AD 821

Åsa called a council of war. She gathered those she trusted most, including Olvir, Jarl Borg, and Heid. Ragnhild was there as well, with her sworn men Einar, Thorgeir, and Svein.

"We'll be seeing the Danes soon, now that the spring storms have left the Skagerrak," Jarl Borg observed over his mead.

"We have some time, though," said Åsa. "Knut reports that Rorik has his hands full, caught between his brothers, his uncle, and the Franks. He'll be busy for a while."

"You have a strong ally in Olaf, and you have us," said Ragnhild.

"Yes, I still have the best allies anyone could have," said Åsa. "Hrolf is dead, and Solvi vanquished. We have won a lot. But we are down to sixty-three fighters. Even with Olaf's warriors, the Danes outnumber us so greatly we have no hope of surviving their attack."

"We'll need more men," said Ragnhild. "You can get them at the midsummer assembly."

"To do that I need silver," Åsa said.

"Olaf will give you whatever you ask," said Heid.

Åsa colored. "If I ask him for silver, he will expect a commitment I am not prepared to make right now."

"My father has plenty of silver," said Ragnhild.

Åsa stared at her. "I doubt if Solvi will offer to make restitution."

Ragnhild gave her an evil grin. "I wasn't suggesting that he would give it willingly."

Åsa caught her breath at the girl's audacity. "We don't have the warriors for a raid on Solvi," she stammered, mind working furiously.

"We don't need to attack them," Ragnhild replied. "I'm his daughter. I know where his hoard is buried. I can sneak in and take it. Just give me a ship and crew. Olvir can guide us down this coast, and once we round to the western side, Einar, Thorgeir, and Svein and I know the way."

Still astonished, Åsa turned to Einar. "You would rob your former king?"

Einar glanced at Thorgeir and Svein, who both nodded. "Lady, after the way he has betrayed us, we owe him no loyalty. And he owes you reparation for the damage he caused, the livestock he slaughtered, the stores he depleted."

Åsa realized they were sincere. She looked around the group. Heid beamed her approval at Ragnhild while Thorgeir and Svein nodded grimly. When she caught Olvir's eye, she saw a predatory gleam in it.

"Very well. Choose a ship."

They trooped down the trail to the beach, where the two Danish warships captured the year before lay beside Solvi's abandoned vessels. These were all too large for this stealthy raid.

"Let's see what's in the boathouse," said Olvir.

It was a huge building nearly as big as the great hall. As Olvir and Einar hauled the great doors open, a shiver ran down Åsa's spine. She had not been in here since before her father's death, and it didn't appear that Hrolf had during his brief stint as lord here. In the dim, cavernous reaches, the shapes of hulls and fierce beasts lurked. These ships had once been famous, Harald's pride, the stuff of legend. Their names floated into her mind like ghosts. *Sea Stallion. Wave King. Ran's Lover. Night Raider.* But Harald had given up raiding to please his queen long before Åsa was born, and for years the proud ships had lain moldering in the dank boathouse. Hrolf had obviously not brought them out in his brief time here. Harald's daughter lacked the men to crew them, and so they must sleep on.

Einar and Olvir looked over the smaller vessels, settling on a twelve-man karvi called *Wave Skimmer.* It was in good repair, with a complete set of oars and four spares. *Wave Skimmer* had been Harald's favorite of the small ships. Åsa remembered many journeys in it, sitting between Harald and Gunnhild while Gyrd annoyed the rowers with questions. Her last journey had been with Harald and Gyrd.

Einar and Olvir dragged *Wave Skimmer* out onto the beach, where they went over it carefully. They spent the day recaulking the seams with wool and pine tar and overhauling the sail and rigging.

Ragnhild chose a dozen of the strongest rowers and decided they could depart in two days. They equipped the ship with wooden spades for digging, a dozen bows with thirty arrows each, casting spears for each member of the crew along with hunting knives and short axes. On this seagoing venture they left their heavy chain mail behind, dressing in jackets of quilted linen. The fabric was coated with a hard pine resin varnish, thick enough to deflect an arrow or a blade but still lightweight and allowing freedom of movement.

"I hope we won't need to fight," Einar told Åsa. "We'd be

outnumbered. Swords will do us little good. We are best off with arrows and casting spears to keep them at a distance."

They loaded provisions, a cask of ale, dried meat, and barley for two weeks.

"If we have to row the entire distance, it will take a week to get there," said Einar. "Once we come out of the skerries, we should catch a good breeze that will speed our trip. But it's best to be prepared."

On the eve of departure, Åsa and Heid sacrificed a goat to the sea goddess, Ran, for a safe passage, and for help from Odin, the god of deception. They feasted late into the night.

Afterward, Åsa lay awake, her mind seething with misgivings. Ragnhild was so confident, too cocksure of her audacious plan. Åsa hoped the experienced húskarlar would keep the girl out of trouble. She winced at the thought of Ragnhild falling back into her father's hands. Even worse would be the fate of the loyal men with her if they were captured. Åsa couldn't even think about how Solvi would deal with their treachery.

Åsa bolted upright, pouring sweat. She couldn't let them go through with it. It wasn't worth the risk. She drew a woolen shawl around her shoulders and ran barefoot into the pre-dawn chill down the trail to the beach.

But they were already gone.

# CHAPTER 19

Southeast Coast of Norway
May, AD 821

The late spring sun was gentle on Ragnhild's shoulders as Olvir guided them through the rocky islets that formed an inside passage. It was exhausting work fighting tide rips and capricious currents, but they were grateful for the shelter the archipelago provided from the open sea.

As evening fell, Olvir directed them to a deserted island to make camp. They built a fire and ate a quick meal of dried meat and flat bread. Nobody seemed to have the energy for conversation, and Ragnhild crawled gratefully into her sheepskins, falling instantly asleep.

In the morning a dense fog closed in, and Ragnhild stationed herself on the bow to guide them through the shoals with hand signals. Peering into the depths for submerged rocks took a toll. She was grateful when the fog burned off in the early afternoon and she could take her place at the oars.

They beached that night in a hidden cove near the cape of Lindesnes, the most southern point of land. From there the next landfall to the south was Daneland.

In the morning the weather was still flat calm, allowing them to round the southern headland under oars and gradually turn north up the west coast. Ragnhild began to recognize the landscape. Olvir deferred to her and Einar's local knowledge. They stayed inside the archipelago, plying their oars through the rocky channels.

Well before evening, Ragnhild started looking for a good place to land. "I think we should put in at Twin Rocks," she said to Einar. "It's close, but not too close."

"A good choice," he replied.

Ragnhild stayed on the bow, watching for the distinctive rocks that marked the entrance. Once she sighted them, she guided them in to land in the deserted cove. They dragged *Wave Skimmer* far up onto the beach, hiding it in the undergrowth.

"We're close to my father's steading," she said. "No fire tonight, and we must stay quiet."

They ate a cold meal of smoked venison and flatbread left from the night before. Most of the crew burrowed under their sheepskins early, but Ragnhild sat up late with her three sworn men. They gazed out on the familiar landscape, each lost in their own memories.

Ragnhild held a short length of rope, which she tied in a slipknot. "Are you certain you want to go through with this?"

"It will be strange, raiding the home we once defended," Einar admitted.

Ragnhild worried the knot. "You can stay here if you want no part in it. We can pick you up on our way back."

"We made up our minds to do this before we left, and that has not changed," said Svein.

Einar nodded in agreement. "We support you and Queen Åsa now."

"You know if we're caught, my father will show you no mercy." Ragnhild pulled the tail of the knot, slipping it free.

"Then we'd best not get caught." Thorgeir's teeth gleamed in the starlight.

The four of them sat in silence, then one by one the men slipped off to their beds, leaving Ragnhild with her piece of rope.

They rose at dawn and quietly equipped themselves with wooden spades as well as throwing spears and hand axes they hoped they would not have to use. The rowers stayed behind to guard the ship, while a small party made up of Ragnhild, Thorgeir, Einar, Svein, and Olvir went after the treasure.

Ragnhild led them silently through the forest she had known since childhood. Familiar landmarks tugged at her. She wanted to turn down the path to the settlement, but she forged onward through the unmarked woodland.

The morning grew warm, and she began to sweat.

"Are you sure we are going the right way?" whispered Olvir.

"Be still!" she hissed and kept going.

Near midday they stopped beside a brook to drink and rest. A cloud of gnats rose up from the creek bed to torment them.

"Are we almost there?" asked Olvir.

"Yes," said Ragnhild, snorting out the gnats that swarmed her nostrils.

"Are you sure?" he persisted.

"I'm sure!" Doubt needled at her. She had not reckoned that it would take this long to find the spot.

"I'm afraid we won't have time to get the hoard back to the ship before dark." Olvir's voice was fraught.

"We'll get there." Ragnhild got to her feet and stomped into the brush, leaving the others to scramble after her.

Worry gnawed at her stomach as she made her way through the undergrowth. It had been five summers since she had come to this spot. The trees and brush had grown a lot. She had been just ten winters old, Harald fourteen and Orlyg twelve, when her father had led them through the forest to the place where he'd buried his hoard. It was marked by an ancient oak that had been split by lightning in some long-ago storm. Half the tree was a bare, dead silver, the other half still bore leaves.

"When I am gone, you will share the treasure buried here and divide my kingdom among you," Solvi had told them. "Harald, I want you to rule Solbakk, Orlyg the islands, and you, daughter, will have Gausel as your mother wished."

That was long before he had made his deal with the Irish king. Her brothers would have split the kingdom between them after she'd married the Christian. She supposed her share of the hoard would make up her dowry. By Norse law, a woman's dowry reverted to her if she were to divorce or become widowed. Ragnhild wondered if the Christian law allowed a woman to keep her dowry if she killed her husband.

She halted abruptly, her knees weak with relief. There it was. The half-dead oak was smaller than she remembered and overgrown with brush, but recognizable.

"This is it," she said. "My father's hoard is buried here."

The hoard had been buried long enough for young shrubs to grow in, but the roots were shallow and their wooden spades turned the soil.

They worked in shifts through the morning, digging a hole the size of a child's grave. Shoulder deep in the pit, Olvir asked, "Are you sure this is the right spot? We have dug nearly to Nifleheim."

Ragnhild's insides quavered. Had she been mistaken? She looked up at the half-dead oak. There could not be another like it in this forest. "Keep digging."

The men groaned but went back to work.

A horrible thought struck Ragnhild. Was it possible her father had moved his hoard? Could he have moved it after she had sworn to Åsa? No. The shrubs that grew here had not been disturbed for years. Yet her certainty wavered.

Then Olvir drew back, spade poised in the air. "Bones!"

"Human bones," said Thorgeir. The men scrambled out of the pit.

"This is a grave," breathed Olvir, staring down at the bones.

"A slave to guard the hoard," said Einar.

The men did not move. No one wanted to risk a curse by the living dead.

"The draugr will not attack a rightful heir," said Ragnhild. She jumped into the hole. Careful not to touch the bones, she began gingerly scraping the dirt away with her spade. When the human skeleton was completely uncovered, she used her spade to lift a section of the bones to the top of the pit and slide them off onto her cloak.

Once the skeleton had been removed, Einar climbed back into the hole to help her broaden the area.

In a mercifully short time, Ragnhild's spade struck something hard.

"There it is!" she said, relieved at the sight of oak.

They scraped away the dirt to reveal an oaken chest bound with iron. The chest was no bigger than a mead cask but surprisingly heavy, and it took Einar, Thorgeir, and Svein working together to pry it up enough for Ragnhild to feed ropes under and pass them to Olvir. He tied them around the chest, and all five of them took a strain. At first the chest stuck fast in the dirt, then suddenly it burst free. They dragged it out of the hole and heaved it onto the ground.

Einar beat the pin from the iron lock with the back of his axe and Svein used a spade to pry the lid open. Gold and silver glimmered in its depths. The chest brimmed with silver coins and Irish gold crosses set with gemstones.

Ragnhild broke the awed silence. "No wonder it was so heavy. Years' worth of looting the Irish. Well, he stole it from them; now we steal it from him."

Einar tore his attention from the treasure and gave the sky a worried glance. "It's getting late."

Ragnhild wrapped the skeleton in her cloak and climbed back down into the hole. She arranged the bones in the bottom of the pit with a silent prayer to Hel, goddess of the dead. The men helped her out, then they shoveled the soil back into the hole and tamped it down. Despite their efforts, a shallow depression remained where the chest had been. They did their best to disguise it by replacing the uprooted plants and smoothing the trampled earth, but Ragnhild could see that it was obvious the ground had been disturbed.

"Let's hope no one comes here until we are well at sea," said Einar.

He replaced the pin in the oak chest's hasp and bound it securely with ropes. They rigged the ends between the four men and set off, following Ragnhild back the way they had come. Despite their efforts at stealth, as they lugged the heavy chest they tramped through the forest like oxen, leaving a broad trail of flattened brush and broken branches.

Ragnhild kept glancing behind her, expecting to see her father's men in pursuit. The brush rustled, and her heart flopped like a fish on the line. She signaled the men to halt, holding her breath as the branches stirred, closer and closer.

She could see her men's heads on poles. Solvi would ship her off to the Irish king, this time leaving no chance of escape.

Her eyes bulged as the brush parted and a head emerged from the undergrowth. Her heart thrashed so hard in her chest that it took her a moment to realize it was a deer.

Her knees quivered in relief as the doe bounded off, followed by a fawn. With a shaky laugh, she led on.

When the brush rustled again, she ignored it. *Another deer.* The branches parted and startled eyes peered out at her.

Human eyes.

They all stopped in their tracks, staring at the man. It was Frode, one of her father's warriors.

"Lady Ragnhild?" he said incredulously. "Einar?" His eyes strayed to the treasure chest.

Einar's hand went to his axe, but he hesitated for an instant. Ragnhild watched understanding dawn in Frode's eyes, then he was gone, crashing through the underbrush.

"I'll get him," said Olvir, drawing his own axe.

"We can't get separated," said Ragnhild. "Let's just go." She was not sure if she had said that only to spare Frode's life.

No longer trying for stealth, they increased their pace. Even so, the sun was low them when they sighted *Wave Skimmer*. The crew emerged from the trees, greeting them with smiles that broadened when they saw the treasure chest.

"We've been spotted." said Olvir. "We must go, now!"

The crew heaved the chest onto the floorboards and shoved the karvi into the water. They slipped over the gunwales and took up their oars, threading their way back through the skerries while Ragnhild kept a nervous lookout from the stern.

They had been underway for an hour when movement in the distance caught her eye. In the late afternoon light, she saw what she feared the most. "There's a ship back there."

The rowers applied themselves to the oars with vigor, and their smaller, more maneuverable vessel managed to maintain the lead as they wended through the skerries. But the inside passage came to an abrupt end and they broke into open water, where the pursuing ship's superior length and bigger crew gave it a strong advantage. Before long, the pursuers halved the distance between them.

"They outnumber us drastically," said Einar. "If they catch us, it will not be a good death."

"For everyone but me," said Ragnhild. "Remember, I'm worth my weight in silver." She bent her bow. "I can try to make them drop their oars to raise their shields."

She nocked, drew, and fired a test arrow.

The first arrow fell short. As the pursuing ship drew closer, she marked the range and held her fire until she could make out the man in the prow. She aimed for his throat and let the ship close a little more until his features became clear. His blond hair shone, his beard glinted gold.

A shock of recognition jolted up Ragnhild's spine.

Harald Goldbeard. Her eldest brother.

"Don't give them a chance to fire back," Einar warned.

Ragnhild shifted her aim a fraction and loosed. The arrow flew by her brother's face and he stopped mid-shout, staring at her open-mouthed.

For a moment they glared at each other across the narrowing gap. Then she nocked and took deliberate aim at his face. As she fired, Harald brought his shield up to catch her arrow. He bawled an order. The crew boated their oars and shields flew up. Immediately the ship lost headway.

"They're slowing!" Ragnhild cried, shooting one arrow after another. Her arms burned and her fingertips were raw.

The gap widened as Harald's crew began to fire back.

Then Ragnhild's bowstring snapped. There was no time to restring. As she reached for a new bow, Einar grabbed another, slipping the rope loop over the steering oar to hold their course.

"It's Harald," she warned as he nocked an arrow. He nodded and took aim.

"Shields!" Einar dropped the bow and snatched a shield from the rail as a flight of incoming arrows hissed down on them.

Ragnhild grabbed a shield and flung it up as an arrow thwacked into it. A cry made her turn and she saw Thorgeir fall, clutching an arrow in his shoulder. Ragnhild started toward him.

"It's in the meat," he said through clenched teeth. "We'll get it out later. Just leave me and row."

Ragnhild took up Thorgeir's oar with the others. As they pulled away, Ragnhild heard her brother shout at his bowmen and her chest tightened. The gap widened between the ships as her brother's men scrambled to regain their oars.

Einar returned to the steering oar and barked out the strokes as they rowed for all they were worth. Ragnhild kept her shield at hand, ready to snatch up if Harald sent another volley, but they made it into the cover of the skerries.

Ragnhild rested her oar. Her fingers throbbed and her arms quivered. As the sun neared the horizon, Einar eyed their pursuer as the bigger boat negotiated the passages.

"If we can stay ahead of them until dark, we should be able to lose them under cover of night."

The sun sank below the horizon and they spoke no more. The crew stuffed rags in their oar holes to muffle the sound, and they rowed silently, the only sound the gentle slap of the oar blades in the water. Thorgeir lay on the floorboards, so quiet Ragnhild feared he was dead.

They rowed through the short summer night without sighting their foes. As the sky began to lighten, they put into a little estuary and hid the boat beneath overhanging branches.

Einar joined Ragnhild at Thorgeir's side. "He breathes," she said.

"We cannot risk trying to get the arrow out now. Even Thorgeir would scream."

Ragnhild shared out food and drink, and the crew rested as best they could. Through the leaves she watched the sun rise, straining for sounds of their pursuers. From time to time, Thorgeir moaned and shifted.

When the sun was fully up, Einar said, "They must have passed us in the dark. Let me take a look at the arrow."

Thorgeir bit a stick in half as Einar cut away the arrow shaft as close to his shoulder as he dared, but the wounded man made no sound.

"I don't dare dig the arrowhead out. I could do more damage than good, and it could be all that's stopping him from bleeding to death," said Einar. "We'll have to leave it in until we get back and pray it does not fester."

They bathed Thorgeir's shoulder in icy seawater, cleansing and numbing the wound, and tucked him into the warm fleece of his sleeping bag. With a groan, he slumped down and closed his eyes.

Ragnhild took the first watch, peering through the foliage for signs of her brother's ships. Thorgeir appeared beside her, his face gray. "I might moan in my sleep," he said. "Best I stay awake."

They kept a silent vigil. Ragnhild couldn't have spoken even if it were safe. Her chest felt as if it was full of mud, so heavy she found it hard to swallow. She knew Thorgeir might die from his wound, and it was all her fault. They had to get him back to Heid before the wound could fester.

Near mid-morning Thorgeir nudged her and pointed at a ship approaching under oars, making its way close in along the coast, combing the shore. She woke the crew silently and they crouched in the boat, weapons ready. They held their breath while the ship passed, close enough that Ragnhild could make out the fury on her brother's face.

After the enemy ship had been out of sight for some time, Einar signaled them to emerge from the estuary.

"You must rest, lady," he said.

Ragnhild crawled under her sleeping skin, where she tossed and fretted. It had shaken her, seeing Harald. The look of hate he had given her put her guts in an uproar. They had always been on the same side before. He had taught her to use the bow she had drawn against him.

Eventually the rhythm of the rowers lulled her into an uneasy sleep.

She woke to shouting.

Ragnhild peered over the gunwales to see Harald's ship looming on the horizon. Her brother had doubled back. He was heading right for them.

Heart pounding, she scrambled out of her sleeping skin and grabbed her bow. She snatched up an enemy arrow from the bottom of the boat and nocked.

"Spears!" Einar barked. The men boated their oars and snatched up their casting spears. As Harald's ship bore down on them, they let fly. Einar and Ragnhild loosed their last arrows. Ragnhild saw her brother duck behind his shield, but scream from the enemy ship told them at least some of their missiles had found marks among the crew.

"Row!" cried Ragnhild, shouldering her bow and grabbing a shield in each hand as Einar did the same. The crew were already back at their oars and pulling hard while Ragnhild and Einar sheltered them from the hail of arrows. Ragnhild picked up those that fell into the boat and fired back.

Hard as they rowed, the bigger ship continued to gain. With no more arrows or spears, there was nothing they could do but watch as Harald bore down on them. In the distance, Ragnhild could see the chain of islands where the inside passage resumed. If only they could make it there, they could elude the bigger ship in the skerries. But their pursuer was gaining too fast.

Ragnhild watched her brother close in. "I am so sorry I got you into this mess."

"We are glad to give our lives in your service," said Einar.

She looked down at Thorgeir, gray-faced and still in his sleeping skins. "I can't let that happen." She had one more ploy that might work.

Ragnhild pulled off her heavy quilted jacket and leaped onto the gunwale.

"Keep going!" she shouted at Einar. "He's my brother. He won't let me drown." *I hope.*

Drawing in a great breath, she threw herself overboard with a cry.

The icy water drove the breath from her. She heard Harald's shout, confirming that he had seen her in the water. As her body recovered from the shock, she began to swim away from both ships, splashing energetically to draw attention. Soon her brother would have to make the choice between rescuing her or pursuing his quarry. She hoped he would decide that her value was greater than her father's hoard.

She swam on. The cold water began to sap her strength. Looking over her shoulder, she saw that Harald's ship still pursued Einar. Had her gambit failed?

She plowed on through the frigid water, though her limbs were numb and her strokes increasingly feeble. The lassitude of cold crept over her and knew she had passed the point of no return. She was too far out to swim to safety before the frigid water overcame her. If Harald didn't pick her up soon, the cold would kill her.

She had heard it was not a painful death.

She forced a few more lazy strokes, but they went awry, barely raising a splash. It didn't matter. This was better than seeing Einar's head on a pole. Better than marrying the Irish king.

A shadow loomed and a big hand seized her arm.

"You brat!" Harald scowled as he yanked her from the water and dropped her in the bottom of the boat. "Father is going to whip you when we get home."

Ragnhild lay shivering on the floorboards. A whipping was the least of her worries.

~

Tromøy

ÅSA WAS WAITING on the shore with her húskarlar when the raiding party arrived four days later. The crew drew the boat up

173

on the beach and carefully lifted Thorgeir over the gunwales. The shore party made a stretcher of their cloaks for the wounded man. He was unconscious, and he moaned faintly when they moved him.

"He took an arrow to the shoulder," said Olvir. "I dared not remove the arrowhead. I fear it may be festering."

Åsa examined Thorgeir. His face was sickly pale and beaded with sweat. "How long has he been unconscious?"

"Since last night."

"Take him to Heid. Let us hope she can heal him," Åsa bade the húskarlar. They set off, bearing the wounded man up the trail with care.

She turned to Einar, who did not meet her eyes.

"Where is Ragnhild?"

"Solvi has her. She sacrificed herself to let us get away."

Åsa's nostrils flared as she stared at Einar's bowed head.

The boat crew heaved the oaken chest onto the sand at her feet. Olvir stepped forward and opened it. At the sight of the glittering contents, Åsa drew a sharp breath.

"We will go after Ragnhild as soon as you have rested," she said.

"We don't have enough men to go against Solvi," Olvir said.

Åsa glared at him. "Are you telling me we must leave her to her fate? That I will not do. We must think of a plan to rescue her."

There was a lengthy silence. At last, Einar stepped forward.

"Speak, man," Åsa said.

"Lady, there is an island lying out some distance from the entrance to Solvi's harbor. It is unguarded, and it could become our base to spy on them. From there, we may be able to find a way to recover Lady Ragnhild."

"Good. Gather fresh men. We'll take two of Solvi's ships with full crews. Be ready to leave at dawn."

# CHAPTER 20

Solbakk, Rogaland
May, AD 821

Harald dragged Ragnhild, still wet and shivering, into the great hall. From his high seat, Solvi glowered down on her.

"Well, daughter, what have you to say to me?"

Ragnhild could not bring herself to answer.

"Speak, girl!"

Ragnhild smiled faintly. The men had gotten away with their lives and the hoard. They would be safe in Tromøy soon.

Solvi turned on his eldest son. "You let them get away with my treasure!"

"Father, it was either that or let her drown."

"I'll get my treasure out of her," Solvi bellowed. "We'll ship her off to the Irish king. Lock her in the bower."

Harald grabbed her roughly and hauled her away. He towered

over her, and his grip was hard as iron. She didn't bother to struggle.

"You shouldn't make him so angry," he said.

"I can't seem to help it," Ragnhild said. "I think he hates everything about me."

"If you did your duty by him, he'd treat you very differently."

She glared up at her brother. "Would you become a slave to an Irish master to make him happy?"

Harald glowered and looked away. As the eldest son, it was not a choice that he would ever have to make.

They had reached the bower. He yanked the door open and shoved her inside.

Katla, her nurse, put down her spinning and hurried over. Her plump arms enfolded Ragnhild and tears rolled down her cheeks. "You're home, lamb," she cried softly, stroking Ragnhild's hair.

"Not for long." Ragnhild's voice cracked in spite of herself.

"You've had a hard time. Let me look after you." Katla gently peeled off Ragnhild's sodden tunic and breeks. She wrapped the shivering girl in a down comforter and led her to the bed. "Now you just rest while I make you something warm."

Katla fed her a hot brew, and she stopped shaking. The old fóstra always knew how to make her feel better. Ragnhild's mother had died birthing her, and Katla had raised the little girl.

She fought sleep, but exhaustion and the drink, which was surely a sleeping potion, dragged her down into unconsciousness.

When she woke, Katla was packing.

"I'm glad to see you are rested, lamb. As soon as you get your strength back, you'll set sail to the Irish kingdom," the nurse chattered happily.

Katla carefully laid out an array of clothing on the bed. "I embroidered these just for you, my lamb." She proudly held up a pleated linen shift, elaborately embroidered. Beside it lay a finely woven blue wool overdress, trimmed with a tablet-woven band, and fur-lined cape of a thicker weave. Katla folded each item carefully before tucking them into a trunk.

Ragnhild's spirits plummeted. Her father was not going to waste any time. There would be no chance to escape.

Katla left off packing and went to Ragnhild, enfolding the girl in her plump arms. "I know you don't want to go, lamb, but you will be happy. I promise. Marriage is good for women."

Åsa would come for her. By now, *Wave Skimmer* should have made it back to Tromøy. She had to delay her departure for a few more days to give them time to come for her. Maybe if she were sick…

Ragnhild tried an experimental cough.

Katla's face wrinkled with concern. "Poor lamb, have you caught a chill?"

Ragnhild nodded weakly and sank back on the pillows.

She managed to stay in bed four days, choking down Katla's medicinal brews. With her spirits so low, the ruse didn't take much effort. But at last her father commanded that she be made ready for the voyage, healthy or not. Katla roused her and fed her some thin gruel, then helped her out of bed. Ragnhild stood, shaky and chilled in her linen shirt.

"Now, lamb, you'll be all right. You will come to like your new home and husband."

Ragnhild fought down panic as Katla pulled the woolen tunic over her head. The old nurse murmured soothingly as she fastened the leather belt around her waist and helped her into woolen breeks. The voyage to Ireland could take a week or more in open seas. Although this time of year the weather was fair, she had to be dressed for anything.

A team of húskarlar waited outside the door. They escorted her to the shore, where Harald and her younger brother, Orlyg, stood by the fine new ship that Solvi had ordered built especially for the marriage. It was of the best oak, rowed by thirty men. The stem and rails had been carved by the finest woodcarvers, the graceful serpentine design picked out in red and blue paint against a black background. It was the centerpiece of a breath-taking dowry.

To Ragnhild it looked like a coffin. She didn't bother to struggle as her father's men led her aboard the ship. She stared out to sea in misery as they shoved off from the beach, escorted by one other ship to protect them in the long crossing and bring the bridal escort back home.

She kept reminding herself it was worth it to save her crew.

A PEREGRINE FALCON perched in a tree, watching the procession. As the wedding party boarded the ship, the falcon took flight.

The peregrine circled round to the western side of the offshore island, where two ships lay under their awnings in a small cove. Each was crewed with thirty warriors. Åsa hoped the small force would be enough for this raid. Surprise was critical to give them the advantage.

The night before, Einar had guided them in through the sker-ries to make landfall. Now they were armed and waiting.

The falcon flew under the ship's awning, lighting beside the prone form on the sheepskins. Åsa reentered her body and sat up, calling for Einar.

"We are in time. The bridal party is embarking now, and Ragnhild is among them. As you predicted, he is only sending two ships to Ireland," she told him.

Einar nodded. "Solvi owns the western sea. The wolf has no fear of sheep."

Åsa grinned. "Let's give him something to fear."

The ship's crews took in their awnings and shoved off.

They lurked out of sight behind the headland, positioned to swoop down on their quarry as soon as the bridal party cleared the island. Their position gave them the windward advantage, and their attack would be well out of sight of the mainland and any help from Solvi.

As the Solbakk vessels emerged from the shelter of the island, they were bucking a foul tide as well as contrary winds that forced them to remain under oars. Åsa's ships hoisted their sails and surged out from behind the headland to intercept them.

Åsa's eyes widened at the sight of the finely carved and painted bridal ship. "That's where Ragnhild will be," she shouted. "Don't damage that ship!"

As the Tromøy fleet ran down on their quarry, their archers loosed a hail of arrows boosted by the favorable breeze. The Solbakk men were still rowing against the foul wind and tide, unsuspecting targets. By their screams, it was apparent that first volley took a toll on the enemy. As Åsa's ships closed, a few of the Solbakk archers returned fire, but the adverse wind robbed the arrows of force, and they dropped harmlessly into the water.

RAGNHILD WAS SULKING in the stern next to Harald, who had the helm, when the arrows hailed down on them and men screamed and fell. Her heart surged when she recognized Åsa and her crew.

As her brother flung up his shield, she threw herself at him and shoved him over the side. Off balance, he tumbled into the water with a cry. Ragnhild grabbed hold of the tiller and veered toward Åsa's ship. The men had abandoned their oars during the attack, and now they stared at her in confusion. One of them rose and started toward her.

With her free hand, Ragnhild picked up a casting spear and jabbed it at him. "This ship is mine. I am in command now. You may swear to me or follow my brother." She nodded at Harald, who was treading water while the other ship came to his rescue.

The warrior froze for an instant. Ragnhild could see him add up the factors. As her dowry, the ship did indeed belong to her, and they had been trained all their lives to obey the king's daughter. But they had their orders from her father, and they feared him far more.

From the corner of her eye she saw the flash of a heaving line as Åsa's grappling hook came over the side. She reached out and latched it firmly to the gunwale. Åsa's other ship came down on the other side.

Åsa's crews swarmed aboard wielding spears and axes. Solvi's escort ship had stopped to pull Harald from the water. Now the crew began to row toward the battle, but they were slowed by wind and tide.

Ragnhild swung her spear and hit one of her father's warriors squarely, knocking him overboard. As he hit the water with a cry, Ragnhild poked another warrior in the back with her spear tip. The man was fighting Einar, but he whirled on her, fury blazing in his eyes. Einar took the opportunity to shoulder him overboard after his shipmate.

With boarding parties on both sides, Harald's men were outnumbered two to one. They managed to put up a creditable defense, but soon Tromøy's warriors forced them all overboard after their leader. Fortunately, they wore linen battle jackets rather than chain mail, so they stayed afloat while Solvi's other ship came to their rescue.

Soon the Solbakk ship would have a double crew, matching Åsa's numbers. The battle had been bloodless so far. Fighting men they'd known all their lives, Ragnhild, Einar, and Svein had shown restraint, and Åsa's men had followed suit. But Ragnhild knew if her father's men caught them, they would not show the Tromøy crews the same mercy.

"We'd better go now," Ragnhild called.

Åsa's warriors scrambled back aboard their ships, leaving a few behind to handle Ragnhild's dowry ship. She took the helm while her new crew cast off the grappling hooks and hastily raised sail.

Solvi's escort ship was busy hauling survivors from the water. By the time they had gotten everyone aboard and raised sail, Åsa's little fleet had cleared the islands and was in open sea with a healthy head start. The Solbakk ship pursued them doggedly, but the vessels were all evenly matched for speed, and they couldn't close the gap.

As evening came on, Ragnhild watched her father's ship tack for home.

~

Tromøy

RAGNHILD KNEW she should be happy to be back on Tromøy, but the visit home had grieved her more than she cared to admit. For the first time, homesickness gripped her. Seeing Katla back in her old room had given her pause. Her foster mother was getting older, and Ragnhild realized they would probably not meet again this side of the rainbow bridge.

And then there was Thorgeir. Heid had succeeded in removing the arrowhead from his shoulder. It had not lodged in the bone, but nevertheless a vicious infection set in. He writhed in a delirium, sweating and gray-faced, while Heid's women applied poultices of honey and cobwebs and chanted over him three times a day.

Heid was tight-lipped about his prognosis. Guilt festered in Ragnhild's heart, as poisonous as Thorgeir's wound. She had been so cocksure as she led them on the raid, but it had not been as simple as she had imagined. If it cost Thorgeir's life, how could she live with that?

Ragnhild never left him, sleeping on a pallet on the floor next to his bench, eating only when someone brought her food.

Åsa brought her a bowl of porridge. Ragnhild took the bowl but couldn't eat. Åsa gave her a worried glance, and Ragnhild forced a smile, bringing the spoon to her lips. But her throat seemed to close up.

Åsa sat down on the bench beside Ragnhild. "You have grown so thin and pale, I fear I will lose both you and Thorgeir."

"My decision nearly killed Thorgeir," said Ragnhild, fury seething in her voice. "I am just a foolish girl. I should never be allowed to make important decisions that affect the safety of others. If he dies, I'll never forgive myself."

Åsa said gently, "A leader must make decisions, and sometimes risk the lives of others as well as her own. Just because Thorgeir was wounded doesn't mean your decision was wrong."

Ragnhild's shoulders hunched as she bent over Thorgeir, her face lost in shadow. Åsa sighed and rose, leaving the shield-maiden with her misery.

WHEN ÅSA ENTERED HER BEDCHAMBER, her son jumped down from Brenna's lap and ran to her. She picked him up and they went over to see Stormrider, tethered on her perch. Heid's cat, Flosi, purred on the sorceress' lap as she sat by the fire. Though they never looked at each other, Åsa could sense Stormrider's hyperawareness of the cat. For her part, Flosi kept to her side of the chamber, and the two predators coexisted in a sort of armed truce.

Halfdan's eyelids were getting heavy and Åsa was tucking the little boy into his cradle when there came a pounding on the chamber door.

"Mistress! Come quickly!" It was one of Heid's apprentices. With a groan, Heid set Flosi on the floor and hoisted herself out of her seat. She threw on her cloak, grabbed her medicine pouch, and hobbled to the door, Åsa on her heels.

In the bower hall, the women gathered around Thorgeir. His body jerked, his back arching in violent convulsions. His mouth contorted into a silent scream, his face purple and glistening with sweat. Heid thrust a stick between his teeth while the women chanted furiously. Ragnhild's voice rose above the rest, echoing in the rafters of the bower. His seizure heightened until it seemed his body would tie itself in a knot.

"Don't leave me, Thorgeir," Ragnhild pleaded. "I have need of you!"

When it seemed the warrior would break in half, his convulsion suddenly released and he fell back on the mattress, limp as a sack of barley.

The room went silent.

Heid bent over him, wiping the sweat from his now-blanched face. "His fever has broken. If he survives the night, he will recover."

Åsa and Heid dozed when they could on the benches as they took turns checking on the fallen warrior. Ragnhild kept watch the entire night, her body rigid and her head bowed. She stared at him as if she could drag him from Hel's grip.

In the morning, Thorgeir still breathed. His face had a little color in it.

"He'll do," said Heid tersely. "Feed him if he wakes." She tottered off to bed.

At midmorning, Thorgeir's eyes fluttered. Ragnhild managed to coax a spoon of broth between his lips.

Under Ragnhild's ministrations, the warrior began to make a gradual recovery. As Thorgeir regained his health, the girl's spirits seemed to lift. She spent much of her time taking him on long, slow walks and working with him to build his strength.

Gradually the shield-maiden seemed less haunted by her guilt. She rejoined Tromøy's ranks in the hall, though she was far quieter than she had ever been. Åsa longed to hear Ragnhild's brash teasing rise above the other voices. She could not fathom how the girl would ever regain the confidence she needed to appear on the practice field.

# CHAPTER 21

Skiringssal, Vestfold
May, AD 821

Olaf greeted his guests as they arrived on horseback. Eystein of Oppland was a big, bluff warrior king who reminded Olaf of his own father. Eystein was accompanied by thirty húskarlar of imposing size and weaponry. Olaf felt himself quail involuntarily.

*I am king here,* he reminded himself sternly.

Eystein turned to assist a woman, muffled in a hooded cloak, who dismounted gingerly.

"This is my daughter, Sonja."

Olaf caught a glimpse of pink lips and a creamy cheek. Blue eyes glimmered briefly from the depths of the hood before blonde lashes descended over them.

As Olaf escorted them to the Shining Hall, Eystein's húskarlar gaped openly at the roofline, which rose high above the trees. Silver-gilt dragonheads jutted from each gable, glinting in the sun. Even Eystein gave the construction a speculative glance. As he ushered him through the massive oaken door, Olaf noted that he was a bit taller than Eystein.

The visitors stared at the intricately carved entwined beasts that graced the door frame. Inside the great hall, they craned their necks to stare up at the lofty ceiling that soared into the gloom, supported by pillars shaped from whole tree trunks, each elaborately carved and painted with scenes of the gods.

Calling for mead, Olaf seated Eystein beside him on the high seat, and his daughter in the seat of honor opposite.

Sonja threw back her hood, drawing the gaze of every man in the room. Olaf gave her an appraising look. She was a pretty girl, but compared to Åsa, her sky-blue eyes seemed vacant, her flaxen hair too pale.

She must have felt him staring, for her eyes flicked up to his for an instant before she looked down again at her hands clasped in her lap.

Olaf looked away quickly, feeling the flush rise in his cheeks. He had not meant to embarrass her. He was relieved when the old widow trudged in with the mead horn. though she looked more slovenly than usual. He took the horn from her and raised it in a toast.

"I am honored by your visit," he ventured, drinking and handing the horn to Eystein.

"We don't get down here often enough," said Eystein, accepting the horn and taking a long draught. "Not since we helped your father take this hall back from the Danes."

"A debt I have not forgotten. You are always welcome in my halls," said Olaf, reminding Eystein that he was the Lord of Borre as well as Skiringssal.

Eystein grinned and leaned forward. "I hear that Alfgeir's taken back Vingulmark now that Gudrød's dead."

Olaf stifled a cringe and answered boldly, "Alfgeir had a right to take my mother's dower lands once both she and my father were dead."

"Some would say her son should have it."

Olaf felt himself flush. They both knew that Olaf lacked the warriors to stand up to Alfgeir. He hoped Eystein would be done with this needling and get down to business soon.

"You need to be strong in the North, like your father was," Eystein continued. "Make old Alfgeir think twice about grabbing any more of your land."

Olaf wondered at what point he would be forced to take insult to this line of talk and draw his sword on his houseguest.

Eystein handed the mead horn back to the widow and eyed his daughter. "You are in need of a strong alliance. You should make an advantageous marriage."

So that was it. "I'm not seeking a wife as yet," said Olaf stiffly.

Eystein slapped his knee. "Redbeard's daughter will never marry you. She's too independent, that one. And if she did marry you, what good would she do you? Look at what she did to your father."

Olaf felt his heart squeeze as the jab hit home. As if realizing he had gone too far, Eystein hurried on. "Agder," he spat. "All they have is soapstone and bog iron."

"Tromøy controls the seaways of the Skagerrak." Olaf's voice grated in his throat.

"As long as the Danes allow it," Eystein corrected. "It's just a matter of time before they swoop in and take the girl. I hear she's had a marriage proposal from one of the brothers. You don't want to get in between them." It was as if Olaf's father were here again, telling him what to do.

"And look at Sonja here," Eystein continued. "She's docile as a lamb. Her mother was a good breeder while she lasted."

Olaf watched the girl's downcast face turn red under her father's scrutiny. Sympathy rose in his chest. He had felt the same embarrassment as a lad when Gudrød had turned his attention on him. It couldn't be easy for her, herded to a strange land, offered as a peace cow to a man who didn't want her.

"She's a lovely girl," Olaf said. "She would be a treasure to any man."

Sonja's eyes flicked up to his. Was that gratitude he saw there?

Fortunately, Eystein saw fit to let the subject drop and turned to a discussion of the Eastern trade.

The next morning Olaf invited his guests to hunt. Sonja eyed the small tiercel his falconer offered her with alarm and shook her head. Under her father's glare, she dropped her gaze in shame. Olaf quickly took the falcon on his own glove, and the awkward moment passed.

When they rode out, Olaf placed himself between Sonja and her father. She clung to her saddle but moved forward doggedly. Olaf led them on an easy trail and stayed with her while her father galloped after his falcon.

There was a long pause while Olaf wracked his mind for conversation. What could he say to such a girl? He saw her glance nervously in his direction and realized she must be wondering the same thing about him.

Emboldened, he said, "I do not think that hunting is your favorite pastime."

"No, my lord," she faltered. He realized it was the first time he'd heard her speak.

Olaf turned to look at her full on. "What do you enjoy?"

She looked down and murmured, "Poetry, my lord."

"I love poetry," he exclaimed. "I studied for years with Knut."

For the first time, a real smile lit up her face. "Knut taught me as well."

"Do you compose?"

"I try, but my kennings are not very original."

"It's not easy to come up with new ones. Most of the good ones have been used—how can you do better than wave-stallion?

Or the goddess of arm-fire?" He blushed, realizing she could construe his remark as a compliment.

They sat their horses, hiding their smiles, waiting for her father.

That night Olaf seated Sonja beside him on the high seat. Eystein took the guest's seat with good grace and watched the two of them with an approving smile.

Olaf offered Sonja the mead horn, and she took it, looking up at him diffidently.

"Perhaps the lady would favor us with a poem?" he asked.

He saw her go pale and instantly regretted his request.

"I meant in company with me." He put out his hand to her and she took it, eyes downcast, and let him lead her to the floor. The húskarlar waited on their benches expectantly.

He started with a simple ballad about the álfir, one of the first Knut had taught him and that he was certain she knew. She took up the lines immediately, and he watched her forget herself as she recited the words with him.

The girl seemed to grow taller as she spoke and her voice strengthened. The warriors listened with rapt attention as Sonja and Olaf told the familiar tale. They came to the finish together, and she met his gaze for the first time. Her eyes shone in the fire-light, and her cheeks were flushed.

But as soon as they had caught their breath, her shyness returned. She looked down and stumbled as she took her seat. Though Olaf did his best to set her at ease, she forced out answers to his questions in a timorous voice, and when her father addressed her, she trembled.

For the remainder of their stay, Olaf took pains to pay extra attention to her. It was the least he could do. Eystein did not bring up marriage again, although the expectation hung heavy in the air. The thought of a lifetime next to this pale girl was so far from Olaf's dreams of Åsa that he could not reconcile it. And yet the thought of leaving her to face her father's disappointment made him uneasy. He remembered how he had betrayed Åsa and abandoned her to his father.

The night before Eystein and his party were due to leave, Olaf passed by the guest house on his way to the horse barn. A rumbling voice drew him closer.

The voice growled on, and he heard a tremulous reply. Sonja. He couldn't make out the words, but the tone was all too familiar. Eystein was chastising the girl. Olaf had heard it often enough from his own father. And he could guess why.

Sonja would be going home in disgrace. He knew what that felt like and realized he could prevent that. He could offer this girl shelter no one had given him.

And why not? Eystein was right. Åsa would never marry him.

He heard a slap and a whimper.

Olaf raised his hand to the guest house door and knocked.

As if Eystein knew he had a slim hold on Olaf, he wasted no time in arranging the wedding. He did well in the dowry and bride price negotiation, for Olaf did not care if they were of equal value as was tradition. After they had reached an agreement, Eystein took over the preparations for the wedding feast as well. An alliance with Vestfold would profit him greatly, and it was obvious he had no intention of letting it get away. The trading port at Skiringssal and Olaf's eastern connections alone would give his landlocked kingdom access to great riches from far afield.

Eystein presided over the ceremony himself on the shores of Skiringssal's sacred lake, with Olaf and Eystein's sworn men in attendance. There had not been time to send invitations to the far reaches. Olaf pushed thoughts of Åsa from his mind. He'd deal with her later.

With his uncanny timing, the skáld Knut arrived at Skiringssal just before the ceremony. Olaf greeted his old friend numbly.

Knut took his hand. "I am so glad to see two of my favorite people married," he said warmly. "You are well suited to each other. You will be happy together." He must have noticed the shadow in Olaf's eye, for he added, "I will take the news to Tromøy."

Olaf crossed the hallowed bands and approached his bride as if he were in a dream. Sonja kept her eyes lowered beneath her fine linen veil while her father spoke the words over them and they exchanged rings on the points of swords. They sat side by side during the feast without exchanging a word. When they shared the marriage cup of honey mead, Sonja met his gaze hesitantly and offered Olaf a tentative smile, and his heart began to thaw.

# CHAPTER 22

Tromøy
May, AD 821

The days lengthened and warmed. Stormrider had finished her molt, and Åsa brought the falcon out to hunt again. She set off riding Gullfaxi, Stormrider on her shoulder and her dog, Flekk, trotting beside. As they left the steading, Ragnhild rode up beside them, armed with her bow. Åsa felt a rush of relief, but she said nothing, fearing the shield-maiden's fragile calm would break if she spoke.

The flax blooms had turned the field into a lake of blue, a soft breeze stirring up waves. Åsa launched the falcon over the field and watched the peregrine soar. She felt the bird's hunger and eagerness to hunt, sensed the updrafts that boosted Stormrider into the heavens. The earth was both far beneath her and right under her feet. Her attention was in two places at once, soaring in the sky with the bird and anchored to the earth by the

woman's body. She felt her mind expand to take in the contra-
dictory points of view.

Ragnhild and Flekk flushed a quail from the field. As the bird
shot up into the air, Åsa felt Stormrider's attention snap to it.
The falcon's wings drew in tight to her body and her head went
down. She dropped on her quarry like a spearhead, and the thrill
of speed coursed through Åsa. In blistering flight, Stormrider
closed on the fluttering quail. Her talons shot out to grip her
prey in an explosion of feathers. She flipped out of her dive and
flung out her wings to brake her speed as she fetched the now-
dead quail to earth.

The falcon tore at the quail, feeding ravenously. Åsa let
Stormrider finish her kill, sharing the raptor's avid satisfaction.
When she sensed the falcon's appetite begin to sate, she
approached and gently slipped her gloved hand beneath the bird.
As the falcon settled, Åsa gripped the jesses with her free hand.
She lifted Stormrider in one smooth motion, where the raptor
preened for a moment before lofting onto Åsa's shoulder. They
rode contentedly home, Ragnhild and Flekk beside them. Åsa still
said nothing to the shield-maiden, but the lift of the girl's shoulders suggested that Ragnhild had forgiven herself for Thorgeir's
wound. In time Åsa could restore the girl's self-confidence.

ÅSA RECEIVED Knut in her great hall. She invited him to sit beside
her on the high seat and called for ale. The inhabitants of
Tromøy crowded the doorway, hoping for news of outlying areas
and perhaps a tale.

"My lady," he said, "I have news that I would share with you
in private."

She nodded and spoke to the crowd. "Please leave us for now.
When Knut and I are finished with our private business, we will

feast and he will give you all the news." The folk backed out, drawing the great oaken doors closed.

When the servant had served ale and departed, Åsa asked, "What news of the Danes?"

"They are negotiating with the Franks, lady. Harald Klak wants to return from exile in Frisia."

"How long will that keep them occupied?"

"It's hard to say, lady."

"I will attend the All-Ting at midsummer, and recruit warriors there."

"That's good. I wish you luck." Knut sipped his ale, then said, "I have just come from Skiringssal."

"Is Olaf well?" she asked anxiously.

"He is married." Knut knew there was no easy way to tell her. He watched her face pale, the ale horn in her hand trembling. She kept her expression impassive, although Stormrider, tethered to the pillar, shrieked and bated.

Knut eyed her with sympathy. "He married Sonja of Oppland."

"I am happy for them," she said woodenly.

"It's a good match," he told her gently.

She nodded, blinking back her tears.

"You made your choice. Don't blame Olaf for making his," said Heid that evening in the bower as they dressed for Knut's welcoming feast. "We got the boy, and that's all we needed from him."

"All you needed," said Åsa. "It never occurred to you that I might need something more."

"You're a queen. I'm sure you will not lack for lovers," said Heid complacently.

As she slept that night, Åsa rose up in the falcon body and

woke to find herself perched in the rafters of the Shining Hall, gazing down on Olaf's bed. She felt the familiar tug on her spirit to slip out of the bird's body. Then she saw the second head upon the pillow. As she watched, Olaf's hand reached out and stroked the woman's pale hair. The falcon's throat constricted so that she could hardly breathe. She twisted away and shot through the smokehole like an arrow.

The way home seemed to take longer than ever before. The air was heavy, and the falcon struggled to lift her wings. When at last she sighted Tromøy's hall, she thrashed her way to the bower roof and landed heavily on the rafters. She looked down upon her sleeping body, lying on the bed.

Something called to the falcon to go back out into the night, to fly off into the wild and never return to the troubled human existence.

She turned and sidled to the smokehole. Peering out at the stars, she spread her wings, ready to launch through the hole.

Then Halfdan whimpered in his sleep.

The falcon instantly flowed back into the sleeping body. Åsa rose to pick him up.

# CHAPTER 23

June, AD 821

The lookouts reported a Danish longship on the outer shores. Åsa mustered her warriors. Although she did not expect an attack, it was best to show strength.

She stood before the hall in mail and helm, surrounded by her húskarlar, Heid at her side, and watched the Danish delegation labor up the hill in their armor. She could have sent a cart, but it was better that the envoy be tired when they met. Greeting Gorm briefly at the door, she escorted him inside. She took the high seat, Heid beside her, and kept him standing.

"What brings you back to my shores?" she asked, as if she had no recollection of the marriage offer and her delaying tactics.

"My lady, King Rorik sends his replies to your questions," Gorm replied patiently.

"Oh, of course. I am eager to hear his answers. And how go things with Rorik? Any word from his brothers in Sverige?"

Gorm could not completely hide his discomfiture at this remark. "There have been…negotiations," he said vaguely.

"I hope they have been friendly ones. And how go his relations with the Franks? And his uncle, Harald Klak?"

Gorm gave her a stone face. "As I said, I come with your answers. Firstly, King Rorik would wish you by his side, and he requires that you produce him an heir. He would appoint a regent to rule Tromøy in your son's name until he comes of age."

"And what of my son and heir, Halfdan?"

"He would be fostered by the regent and grow up on Tromøy."

"And who would this regent be?"

"My lord has a man in mind, an able man."

"I'm sure he does." Anger coursed through her veins, bringing her to her feet. "So, your king wishes to take me from my lands and give my kingdom and my son to the care of some unknown man. Meanwhile, I would be no better than a prisoner, unable to protect my son or my lands." She glared at him. "This stinks of Frankish influence. I thought that Rorik still held to our ways."

Gorm cleared his throat again. "My lord Rorik has adopted some of the Frankish ways. They are a powerful neighbor, and it is important to keep their goodwill. But I assure you, these are only for appearances. He is still true to the old ways."

Fury seared through her, giving a knife-edge to her voice. "Yet he would have me give my father's kingdom over to Danish rule and make my son his hostage."

Gorm's mouth opened, then closed. Åsa raged on. "I think Rorik has become nothing more than a Frankish puppet-king. And I would become a pawn in their game. Your master leaves me no choice but to decline his offer."

The envoy paled. "My lady, Rorik does not like his generosity to be refused. I fear his retribution will be swift and cruel."

"Does he think I am a helpless woman who will fall gratefully into his arms? Has he forgotten that I defeated him only last year in Borre? That two of his good ships lie on my shores? This audience is over."

"But lady, I beg you to reconsider..."

"Olvir, show our visitors to their ship."

Gorm gaped at her as Olvir took a firm grip on his arm and levered him toward the door. "I pity you, lady..."

Åsa fought the familiar grip of fear in the pit of her stomach, balancing her head carefully on her neck and keeping her back straight as a spear until the Danish contingent were out of sight. They'd be back in force, but she'd be ready.

Skiringssal

OLAF TREATED Sonja as kindly as he knew how. Her lack of fire disappointed him, but it also aroused his sympathy. Though she wore the keys on her belt, she crept about the house like a wary mouse, keeping to the shadows as if afraid of capture and extermination.

The first night in bed, she had held herself stiffly as a hard-forged sword. But Olaf kept his voice soft and his hands gentle, and one night as he stroked her hair, she met his gaze and smiled.

The bashful girl began to take charge of the hall and the daily operations. Olaf approved of her decisions, although he would never have openly disagreed with them. The wife's authority over the household was as absolute as her husband's over the warband.

She rose at first light and briskly took up direction of the daily farm work. There was a quiet happiness about her that spread to the entire household. Under her direction, not a weed dared poke its head above ground in the fields, the cows seemed to compete to give the richest milk, and the sheep grew in their fall coats early. The wild birds laid their eggs in convenient places and avoided eating the berries growing closest to the hall, which were the plumpest and the earliest ripening. Wild apples grew low on the tree, and flowers bloomed that had never been seen before.

Olaf began to feel better about his decision to liberate her from her father's shadow and give her a household of her own to rule. With a gentle but steady hand, Sonja transformed Skiringssal from a stronghold to a home. She traveled to Borre to ensure the operations there were satisfactory. She brought to Vestfold a sense of security Olaf had not felt since his mother died.

If there were times he looked to the south with longing, he made sure she never saw.

~

Tromøy

Åsa MADE ready to attend All-Ting, the great assembly at which all the free folk east of the mountains gathered during midsummer every three years.

Olaf would be there. Her stomach knotted at the thought of facing him, yet she must establish her position among the rulers of the land. Failure to appear would be the act of a coward, and yield her place as an equal.

The yard rang with shouts as the household prepared for the journey to the sacred site. Toki sent his men scurrying to load pack horses with tents and bedding, cooking gear, food, and ale, as well as soapstone pots and whetstones to trade. Heid fussed as slaves loaded her tent, her chair, and her folding bed into a utility wagon that would come behind her own elaborately carved cart. The carts would slow the travelers down, but it was the only way the crippled sorceress could make the journey, and no assembly could be complete without her.

Three male animals were selected to bring as sacrifices: a goat, a ram, and a yearling calf. From Solvi's hoard, Åsa selected a judicious number of bronze and silver arm rings and cloak pins to entice warriors to join her, and packed them in a leather bag.

In addition to Tromøy's steward, Toki, and his staff of serving men, Åsa took six of her húskarlar, Heid and her nine apprentices, and Jarl Borg, who held his own position at the assembly. She left Olvir in charge of the majority of her forces along with Ragnhild, Einar, Thorgeir, and Svein. Brenna stayed behind with Halfdan.

Early in the morning the party mounted their sturdy mountain ponies and drank the stirrup cup, then set out for the ferry landing. Heid drove her cart, her apprentices walking alongside, voices raised in song. The entourage took three ferry trips to get everyone across, but by late morning, all were assembled on the mainland. They set out on the three-day trek through the forest and into the mountains along trails their forefathers had followed since ancient times.

Åsa rode Gullfaxi at the fore beside Jarl Borg, Stormrider perched on her leather-clad shoulder and the treasure bag tied to her saddle. She had made this journey many times with her father and brother, but she had never expected to attend as head of the family.

Though the sorceress had her tent and bed set up each night, the rest of them camped rough, sleeping in the open, wrapped up in hudfat, sheepskin sleeping bags, close to the fire. In spite of the long days' rides, Åsa lay awake at night, staring up at the stars. How would she be received at the Ting? It was rare for a woman to take her place among the kings and jarls. She had seen it happen, but only by older women who had gained their power with years of experience. By comparison, she was a child. How would she hold her own in the war of words between the old chieftains? She longed to share her fears with Jarl Borg, but the old lord fell asleep the minute he laid his head down, and she was loath to disturb his rest. During the day's ride there was no privacy to discuss the doubts of a queen. She gritted her teeth and kept her council.

By the time they crested the last mountain and campfire smoke tinged the air, she longed to turn Gullfaxi for home.

The Ting site lay on the shores of a broad lake, fed by a waterfall that tumbled down the rock face of the sacred hill. Here the landwights' laughter seemed to ring in the rushing water, and Åsa felt the sprites' eyes evaluating her. What made her think she was worthy to represent the kings that had gone before her?

The site already thronged with warlords' encampments, their banners streaming over a sea of tents. Beneath the stares of the chieftains, kings, and jarls, Åsa led her party to her family's historic plot and bade them pitch their tents. She felt eyes on her and whirled to spot Orm, King of Telemark, an old rival of her father's. He scowled at her across the field, and she mustered her fiercest glare in return.

Angry voices made her turn back to Toki and Heid, directing the camp's setup.

"You fools, how do you expect me to sleep like this?" The sorceress stood in the entrance of the tent, brandishing her staff over cowering servants.

"And what is the trouble, lady?" Åsa entered the tent.

"The idiots have broken my bed!"

On the floor lay Heid's collapsible wooden bedframe, one of its legs broken.

"We can repair it, lady," said Toki.

Heid turned on him. "Before tonight?" she shrilled.

Toki hung his head. "Perhaps by tomorrow…"

Åsa's heart sank. Heid's twisted body caused her endless pain, and sleep was a nightly battle for her. The journey here had been harder on her than anyone, and the thought of one more difficult night had to be torture for the sorceress.

"For tonight, lady, take my bed."

"How will you sleep, then?" Heid asked. "You must be rested for assembly."

"I am young, and the ground does not hurt me as it does you," Åsa soothed. "Don't worry, I will sleep well."

The sorceress assented, grumbling, and the servants carried off the broken bedframe.

A cooking fire was started, and soon the comforting fragrance of barley porridge wafted over the campsite. After they ate, mead flowed as they gathered around the fire, their voices raised in traditional songs.

That night, Åsa tossed in her hudfat while Heid snored in her bed. Åsa knew that tonight she could not have slept in the most luxurious bed in the world. Too much was at stake. There was no point in fighting the sleeplessness. She rolled up her bedding and slipped out of the tent, taking her swords, for though the Ting site was neutral ground, no one went unarmed. She wandered to a solitary spot where she spread out her sleeping bag and burrowed into it. She lay staring up at the starry sky and began to chant the vardlokkur in low tones, calling on her ancestors to guide her.

As the familiar trance came over her, she could feel the presence of her father and her mother. They were here with her, and all her ancestors that came before them.

She slept.

Dawn came soon, but she woke feeling strong. She rose and returned to the tent to dress. Heid was just rising, sipping a steaming brew that soothed her pain. The sorceress looked better rested, and Åsa was glad she had been able to lend her bed to the sorceress.

She strode across the field to the center where twenty-four chairs stood in a ring facing each other. One of these chairs had seated a member of her family since ancient times.

Her place now.

Men drove hazel poles into the ground, forming a ring around the circle of chairs. They stretched ropes between the poles, marking off the sacred enclosure that surrounded the council. Heid appeared with two venerable sorceresses from other districts, resplendent in their gem-studded cloaks. A male priest joined them, dressed in his godi's robes, carrying a live cockerel by the neck.

The three women gathered by the western pole and began an eerie chant, a vardlokkur from ancient times. As the sorceresses chanted, the priest drew his knife, and in one quick motion, struck off the cockerel's head. Blood spurted from the neck. The godi began to pace backward, circling the enclosure from west to east, spraying the perimeter with blood. He kept up a howling chant as he went. When he had made a full circumnavigation, the priest backed away and stood with his head bowed while the last of the blood drained from the dead bird onto the grass.

Åsa approached the sanctified enclosure with the other council members. As she stepped over the hallowed bands, she firmly quelled the butterflies that fluttered in her stomach and took her father's place among the other lords. She secured Stormrider's jesses to the back of the chair, stroking the falcon's chest to settle her and taking the opportunity to look around. Olaf sat across from her in the place that had once been Gudrød's, far enough away that she could avoid meeting his eye without seeming to shun him. In the morning sunlight he looked more handsome than ever, and from this distance it looked as if he wore an expression she had never seen before. Was it contentment? Her stomach gave a twist. She forced herself to look away from him and survey the other council members.

As she had feared, she was the only woman in the council circle. Most of the men were her father's age, battle-scarred and confident. Their stares made her want to bolt. Instead, she gritted her teeth and forced a smile. The grizzled warlord sitting next to her, Jarl Arn, was an old comrade of her father's. He gave her a quick smile, then rose and addressed the council.

"I'm glad to see Redbeard's daughter take her place among us."

"She's just a child. She should be married and bearing children of her own," growled a jarl seated not far from Olaf.

"Who would dare to marry her? You saw what she did to her last husband," King Orm said.

Åsa's face grew hot as the men laughed. Stormrider grumbled from her perch. Before she knew what she was doing, Åsa was on her feet, shaking with rage.

"Be careful, Orm, for one old king can die much like another." Her words silenced the men, and she addressed the council in a voice potent with anger. "I killed my father's murderer as honor demanded. I accomplished this deed alone, with no help from the likes of you. Now I have taken the reins of my father's kingdom, where I will protect his people and lands to the best of my ability."

Disgruntled murmurs rose from the council. Across the circle, Olaf stood.

"Queen Åsa has proven herself an effective battle leader more than once. She led the defense of Borre against the Danish invasion. She was outnumbered, yet she was able to hold them off until I arrived with Borre's fleet. She routed out a den of outlaws and stood against King Solvi's invasion of Tromøy. She deserves to be in our ranks."

"You're just a puppy yourself," said the jarl beside him.

Olaf colored, but he didn't sit down.

"Don't you have a blood feud to settle with this woman? She killed your father. Why is she still above ground? Are you afraid of her?" Orm demanded.

Olaf could not answer Orm's insult with anything less than a challenge to holmgang, a duel of honor.

Before he could speak, Åsa jumped in, her voice taut with fury. "Gudrød murdered my father and my brother. I killed Gudrød to settle the requirements of justice. King Olaf has no grounds to feud with me." She glared around the council. The men murmured among themselves, but no one spoke up.

"Does anyone here question my right to take vengeance?" she demanded.

She and Olaf remained standing. They did not meet each other's eyes.

At last Jarl Borg rose. The assembly fell silent. He was the eldest of the council and most respected for his knowledge.

"The lady has the right of it," he said in a grating voice. His rheumy eyes swept the council, daring them to disagree. No one said a word. "Honor has been served. Nothing more is due. To speak otherwise risks outlawry."

Some of the lords glared at Åsa, but none of them challenged the old jarl's declaration.

After a tense interval, Åsa and Olaf took their seats.

THAT EVENING, Olaf appeared at Åsa's campfire. She stood to greet him, and they strolled away from the others into the forest.

"Thank you for standing up for me in council," she said, smiling up at him. His hair formed a golden halo in the late midsummer sun. She met his gaze and was stunned at the way his eyes shimmered like the sea on a sunny day, just as she was the first time she had looked into them so long ago.

"Thank you for keeping me out of a holmgang." His eyes crinkled as he grinned. "I would hate to have to trim old Orm's whiskers."

A lump rose in Åsa's throat, and for a moment neither of them could speak. She swallowed hard. "You are married."

Olaf's smile fell. "Yes."

Even if Åsa could have found the words, she could not have forced them from her constricted throat. She could only stare at him, tears prickling at the edges of her eyes.

He looked at the ground. "I waited for you for two years."

"I always thought you would wait for me forever." A tear quivered on her lashes. She blinked it away.

"I am a king. I must have a son."

Åsa's hands began to tremble. "You have a son!" She realized she was shouting and struggled to get her voice under control. "We have a son."

Realization crossed his face like a thunderbolt.

They stared at each other, neither daring to break eye contact.

"Halfdan is your son," she faltered as the color bled from his face and grief bloomed in its place. Her body was heavy, sodden, like wool left in a rainstorm.

Olaf's face was white. He began to pace back and forth before her. "Why did you not tell me? I had a right to know he was my son."

She had never seen him angry. Tendrils of fear poked at her, raising her own fury.

"You betrayed me! I gave myself to you, and you bound me like an animal and delivered me to my father's murderer. How could I ever trust you again?"

"How do you know Halfdan is mine?" he raged.

Åsa's fury rose to match his own. "You know you were my first! When you dragged me back to the wedding chamber with that monster, I tried to kill him or myself. I failed, but Gudrød could not do as he wanted. When he found out I was with child, he knew it could not be his, and it was all the worse for me."

He jerked to a stop and stared at her. In his face she read his shame.

After a long silence, she said, "Your new wife need not know. Halfdan is Gudrød's heir. But he must have half of Vestfold when he comes of age."

Olaf bowed his golden head. He turned and walked slowly away.

~

OLAF AND ÅSA managed to avoid each other for the rest of the week, though her eyes seized on him of their own accord whenever he entered her field of vision.

The day after the council's first meeting, Åsa put it about that she was taking new recruits. After the council adjourned for the day, she took her seat with Jarl Borg by the campfire, Gudrød's Bane shining by her side. All evening they watched as warriors passed by to offer their swords to other lords. As time wore on, Åsa smiled wryly at Jarl Borg. "No one wants to follow an upstart queen."

"Summer days are long," said the old warlord complacently.

As the sun blazed near to the horizon, five sturdy figures approached, and Jarl Borg nudged her. "See here."

The figures drew near and resolved into five robust girls, sisters by their matching brown braids. They huddled together, giggling. Åsa bit back her disappointment and smiled in encouragement, until the tallest of them stepped out of the group and knelt before her.

"Lady, I am called Helga. These are my sisters. We wish to serve you."

"I already have enough serving women," Åsa said.

The girl raised blazing eyes to hers. "We wish to fight."

Åsa hid a smile. "But you are girls."

"We have heard that you train shield-maidens. That is what we wish to become."

"It is not as easy as just wishing for it. It's dangerous, hard work."

"On the farm my sisters and I work hard from sunrise until after dark. We are accustomed to blood and slaughter. We can kill men as well as livestock. We fear nothing but death without honor. Our wish is to die in battle and earn our place in Freyja's hall." Helga's voice rang with conviction, her eyes alive with passion.

Åsa considered the girls' earnest faces. Their hair shone in neat braids, and their cheeks glowed, ruddy with health. Helga was the tallest, but her sisters were all good-sized, with the muscular shoulders of dairy maids who had lugged many a yoke of milk-pails. These girls dreamed of a more exciting life than what they had been born to, just as she had. Who was she to deny them? They already had the strength and endurance of shield-maidens. They needed only to trade the pitchfork for a spear and cultivate the battle skills.

"Aren't you needed at home?"

Helga hung her head. "Lady, our families cannot feed all of us over the winter."

So, that was it. Their parents had sent them away. If they did not find a position, they would be a burden on their families. Food would be short for everyone at home.

Åsa wondered if she was being a fool, but she could not leave them to that fate. And what choice did she have? No one else had come to offer her their oath. She looked over at Jarl Borg, but he only shrugged. The decision was hers alone.

"Come forward, Helga. You and your sisters are welcome in my hird." Åsa hauled up Gudrød's Bane and laid the sword across her knees.

Beaming, Helga and her sisters lined up to kneel and swear on the blade. Åsa awarded them each a bronze cloak pin.

They proudly donned their treasures, then scampered off to move their belongings, their happy chatter rising in the air.

The pins seemed to have made an impression, for over the next days, more young people of both sexes straggled into camp in small groups. There must have been many farm families with too many children to support through the winter. Åsa took them all. Laughter and shouts rang from the goodly crop of tents that sprang up around her camp.

Heid eyed them with a dour expression. "How will you feed them all?"

"I'll find a way. I must have warriors if I am to fight the Danes."

"These are not warriors," Heid scoffed.

"Not yet," said Åsa. "But with training, they will be soon enough."

Heid huffed and strode off, where she could be heard berating her apprentices.

Out of the corner of her eye, Åsa saw King Orm approach. He was surrounded by five muscular warriors, well-armed and sporting silver arm bands. Orm stopped beside Åsa, watching one of Helga's sisters chase a boy through the camp, shrieking, her eyes bright with laughter while others cheered them on.

"I see your hird swells with skilled warriors," Orm said, a sneer in his voice.

Åsa bared her teeth in an unfriendly grin, willing him to move on.

With a squeal, Helga's sister launched into a flying tackle. She landed on the boy's back, bringing him down. They rolled through the crowd, knocking over kettles and buckets, sending the camp into fits of laughter.

"You have a lot of faith in a bunch of backward children," said Orm. Åsa had no answer, for he voiced her own misgivings.

Jarl Borg fixed Orm with his stare. "Faith is what makes a warband. They have faith in their queen, as she has in them." Orm opened his mouth, then closed it and stalked away, followed by his húskarlar.

The next evening Åsa sat at the fire amid her raucous hird when a tall man in a hooded cloak approached her and bowed. Even in his cloak, his bearing proclaimed him a warrior. Åsa was so surprised it took her a moment to find her voice.

"Come forward," she said, beckoning Toki to pour him some ale.

The man put back his hood and stepped into the firelight. His weathered face bore a network of fine lines and several scars, but the sinew and muscle stood out on his arms and legs and a sword hung from his belt. This was a seasoned warrior in his prime, the first such that had presented himself to her. Hope flared in Åsa, tempered with suspicion.

"Name yourself," she ordered.

The stranger went down on one knee. "Lady, I am called Behrt Audunson. I seek your service."

"And why would you serve a woman and not some other lord?"

"No other lord will have me," he said.

The insult left Åsa speechless. To admit such a thing and to imply that she was his last choice--at least he was honest. But of course she would have found this out on her own.

She drank from her ale cup to recover her voice. "Why should I take you when others will not?"

"I am well-seasoned in war, lady. And loyal."

"You sound like a dream come true. Why would the others not have you?"

"I am a Christian, lady." Behrt's voice carried throughout the circle. Åsa's warriors drew back in unison and touched the Thor's hammers they wore beneath their tunics.

"Oh, come now," said Åsa. "It's not contagious." She turned

back to Behrt. "You look to be Norse born, yet you say you are a Christ-follower. How ever did such a misfortune befall you?"

"I was born on the Sognefjord," Behrt said. "When I was a boy, my older brothers took me a-viking across the sea to Ireland. The raid failed, and all of my brothers were killed, along with the rest of the crew. I was but a child, and the Irish made me a slave. The Irish lord who became my master indoctrinated me into worship of the White Christ. As I grew older, he saw that I was devoted to him, and to his faith. He made me a free man and a member of his household guard. I served him faithfully for many years."

"And why is it you serve him no longer?"

"He died, lady. Now, the Irish won't have me because I am of Norse birth. The Norse don't want me because I am a Christian."

Another misfit. Åsa's hopes sank, yet a flicker of sympathy stirred in her at the resignation in Behrt's eyes.

"I see. Have you other skills besides arms?"

"I can train horses, and I have some skill as a smith."

Åsa's heart leaped at his words. She needed someone like him. Ulf was getting old, and with the loss of Bram, he needed a strong helper to make all the weapons her new húskarlar would need. And someone good with horses...

"We worship the northern gods here," she said sternly. "I will take you, but you must keep your religion out of the way."

"Indeed, lady, I will do so." His expression was earnest, and a flicker of hope sparked in his eyes.

Åsa drew her sword and laid it across her knees. Behrt leaned forward and laid his hand on the blade.

"I am Behrt, son of Audun, a free man and Norse born. I served my master as a warrior for ten years and have fought in many battles. I now offer to serve you faithfully with my life."

When he looked up, his eyes were glowing.

"Find a place among the warriors, Behrt Audunson," said Åsa, awarding him a silver arm ring of twisted silver terminating in serpents' heads. She raised her voice so all could hear. "No one is to bother this man. You will accept him as one of us." She listened for grumbling, but the hird was silent.

"Are you mad?" said Heid when they had retired to Åsa's tent. "A Christian?"

"He's an experienced warrior, and we are in desperate need of his skills, in case you hadn't noticed."

"The gods will be furious," Heid warned.

"The gods will be tolerant," Åsa replied. "It's you who are furious. And you heard him, he's good with horses and he can help Ulf."

"That would be as bad as Hrafn, meddling with the weaponry," Heid spat.

"If he becomes a problem, I'll turn him out. But for now, we need his skills."

Heid looked as if she had a lot more to say on the subject, but she clamped her jaw and turned away.

Behrt's allegiance and the quality of his armband drew a trickle of more experienced warriors to Åsa's fire. She swore them in with a flicker of triumph and relief.

# CHAPTER 24

The Ting ended, and Åsa led her ragtag hird back across the mountains to Tromøy. She had gained sixty-five recruits. Solvi's hoard had attracted seven men with weapons of their own. The most experienced warrior by far was Behrt the Christian. The rest were young, untried, fresh from the farm, twenty-four of them girls.

The solstice had passed during the Ting, and the summer days were long. They trooped over the steep mountain trails, strong voices raised in song. Their high good spirits and energy buoyed Åsa's hopes for the future. Hadn't she been the same just a few short years before? Under Jarl Borg's tutelage, she and her brother had become proficient with all weapons. This was a much larger challenge, but she had experienced warriors to assist in the training. To speed things along, she would spread the novices among her húskarlar for mentoring. How to feed and house them all was a problem she'd need to solve.

The party reached the ferry in the late afternoon of the third day, hot and tired from the journey. The sun had warmed the water, and the youngsters shed their clothes and splashed, shrieking, into the narrow channel that separated Tromøy from the mainland. Even the horses eagerly waded in and swam across. It was a relief not to try to coax them onto the hated ferry. The wagons and gear were loaded onto the flat-bottomed boat, accompanied by Heid, Toki, and Jarl Borg. The Christian, Behrt, and Olvir poled the raft across while everyone else swam.

Åsa could not resist stripping down to her linen shift and diving into the chill water. As she swam, her worries floated away with every stroke. On the other side, she pulled herself up on the bank to dry off in the late afternoon sun amid her boisterous crew. Tromøy would sound more like a bird rookery than a royal steading, but their liveliness made her smile, and she was glad to be surrounded by people close to her own age. For now she dropped her worries and joined them in another song.

As the sun descended in the sky, they put their damp clothes back on and hitched the horses to the carts. They followed the forest trail across the island to the south end, where Åsa's steading lay.

As they emerged from the woods into the yard, Brenna appeared in the bower door to greet them, Halfdan in her arms. Åsa's heart leaped when she saw her son, and she hurried to take him from Brenna. Halfdan squealed in delight and threw his chubby arms around her. She stood there a moment, inhaling his baby-scent of fresh grass, holding his petal-soft cheek to hers.

Ragnhild threw down her arms and raced up to the group. "You have brought us…" she trailed off, gawking at the crowd of farm girls and boys.

"New recruits," Åsa finished with a meaningful look.

Ragnhild searched the new faces, her gaze pausing on Behrt with interest until her eyes fell on the crucifix on his helm. She scrunched her nose in a scowl and quickly looked away. But Behrt's gaze remained fastened on the shield-maiden.

The lookout had brought news of their approach hours before, and Brenna already had the welcome feast underway. Two goats roasted over a spit in the courtyard while the smell of fresh-baked bread filled the air. Benches and trestles had been set up outdoors, Åsa's high seat at their head.

The farmstead rang with chatter as the new lads filled the long-empty barracks, while the twenty-four farm girls crowded into the bower. They stowed their belongings and trooped back to the main yard for the feast.

There were not enough seats for all of them, so they settled down in clusters on the ground around the fire. Åsa's father's hall had accommodated a hird of this size before Gudrød burned it, and she vowed to have a seat for every one of her new warriors before winter.

Servers lugged buckets of ale, and wooden cups were shared around. Before long, laughter and song mingled in the air with the woodsmoke.

Åsa presided from her high seat with Halfdan in her lap, loath to be separated from her son. The little boy eyed the boisterous newcomers with lively interest, and the young people were fascinated by their tiny lord.

When the food arrived, silence reigned until the hungry travelers had eaten their fill. Then the ale made the rounds again, and the celebration continued late into the night. As wrestling matches and good-natured flytings broke out, Åsa slipped off to the bower with Halfdan. Heid was already in her bed, her ravaged face relaxed in sleep.

Åsa gave her new recruits two days to rest from the journey and settle in. She had little time to waste in making ready for the Danes' attack. The news at the Ting had been that Rorik and his brothers were still embroiled in the dispute over the throne with their uncle, Harald Klak, who had the support of the powerful Frankish emperor. Åsa wished she had spies to send across the water, but that took a special kind of person, traders who could cross borders without being noticed and blend in anywhere. There was no one on Tromøy with that kind of sophistication. Knut was the only one, and while his information was invaluable, he was only one man, and an old one at that. He served many far-flung districts and could not be everywhere at once.

By now, traders coming through Skiringssal could have carried news of her growing reputation across the Skagerrak to the Danes. Rorik would not fear her. If anything, the news would make him more eager to put her under his control before she became too powerful. And if stories of Solvi's treasure had somehow reached them, Tromøy would be an even more tempting target.

The recruits settled in very quickly, and when she mustered them on the third morning, they were fresh-eyed and strong. She assigned Einar, Olvir, Thorgeir, and Svein to whip the new boys into shape while she and Ragnhild took on the gaggle of farm girls. These girls were as strong as the boys, with callused hands and wiry muscles from hard work on the farm.

"Danes are not just thick barley or tall goats," Ragnhild told them, thrusting her spearpole at Thorgeir. Recovered completely from his wounds, he retaliated with a sweep of his own weapon, which Ragnhild dodged neatly. "They fight back, and their blades are as sharp as yours. They won't hesitate to gut you, and if you want to live, you will get them first."

From the first, the girls trained viciously, awarding each other cuts and bruises that kept Heid and her apprentices busy with bandages and splints. Helga and her sisters were the boldest of them, hurtling into the fray with swinging sticks and howls of fury.

Åsa had more benches built. The two dozen new girls crowded onto them around the outdoor fire beside their male counterparts, Ragnhild seated at their head across from Olvir. To ensure equality and respect, Asa seated the women with the men from the beginning. They would need this bond in battle, when warriors must sacrifice their lives for their comrades.

It seemed to be working as laughter and chatter rose from the benches while trestles were set up and the ale was served out.

Tromøy supported close to one hundred noncombatants: servants, craftsmen, farmworkers, their children, and Heid with her nine apprentices. Counting those who had joined Åsa at the Ting, Tromøy's army had swollen to one hundred twenty-eight: ninety men, and a total of thirty-eight women in various stages of training.

With more than two hundred hungry people, as Heid had feared, Åsa was hard put to feed them all. She came up with a scheme of dividing the trainees into six squads, each led by an experienced warrior. Einar, Thorgeir, Svein and Olvir divided up the men, while Ragnhild and Åsa formed the women into two squads, mingling the two dozen new farm girls with the experienced women.

Each day three groups would train while another helped tending the fields, pulling weeds and scaring off the birds, and the other two squads augmented the food supply by hunting, fishing, and foraging wild vegetables. This brought in enough to keep the horde of active young people nourished for now. But winter would be another matter.

In the long summer evenings, the recruits worked on their battle gear. The farmers possessed no armor, but Olvir, Einar, and the other húskarlar showed them how to pad their jackets with layers of wool and coat them with hard pine resin varnish to deflect a glancing blow from an arrow or sword.

Under the húskarlar's tutelage, the young people carved longbows from yew saplings, steaming the green wood over the fire, then bending the staves over barrels to put a curve in each bow. Evenings were spent fletching arrows and braiding bowstrings.

Ragnhild and Åsa trained their shield-maidens to draw the longbows along with the boys, building their strength until they were able to fire arrow after arrow without pause. They organized competitions against the boys, and the girls proved themselves to be deadly shots.

The húskarlar trained the recruits to use their shields as

weapons, ramming the boss into an opponent's face and hitting with the rim. They learned to make their own shields from thin pine boards. After trimming the boards into circles and cutting holes in the center, they glued on a layer of linen, followed by one of rawhide. Then they stitched bands of rawhide around the rims for reinforcement. The last step was to take the shields to the smithy, to have iron shieldbosses riveted to the centers.

Åsa had sent the Christian warrior Behrt to work in the smithy. Ulf needed an experienced helper, and Åsa felt it best to keep the Christian separate from the others until they got used to him. He slept in a cot by the forge, though he ate at the campfire with everyone else.

Behrt was in his prime, middling tall, strong and vigorous but quiet. He was handsome by any measure, with his neatly trimmed brown hair and beard, but for the look in his gray eyes. Åsa found she could not meet his gaze for long without a strange sadness rising in her chest. She would turn away, choking down a lump in her throat, glad he had found a place with Ulf. She often saw Behrt standing outside the smithy in the sunshine, watching the recruits train.

It seemed to her that his gaze followed Ragnhild more than any other.

Ulf kept his new assistant busy making weapons for the new recruits. The smithy rang with hammer blows late into the night as they turned out dozens of arrowheads, spearheads, and shieldbosses. Ulf seemed very happy with his new helper.

"I've fought beside Christians before," he said to Åsa, "as well as against them. They're just people. Behrt is a skillful and diligent smith, and strong. He has nearly doubled my production."

"Just keep him out of Heid's sight," Åsa said.

"And keep that old witch out of my smithy," growled Ulf. He still had not forgiven the sorceress for her interference with Hrafn. The fact that she had been right about the old wizard made the affront even more unpardonable.

~

ÅSA PACED along Tromøy's rocky shore, surveying her fleet. Twelve good ships lay drawn up on the beach. Five of them were her father's, dragged out of the boat house this morning.

Einar ran an experienced eye over them. "The planks are sound, but the seams have dried out. We'll replace the wool roving, give them a new coat of pine tar, and they'll be ready to take to the seas again."

Heid's grand vessel, *Freyja*, was in perfect condition, but it was sacred to the goddess and not to be used for war. Ragnhild's dowry ship, which she had named *Raider Bride*, was also in excellent shape, as were the others captured from Solvi. The Danish ships were another matter. Their gunwales had been hacked by axes, and several strakes of one had been cracked during a collision in the battle.

"We can smooth out the axe marks," said Einar. "But these strakes will have to be replaced."

"Very well. You should find suitable oaks in the grove." Åsa was glad that Hrolf had not touched the oak grove her father had husbanded for decades to provide the green wood needed to build and repair the longships' flexible hulls. "You might also check the holding pond. My father may have preserved something you can use." Wood submerged in water retained the moisture that allowed it to be easily worked and steamed over a fire to form a ship's curve.

Ulf and Behrt set the farm boys to forging dozens of iron rivets to replace the rusted ones. The others who were not training for battle sat in the sunshine, braiding new ropes from hemp or horsehair.

Heid and her nine apprentices laid the vast sails out in a sunny meadow and went over them carefully, reweaving holes and stitching on new ropes. They commandeered the bower on the long summer days, where they wove Åsa's banner with a falcon symbol. The work was done in seclusion, accompanied by chants and spells no man was allowed to hear.

During all this preparation, the flax had finished blooming and gone to seed. The plants had turned from green to yellow, indicating the fibers within were at their strongest and finest to make the best linen. Åsa rounded up all of Tromøy's folk and led them out to the field to harvest. Even the shield-maidens and warriors abandoned their swordplay to pull up the plants, roots and all.

They left the harvested flax in the fields to dry under the summer sun while they resumed battle practice. After a week, the women took up big iron-toothed combs to thresh the seeds from the stalks, and stored them in sacks in the granary. The flax stalks they hauled off to a still pond downwind of the hall and set them to soak for another week.

When Åsa appeared on the practice field with a handful of straws, everyone groaned. They dutifully lined up and drew their straw.

The short straw fell to Helga. She sighed and trudged off to the foul-smelling pool, where she fished in the mire to see if the tough outer stems had rotted off. She returned shaking her head, and the next day someone else had to go and check.

On the day a girl returned from the pool to report that the stems had fallen away, all the women descended on the pond to gather the slimy, reeking stalks. They rinsed away the odor in a swift-running brook and lugged their sodden harvest back to the yard, where every woman and girl joined in beating the plants with wooden clubs to break the woody outer husks. Then they laid the stalks on a board and scraped the husks away with scutching knives to expose the soft inner fibers. These they combed through a fine-toothed heckle until they lay straight and silky, ready for the winter spinning.

Once the flax was safely tended to, the women rejoined the men in training. After a hard day of drilling, Tromøy's warriors gathered around the bonfire. While they awaited their dinner, the ale made its rounds, and soon the volume of laughter and chatter rose in the air.

"What are you staring at, Christian?" Silence fell swift as an axeblow. Ragnhild was pointing her eating knife at Behrt, who was seated across the fire next to Ulf. All eyes watched as a furious blush surged over the Christian's face, but he kept his gaze fixed on his trencher.

"Keep your eyes to yourself, or I'll poke them out and feed them to you," Ragnhild growled, turning back to her ale. Conversation trickled back, although voices remained subdued.

A few minutes later, Åsa noticed Behrt was staring at the shield-maiden again. Ragnhild seemed oblivious to it as she joked with the others.

As Åsa left the fire for the bower, she saw Behrt walking alone to the smithy. Just then, a group passed by, laughing and chattering. Ragnhild was at their center. At the sound of her voice, Behrt's head turned toward the shield-maiden.

He looked so forlorn, Åsa changed course to catch up with him. At her approach, Behrt tore his gaze from Ragnhild and gave his queen the proper greeting, bowing low.

"Good evening, Behrt."

"Good evening, lady." He straightened up and waited.

She could think of nothing to say that wouldn't embarrass him, but she felt better now that he was not alone.

The Christian was silent too, but it was a silence that didn't beg to be filled. They walked together to the smithy, where the glow of the forge greeted them. Ulf's burly form was silhouetted by the firelight. He nodded in greeting without taking his eyes from the metal bar he had in the fire, watching it change from red to orange. He drew it out with the tongs and laid it on the anvil while picking up his hammer. Behrt moved to help him, and Åsa felt better to see him occupied. She turned to go.

From that night on, Åsa made it her habit to walk Behrt back to the smithy. Gradually, their silence turned to talk. At first, she asked him about the progress he and Ulf had made in the smithy, how many spearheads or axeheads they had forged, how their supply of charcoal was holding out. She in turn told him everyday things about the harvest or hunting, or how the recruits were progressing.

One night Åsa was chattering along, trying to fill the silence. "The farm girls are transforming from dairy maids into shield-maidens. Ragnhild is working miracles with them."

"Women should not be fighting," said Behrt.

Åsa stopped short and stared at him. "And why not?" she demanded.

"It is against God's will," he said.

Åsa snorted. "Not my gods. I'll thank you to keep those opinions to yourself. I can't have morale damaged." To cut off any further argument, she changed the subject. "The boys are coming along very well too, but my experienced húskarlar are hard pressed to train them all. As soon as Ulf can spare you I'll need you to take on a squad."

"Thank you, lady." Behrt nodded.

When the day came that the smithy had produced enough weaponry to arm all the recruits and Ulf could spare Behrt for the practice field, Åsa assigned him his own squad of farm boys. She placed him a safe distance from Ragnhild and her farm girls, but Åsa often glimpsed him staring across the field in their direction.

If the shield-maiden noticed the Christian's attention, she didn't show it.

RAGNHILD DROVE her farm girls harder than ever, and they gained prowess quickly. The day came when Helga's spearshaft swept Ragnhild's legs out from under her. The shield-maiden landed hard on her backside, shock jolting across her features. Weapons were lowered as the girls gasped in unison. Helga froze, her eyes wide in her pale face.

Ragnhild threw back her head and laughed. Åsa strode forward to haul her to her feet.

"I think they are ready to fight the men," Ragnhild said, brushing herself off.

The next day the women met the men in the practice yard, and it began as expected. They minced across the field toward each other, practice weapons outstretched. When they got within reach, they waved their spear shafts tentatively, pole ends clacking faintly.

"Fight, you cowards," Ragnhild bellowed, striding onto the field and knocking a husky boy down with her spear shaft. Her second whack bloodied his nose. "Come on!"

First blood seemed to break the spell. Roaring, the girls charged down on their opponents. Spear poles smacked into flesh.

"That's more like it!" Ragnhild shouted, banging her sword on her shield and grinning.

After a few whacks, the beleaguered boys shook off their reluctance and fought back. A free-for-all ensued. The air resounded with thuds and curses, resulting in blood and bruises on both sides. Satisfied, Ragnhild called an end early before bones were broken.

The next day she set her shield-maidens against the males again with even more gratifying results. Ragnhild called encouragement as her recruits stormed onto the field, whacking the boys enthusiastically with their sticks.

"They fight like Valkyries," said Åsa. Pride welled up in Ragnhild.

In response to the women's fierce attacks, the male trainees defended themselves with equal vigor, no longer squeamish about hitting a girl. It was a satisfying session.

Jarl Borg was equally impressed. "Another week of this and I'll begin drilling them in formation."

When the day came, the old jarl appeared on the field, resplendent in chain mail and helm. He lined the squads up in two long shield walls and called the leaders out to the center of the field to demonstrate techniques. Ragnhild showed them how to hook the top of Einar's shield with her axe and pull it down so that Åsa, who wielded a spear behind her, could strike the exposed enemy. Einar in turn showed them how to slash low at Ragnhild's unprotected calves with his practice sword. She let him sweep her legs out from under her and crashed to the ground with dramatic realism.

The squad leaders moved down one after each turn, so each person sparred against a different opponent, and eventually Ragnhild found herself face to face with Behrt the Christian.

She fought down the rage that roiled up in her at the sight of the crucifix that dangled from his neck. She wanted to choke him with it. Even though she had done her best to ignore him, she was only too aware that he watched her. It made her feel like a mouse with a falcon hovering overhead, ready to stoop. No matter where she ran, his raptor's gaze found her.

She was not a mouse. "Hello, Christian," she hissed. "I hope you're ready for a beating."

Behrt smiled at her mildly and nodded.

While he was still smiling, Ragnhild jerked her pole up in a vicious slash to catch him under the chin. But her spear pole collided with Behrt's shield. He'd managed to bring it up to meet her blow. His pleasant smile was still in place.

Infuriated, Ragnhild whirled, swinging her stick in a circle with enough force to knock him off his feet, shield or no. But as she came around, their eyes met for an instant. Ragnhild yanked her pole back to just miss him.

"Move on!" barked Jarl Borg. Averting her gaze, Ragnhild moved on to Svein with relief.

After the demonstration was complete, Borg sent the squad leaders to rejoin their trainees to spend the afternoon practicing the techniques.

It had been more than a year since Ragnhild had practiced battle formations with a full army. As she fought beside Einar, Thorgeir, and Svein, she felt like she was home. Only this was a home where she was valued for her battle skills, not just tolerated by her father and brothers until she could be married off to the highest bidder.

After the recruits had become familiar with the techniques, Jarl Borg herded them together into squares to form a shield fort. The outside ranks locked their shields to make a four-sided fortress, and some in the center held their shields above their heads, making a solid tortoise shape. Those within who were not holding a shield thrust their spears out between the shields. The groups took turns attacking each other's forts.

When they were able to form solid shield forts, Borg introduced the swine horn. This was a fortress in motion—much more difficult to maintain.

Ragnhild paced around her square, shoving until she was satisfied that the walls were tight. Then she took her place at the head of her squad.

"Forward!" shouted Borg, and Ragnhild began to move ahead with the rest of the leaders, followed by their ranks. Those in the rear lagged slightly, and the squares elongated into the wedge shape.

"Stay tight to your neighbor," Borg admonished, rapping the shields with the butt of his spear. Eventually he was satisfied with their transitions from rectangle to wedge and he formed them into two lines, facing each other across the practice field.

"Shield wall!" he barked. Both rows pivoted, wood clacking as they overlapped their shields. Borg turned to the southernmost line. "Square!" The line folded on itself until they formed a rectangle with spearmen packed into the center and protected by shields on all four sides.

"Swine horn!"

The rectangular shield wall pivoted until they presented a point aimed at the enemy, with rows angled to either side like the wings of a falcon.

"Charge!"

The wedge began to move forward in a fast march that soon became a run. The formation loosened a little as the leaders surged ahead, but as the front-runners struck the opposing line, those behind them locked into place. The wedge drove into the opponent's shield wall and broke through.

"Split!"

The swine horn poured through the defenses, split into two lines, and doubled back behind the enemy line. The defenders turned to face their attackers, and the line of shields dissolved. Locked together, the warriors of the swine horn formed a new shield wall and attacked from behind, spearmen thrusting between the shields. The defenders tried to flank the wedge, but the double wings met the comers with a tight formation. Before long, the swine horn side had vanquished the last of the straight-line defenders.

"That's the way it's supposed to work," said Jarl Borg approvingly. "War is not a drill. Don't expect this formation to work so well in battle. But there are times when it's the only chance, so we practice. Again! Swine horn!" This time he pointed to the other side.

By now the newcomers were working with the experienced warriors as a cohesive whole, teammates who had grown to trust and rely on each other. The competition between squads was intense but good-natured. Ragnhild made sure her squad was far from the Christian's.

~

"FORM UP!" Ragnhild shouted, and her shield-maidens lined up on either side of her, two rows deep, spears and shields at the ready.

"Shield wall!" she bellowed, and the front line pivoted as one, presenting their shields to the men across the field, who formed their own line at Olvir's command. Jarl Borg stood at the far end of the grounds, hands clasped behind his back, silent for once.

"Advance!" Ragnhild gave the order at the same time as Olvir, and the lines marched toward each other, front rows with shields locked and short swords or axes in their hands, the spears of the second rows bristling between the shields.

Eyeing the men's line, Ragnhild recognized the man opposite her. The Christian had placed himself directly in her path. He smiled at her and an evil grin spread across her face as the two rows broke into a run.

As the shield walls clashed, she rammed her shield boss at the Christian's face. Behrt blinked but dodged the blow. Her shield glanced off his mailed shoulder, leaving her exposed for an instant. The Christian's eyes flicked over her, but he did not take the opening. Ragnhild flushed as she recovered and redoubled her attack. Behrt fended her strikes with minimal force.

A rush of fury drove her to hack at him viciously, but her blows slid off his chain mail like ice in a thaw.

Her face heated up and sweat prickled at her forehead. She was about to make a fool of herself. She drew back, raised her shield, and eased her sword arm down. The Christian waited, his face serene, while she drew a deep breath and got control of herself.

Renewed, she launched herself at him.

He caught her first sword blow on his shield. Hers was ready for his counter strike, but his sword remained by his side. She felt her anger rise again and willed it away.

"Fight, damn you!" she hissed through gritted teeth.

"I do not wish to hurt you."

Rage nearly blinded her. "You think you could hurt me, you lily-livered milksop?" she screamed, swinging the flat of her sword at his helmet.

He retreated before her fury. She drove him back out of the practice field until they were in the barnyard. Pigs and geese scattered before them, squawking indignantly. Behrt continued to fend off her blows, but his sword arm stayed by his side.

She pinned him against the cow byre. He just stood there, staring at her. The condescension in his eyes drove her mad. In a fury she plunged her sword into the woven wall beside him.

"What is wrong with you?" she cried.

He smiled as her arm lowered to her side, leaving the sword quivering in the wall.

"It isn't right to fight a woman. You are the weaker sex, and it is a man's place to protect your kind."

Ragnhild stared at him as the anger burned inside her like a molten tide.

"I don't need your protection!" she snarled. "You're just a coward like your nailed god." She turned and stalked away.

ÅSA WATCHED the shield-maiden turn her back on Behrt, leaving him alone in the barnyard as the pigs and geese returned and resumed their foraging.

As she came beside him, his gaze flicked toward her.

"Never mind," she said. "Let her go. She'll cool off."

"I fear I do not belong here, lady."

"Of course, you do. You are one of us." Åsa's tone made it a command.

He shook his head. "I've been a Christian since I was a child. I am a true believer. It is a faith of peace."

"The Irish are Christians, but I hear they are no more peaceful than we are."

"No, I suppose that is true." Behrt gazed after Ragnhild's retreating form. The set of the shield-maiden's shoulders radiated indignation. "But their women do not make war."

"You chose a hard person to love."

Behrt nodded.

"You know her father promised her to an Irish king without her consent. A Christian."

Behrt looked at her, a question in his eyes.

"She feels threatened by your attention. Your religion strips women of their power and their freedom, makes them subservient to their husbands. To us it is no better than slavery. Ragnhild ran away from home to escape that fate, leaving behind her family and her inheritance to join me. She defeated her own father in battle to remain free. I've never seen anyone fight harder against fate. No one is more determined to rule her own life than Ragnhild."

Behrt swallowed, but when he spoke, his voice was steady. "I suppose that is what draws me to her. She's like no one I've ever known. But I realize she will never love me."

"I know how hard it is to love someone you cannot have."

Behrt's smile was more like a wince. "You are very wise."

Åsa's smile mirrored his. "I speak from experience, my friend."

They set out for the smithy, companions in grief.

# CHAPTER 25

August, AD 821

The barley turned golden in the fields. Toki tested the grain and reported that it was dry enough to harvest while the weather held. Åsa was glad to have so many experienced farm hands.

Every able person turned out to the fields. They took turns at the back-breaking work of scything down the barley close to the ground, then got some relief by gathering the stalks and tying them in bundles. Soon the golden stubble fields were dotted with stooks of a dozen bundles, leaning against each other to dry. Recruits were assigned to patrol the fields, scaring off birds and rodents while the precious grain dried under the sun. If rain threatened, they scurried to cover the stooks with ships' awnings. They knew their lives depended on the barley's success.

The sun shone reliably, and after two weeks, the barley had dried enough to thresh. The ships' awnings were spread out across the fields, and the barley bundles laid upon them.

Everyone who could wield a flail joined in beating the grains from the stalks. The crows went into a frenzy, and anyone not threshing picked up weapons and ran through the fields, clashing swords on shields to drive the birds away.

After the threshing, the stalks were gathered and set aside for livestock bedding while the grains were carefully scooped into buckets. When a stiff breeze sprang up, the barley seeds were poured back and forth between buckets a dozen times, filling the air with chaff that the wind carried away.

When the buckets of grain were clean and dry, the barley was poured into sacks and stored in the granary, where cats patrolled to keep away the mice and birds.

Åsa counted the sacks, her brow furrowed as she calculated whether they would last the winter. There might be enough if the grain could be kept from damp, if the seeds didn't go to mold, and if the cats kept the mice at bay.

She shook the worries from her head. It would be as it would be.

Now everyone was turned to training, for the Danes would have gotten their crops in too.

In spite of the long workdays, Åsa slept little at night. Instead she rose into the falcon's waiting body and patrolled the broad waters of the Skagerrak.

Night after night, the sea was empty.

ON THE FIRST night of the full moon, the peregrine soared out over the Skagerrak. Far below, the sea shimmered and the light revealed a sight that made her falcon's heart stutter.

Dragon ships. Their banners cracked in the breeze, striped sails bellied, driving them inexorably closer.

If this wind held, they would land on Tromøy's beach by dawn.

She beat her wings hard to stay aloft, counting. Seven ships. Fully manned, that could mean more than two hundred men. Tromøy had one hundred and twenty-eight warriors, only half of those with any real battle experience.

This was her own doing. What had she been thinking? How could Tromøy's puny collection of shield-maidens and half-trained boys stand against this overwhelming force? They weren't ready. The Danes would surge over them like a tidal wave, leaving broken bodies and burned buildings in their wake.

Before the rift with Olaf, she had been so sure of her choice to refuse Rorik's proposal. How wrong she had been, and now it was too late.

She beat her way back to the bower and dove into her body, stumbling out of bed before she had full control of her legs.

"Danes!" she croaked as she floundered into the main room. Women threw off their blankets as she rushed out the door and across the yard to the great hall where the húskarlar slept.

"The Danish fleet is coming," she cried. "Seven ships. They'll be here by dawn."

The men tumbled from their sleeping benches and lunged for their war gear.

"Light the beacons," said Jarl Borg.

She turned away, shaking her head.

"Lady, you must put aside your pride for the sake of your people." The old jarl's tone was close to an admonition.

"He won't come."

"He will. You know he will."

"He can't get here in time."

"You have to try. Please."

Åsa had never heard him say please before.

She nodded her head once, and that was all he needed to send a lad running to the hilltop.

Åsa ordered the log boom deployed. Tromøy's defenders

spent the hours of the night sharpening axes and spears, fletching arrows, and cleaning chain mail.

Near dawn Åsa sent her archers to the log boom while the rest armed themselves. Those that owned them struggled into leather armor and brynja, while the rest donned rawhide-coated battle jackets. They strapped on swords, tucked axes into their belts, and slung shields over their shoulders. Spears stood in a barrel by the door, and every warrior grabbed one before mustering beneath the giant ash tree beside the hall.

Olvir took his place beside Åsa at the head of the elite warriors chosen to protect their queen. On her other side stood Kjell, the new recruit she'd chosen to carry her falcon banner. Each of them wore chain mail and helms and wielded the finest weapons Ulf could make. They waited in silence while Heid and her women sacrificed a goat to the gods for victory, sprinkling each warrior with the sacred blood.

As the sun rose, the first dragon ships surged into the bay. Åsa watched them drop sail and sprout oars like spider legs. Soon the water was crawling with them, making their way toward the beach.

The warships shuddered to a halt as they struck the log boom, submerged just below the surface of the water. Arrows whickered from the trees and screams rose from the enemy ships. Bodies splashed into the water as the Danes heaved their dead overboard. Tromøy's archers kept up heavy fire as the enemy struggled to free themselves. Arrows flew from the Danish ships toward shore, but they were firing blind at an enemy they could not see.

At last the Danish ships broke through and resumed their approach. The arrows ceased as Tromøy's archers hurried back to the hall. Åsa had no idea how many of enemy they had killed, but she prayed it was enough.

She surveyed her collection of half-trained young, clad in their fragile weapon-shirts, clutching their spears and shields, faces pale beneath their helms. The seasoned warriors were spread thinly in their ranks.

She wanted to shout at them all to run.

Instead she sucked in her churning guts and stalked toward them.

"Today, we face our enemy," she declared, making her voice ring clear and strong. "Whether we win or lose, this battle will settle matters for all time. We will fight off the Danes, or we will be dead. Either way, they can bother us no more.

"The Norns measured out the thread of our lives on the day we were born. These Danes cannot cut it shorter. So let us fight with honor and die with courage if that is our fate.

"I fought this same enemy on the shores of Borre and won. With your help, we will win again."

The blood surged into their faces as they cheered and clashed weapons on shields.

She could lose them all today.

The first enemy longships grated onto the beach. Danes swarmed over their sides, thick as bees in a hive, the first comers lining up in a shield wall. When the first row stretched the length of the beach, a second row crowded in behind, then a third. Åsa's stomach dropped at the sight, but she showed no sign of her dismay.

Åsa sought out the Danish king's war banner in the triple ranks. The raven embroidered on the blood-red background seemed to flap its wings as the banner rippled in the breeze, sending a shiver down her back. The magic woven into raven banners was said to be invincible. She hoped Heid and her apprentices had imbued her falcon with equal power.

Below his banner, the early sun glinted on the crested battle helm of Rorik, surrounded by his húskarlar, huge men in full war gear, hefting long-bladed spears. Åsa fought the crazy urge to run down the hill and beg him to take her and spare her people. She gritted her teeth. It wouldn't work. She had argued it all out in her mind a thousand times. Her son's life would be forfeit, and Tromøy's people no better than slaves under Danish rule. They'd made their decision together, and there was no going back.

The triple shield wall began to move up the hill.

"Archers!" Jarl Borg shouted.

In the trees around the hall, unseen bows creaked as strings were drawn. Åsa exhaled in relief, knowing her archers were in position. All eyes trained on Jarl Borg. He raised his hand high as he gauged the range. Despite his age, Borg's eyesight was still true. His long fingers dropped and arrows whirred into the air, arcing up and lashing down on the invaders like deadly rain. Danes raised their shields, but many screamed and dropped. The defenders cheered, but still the enemy came on, trampling over their dead. They infested the hillside. Jarl Borg kept the air filled with arrows, thinning their ranks, but Åsa knew soon they would have to engage that enormous host directly.

A shout from the enemy, and the Danish horde halted as their archers nocked. The commander roared his order and arrows darkened the sky.

"Shields up," barked Jarl Borg. Wood clacked as Tromøy's defenders racked shield to shield and jerked the solid wall overhead to weather the arrows that hailed down on the linden. Åsa sheltered herself and Kjell beneath her shield. No death cries came from Tromøy's ranks. Every carefully made shield held up against the battering.

Straining her vision to the side, Åsa caught the gleam in Olvir's eye. He was eager for battle, no matter the outcome. He met her glance and flashed a grin while his farm boys cheered. To her left, Ragnhild and her shield-maidens raised their spears in salute.

They weren't afraid. Why was she? They would stand together, and fall if the Norns decreed. The thought drained her fear away, and the joy of battle rose fierce in her chest.

"I dedicate you all to Odin!" the Danish king cried as he hurled a spear directly at her.

From her battle state, Åsa watched it soar regally toward her, its flight unhurried. She had plenty of time to step aside, reach up, and grab the shaft out of the air as it passed inches from her face.

The spear quivered in her grip. Joy raged in her, and a cheer rose up from her warriors.

"I mark you all for Freyja!" The cry tore from her lips as she hurled the spear back into the Danish horde. The unexpected missile struck the bannerman's helmet, knocking him off his feet and sending the Danish banner to the ground.

Tromøy's troops roared at the omen.

The Danes paused in their onslaught, momentarily shaken, but the bannerman regained his feet and their commanders rallied them with curses and blows. They resumed their march up the hill.

Jarl Borg eyed their triple ranks. "The swine horn is our only option."

Åsa's eyes met Olvir's. Outnumbered as they were, with the advantage of their uphill position, a square-angled wedge might punch through the enemy's defenses. Yet if they failed to penetrate the enemy shield wall, the Danes would quickly swallow them. Åsa shuddered at the risk of it, but Borg was right, it was their only chance. She hoped that their weeks of drilling had been enough.

Åsa pounded the butt of her spear on the ground. "This is our chance!" she cried. "Our chance for peace and plenty. These Danes would take our land, our freedom, our lives. They will keep coming until we stop them. Let's drive them back into the sea. We can do it. The gods are on our side. Tromøy will triumph!"

Their cheer swelled in a deafening wave.

"Swine horn!" shouted Jarl Borg.

They brought their shields down, locked together. Åsa hefted her spear.

Tromøy's strongest warriors surged forward to form the apex. Åsa burned to lead them, but she knew that if their queen fell in the first assault, the battle would be over. She kept her place in the second row, next to Kjell.

They tightened up into a cohesive rectangle of steel and linden. Åsa thrust her spear between the shields in front of her.

"Charge!" shouted Jarl Borg.

For a fraction of a second, Åsa pushed against those ahead of her. Then she hurtled downhill with the others, spear driving forward, a scream ripping from her throat.

Their momentum carried them into the enemy's first ranks. Åsa held her breath as the warriors in front of her crashed through the mass of enemies. Her spearpoint rammed into chain mail, and her victim screamed and fell. She jerked her spear free, then thrust it into the crowd again. She jabbed her spear in and out as she shoved her way through the crowd. They were in the thick of the Danish shield wall, enemies on all sides. Then they broke through so suddenly she nearly stumbled. She pivoted with her line and attacked the enemy ranks from the rear.

The Danes were off-balance, having lost precious seconds trying to recover from the breach and defend three sides. Tromøy's warriors maintained their formation and took their toll before the Danes could regroup. Åsa prayed that it had been enough as the enemy turned on them and the well-ordered shield walls dissolved into the chaos of battle.

As the shields in front of her were pried apart, Åsa drove her spear into an enemy's eye, where it lodged in the back of his skull. She let go of the shaft as he fell and tore her short sword, Lightning, from the scabbard.

A gray-bearded Dane swung his axe at her legs in a crippling blow. She sidestepped and rammed her sword into his belly. His chain mail stopped the point, but the force drove the air from him. He clutched the blade and doubled over with an "Oof!" Åsa slammed her shield boss onto his helmet with a clang that jarred all the way up her arm, then yanked her blade back. The Dane stumbled to his knees, and she slammed Lightning down on the back of his neck, biting flesh and bone. Blood flowed and the Dane toppled.

Her peripheral vision caught a flash of steel and she pivoted again, flinging her shield up to deflect a sword while slashing her blade across the calves of her attacker, bringing him down on top of the first.

Åsa glimpsed Ragnhild at the head of her shield-maidens in a sea of Danes. The women's superior weapons and their hard weeks of training showed as they made the most of their speed and flexibility, but the enemy outnumbered them drastically. Åsa fought her way toward them, Kjell sticking to her like pinesap. Shouts and screams rang out with the clash of steel. The air reeked of blood, and the grass was slippery with it. Bodies made the footing treacherous, the wounded writhing among the dead. A hand reached out of the tangle and grabbed Åsa's ankle. She jerked her foot away, struggling on through the battle mire, eyes on her shield-maidens.

Helga, the eldest of the five sisters, confronted a leering Dane. The girl, quick and strong from weeks of training, drove her blade upward beneath the Dane's beard, and the man's eyes rounded in surprise. Helga tore her weapon from his throat and spun away as he pitched forward. She hacked down on the next foe where his neck met his shoulder, felling him instantly. Pivoting, she swung her shield into a helmet, and the Dane stumbled, dazed.

Åsa ducked an enemy's axeblow while Olvir dispatched him with a sword. She scanned the crowd for Helga. The girl stood in a tangle of fallen Danes, catching her breath. Her eyes sparkled and her cheeks were flushed, the joy of battle upon her.

Helga caught Åsa's eye and grinned proudly. Behind her steel flashed as a warrior swung his axe. Åsa screamed a warning, and the girl turned to meet the attack a heartbeat too late. The Danish axe flashed and took the girl in the neck. Helga fell in a spray of blood, her eyes wide with shock.

Fury shot venom in Åsa's veins, and she hacked viciously at the man in front of her. He fell, but all around her own people were falling too.

Ragnhild held two men at bay, and Åsa saw Helga's killer come at her from behind. He was a huge, black-bearded Dane, fully mailed and helmeted with a long-hafted broad axe. The shield-maiden swung toward the movement, but the third assailant was beyond her range.

Åsa shoved futilely against the mass of heaving bodies between them. She would never reach Ragnhild in time. The three Danes had the shield-maiden cornered and were closing in for the kill. Where was Einar? She scanned the crowd.

The giant Dane swung his axe at Ragnhild and Åsa shouted a warning the shield-maiden could not hear. A warrior thrust his shield in the axe's path, deflecting its path. Åsa recognized Behrt's mail and the cross inlaid on his helm.

The Dane's blow knocked Behrt sideways, but Ragnhild drove him off while the Christian recovered. She held off the other two assailants while Behrt faced the giant Dane.

Åsa fought her way toward them, Olvir and her guard beside her, but they were caught in a crush of warriors too tight to swing a blade. Åsa shoved Lightning into ribs of the Dane ahead of her. He screamed and sagged, but the crowd was too tight for him to fall. Åsa yanked her blade from the corpse, but like the dead man, she was trapped in a seething, shoving mass of bodies. All she could do was watch the battle that raged beyond the mob.

Behrt fended off the huge Dane's blows with his shield while putting himself between Ragnhild and her assailants. The shield-maiden slammed her blade down on one attacker's sword arm as he swung toward Behrt. Her blow slashed partway through his wrist. His sword fell as blood spurted from the wound, and he went down, screaming as he clutched his wrist.

The black-haired giant swung his axe at the Christian's neck.

"Look out!" Åsa shouted.

Behrt dodged but took the blow on his mailed shoulder. Rings popped out of Behrt's brynja as the Dane's axe peeled back his padded battle shirt. A thin line of blood welled on bare flesh. Behrt slashed at the giant's calves. The blade hit metal shin guards, but the big Dane staggered from the blow. Behrt pressed his advantage, driving his blade up into the Dane's midsection. Behrt's thrust failed to pierce the chain mail, but it knocked the wind out of his adversary and sent him stumbling back. The big man kept to his feet and sent his axe hurtling through the air. Behrt ducked beneath the haft and charged, ramming his sword into the Dane's body again, this time breaking through the mail. The giant roared and went down with a thud that shook the ground.

Behrt jerked his sword free and closed in to finish the big Dane. Ragnhild shrieked a warning as her remaining assailant turned and drove his sword into Behrt's back. The Christian went down on top of the giant. Ragnhild threw herself at the backstabbing Dane and knocked him away.

The giant Dane had his hands around the Christian's throat, pulling Behrt close and trapping his arms between their bodies. Behrt dropped his sword and fumbled for his knife as his face turned red, then purple. He got his knife unsheathed and struggled to free his arm.

Ragnhild's opponent thrashed like a wet dog, finally throwing off the shield-maiden. She was on her feet in an eyeblink and after him as he went for Behrt. Ragnhild hacked her sword at him, but he turned his own blade on her.

Behrt got his knife arm free and drove his blade up under the giant's beard. Blood spurted and the Dane writhed, then abruptly went still.

The knife dropped from Behrt's hand, and he slumped on the giant.

Ragnhild fended off her foe with sword and shield, but he drove her backward. The shield-maiden stumbled over a body in the long grass and went down. The Dane was on her in a flash, straddling her chest. Ragnhild thrashed and bucked, but he had her arms pinned beneath his thighs. He grabbed her chin with his left hand and forced it back, exposing her throat, while he drew his knife with his right. Åsa hacked at the men between them, screaming as the blade flashed toward the shield-maiden's throat.

Behrt roused and flung himself onto Ragnhild's assailant, knocking the Dane to the side. The blade skimmed by her throat, drawing a hairline of blood. Ragnhild struggled to her knees and grabbed the Dane, but he jerked away and plunged his knife into Behrt's gut.

Ragnhild found her sword and with a cry of fury, swung it, and took the Dane's head half off. She shoved his corpse aside to get to Behrt.

Åsa and her guard finally managed to hack their way through the crowd, and they surrounded the shield-maiden and the Christian. Ragnhild knelt beside Behrt. His eyes were closed and blood flowed onto the grass.

Ragnhild stayed on her knees beside Behrt's body, oblivious to the battle around her. Beneath her helm, tears made trails through the blood and dirt on her face. But the enemy was closing in, and Åsa pulled the shield-maiden to her feet. Rage flooded into Ragnhild's eyes and she stood over the Christian's body, slaughtering everyone who came near.

Olvir and his men held back the sea of enemy, but more Danes bore down on them, and Tromøy's warriors were falling.

How much longer could they hold out?

It didn't matter. They would fight until the choosers of the slain snatched them up from the battlefield. Åsa could feel the Valkyries hovering, reveling in the sounds of slaughter.

Sword dripping gore, Åsa stalked the throng, seeking her target. Kjell followed with her banner and her household guard formed a buffer around her, their shields and swords fending off attackers.

She squinted through the fury and picked out the enemy pennant, red as blood. Looking down the shaft, she found the one she hunted.

Rorik.

*The cause of my problems. All I have to do is kill him.*

Beneath his banner, the Danish king and his guard were besieged by Tromøy's warriors. But they were the young recruits, and the Danes were scything them down like barley.

Time slowed again.

Åsa's vision sharpened with a falcon's focus. The sounds of battle fell away. Her quarry drew her like a magnet as she hacked her way toward Rorik's banner.

A Dane whirled on her. She swung her sword low, sweeping his legs from under him. As he fell, she ripped Lightning from his calf and shoved it into his throat. Blood spouted as she jerked the blade free and resumed her quest. The warriors that stood between her and Rorik seemed mere annoyances. She dodged them or felled them, leaving Olvir and her guard behind.

And then she was before Rorik. He stood knee-deep among the corpses of her farm boys.

"Rorik!" she shouted.

The Danish king rotated slowly in her direction, his face a mask of surprise. His helmet and brynja were drenched with blood, his beard dripping red as if he had been feasting on corpses.

She took a firm grip on her sword and shield. "I am Åsa, Queen of Tromøy. You trespass on my land."

Rorik's surprise turned into a red-toothed grin as he looked down on her. "There you are, my queen. Have you decided to accept my proposal?"

"Here's my answer." Åsa lunged, ramming Lightning at his gut. Rorik moved aside, and her swordblow barely grazed his chain mail. Her momentum carried her forward, and he swatted her helm with the flat of his sword. The blow rang in her head, and the force sent her reeling.

She staggered but managed to use the impetus to drag Lightning in an arc that connected solidly with Rorik's torso, knocking him sideways. His eyes widened in surprise. He swayed with the blow, his legs rooted like oak trees.

Rorik's shock darkened to a scowl as he steadied on his feet. "I'd kill you now, but I can't wed a corpse."

"I'll never marry you," she said.

"Very well. A corpse you'll be, then." He swung his sword at her and she dodged, but it caught her on the left shoulder with a force that numbed her arm. Her shield fell from her hand. Sensation returned in a throbbing rush of pain that nearly brought her to her knees. Before she could recover, he hit her shoulder again, and she screamed in spite of herself.

Her left arm hung useless at her side.

As she rallied for another strike, he smashed his shield into her helmet with a force that made her stagger. She tripped on a body slippery with blood and went down. As she fell, she slashed at Rorik's legs. Her sword clanged off his shin guards. He lurched but kept his feet.

Åsa glimpsed Olvir and his guard fighting Rorik's guard to get to her. She struggled to get her legs under her but slipped on the blood-slick grass and fell back. She found herself looking into the eyes of a farm boy, glazed in death, his flimsy battle shirt torn and soaked with blood. Beside him lay another boy, his fair hair a red mat. Beyond, more staring young eyes, the corpses of her recruits.

*What have I wrought?*

Her bravado evaporated as she stared up at Rorik, looming above her. This king was more than a match for her. Older, wiser, crueler. She should have taken his marriage offer and saved her people.

Rorik grinned as he raised his sword.

*My deathblow.*

He stood above her, leering at the defeat in her eyes.

A falcon's cry pierced the air. High overhead, Stormrider soared, trailing her jesses.

*Prey. He is our prey.*

Åsa's sight expanded as she allowed the falcon's vision to take hold of her mind. From above, she stared down on the body that lay in a jumble of corpses. She watched the arc of Rorik's sword, which now seemed to drift down slow as a feather.

She rolled aside as Rorik's sword drove into the turf beside her. Rage engorged his face as he put both hands on the pommel and jerked the blade free.

*He is our prey.*

From where Åsa lay sprawled at Rorik's feet, she had a clear shot to his groin. What arrogance the man had to let his guard lapse. As he pulled his sword out of the ground, she rolled forward, driving her blade up between his legs with both hands. The point pierced his breeks and slid into flesh. With another heave, she drove it in.

Rorik pitched forward, screaming. She jerked her sword from his groin as hot blood gushed over her face. He toppled among Tromøy's dead.

She struggled to her feet. She saw her banner, where Olvir and his men still fought Rorik's bodyguard. Åsa shouldered her way into the melee and grabbed the Danish pennant from the bannerman's hand.

"Your king is dead," she rasped.

The bannerman gaped from her to Rorik's corpse. High above, Stormrider rode the air currents.

A horn sounded in the distance. Åsa squinted through the smoke as longships scudded into the bay. Her heart leaped as she recognized the red stripes on the lead sail.

Olaf.

Olvir tore his horn from his belt and sounded an answering call. Every warrior's head turned to see the Danish banner go down. Åsa held her bloody sword above her head while her húskarlar raised a cheer.

The Danes turned toward the sea and stumbled across the corpse-strewn ground toward the boats. Tromøy's warriors scrambled in pursuit.

The leading Danes reached their boats and dragged three of them off the beach, but the Vestfold fleet formed a solid wall of ships, blocking the Dane's escape.

"Launch our ships!" Åsa cried. "We can crush them between us. This is our chance to destroy them. Never again will they threaten our shores!"

Tromøy's warriors heaved their ships into the water. Åsa climbed aboard her father's flagship, *Wave King*, followed by Kjell and twenty-five of her strongest men. Olvir mustered another boat's crew from those húskarlar who could still man the oars, and they struck out after the Danes.

Tromøy's vessels harried the fleeing Danes straight into Olaf's fleet. His first flight of arrows whickered through the air and thinned the enemy decks. Shrieking men fell over the side, darkening the harbor with their blood.

Åsa's dragons rode them down, their high prows surging over the swimmers to ram the fleeing ships. Tromøy's warriors were no fresher than their enemies, but they strove to hold the Danish ships while Olaf's fleet attacked from the other side.

The surviving Danes expected no quarter. They crowded into the bows with spears and long-handled axes, prepared to fight to the death. There would be no dawn for these men.

Olaf's warriors reaped a red harvest with their spears and

axes. When the enemy forces had been decimated, Åsa ordered the last survivors bound. Tromøy's crews towed the Danish ships through the gore-slick water, scaring off the raucous gulls that fed on the bobbing bodies.

The eight surviving Danes were dragged ashore where they huddled together, ready to be sacrificed to the gods.

With a piercing cry, Stormrider lit on Åsa's shoulder as she stood over her captives. "Get them in a skiff," she ordered. As her men scurried off to find one, she smiled down on the prisoners. "You will live. You will take your boat back across the Skagerrak to carry my invitation to your lords. I invite them to visit me here on Tromøy. Tell them I will give them the same welcome I gave their brother Rorik."

Åsa had the skiff stocked with fresh water and a scant ration of food, then made the Danes shove off without rest.

"Do you think they'll make it?" Olvir asked, watching them row the tiny boat out of the harbor.

"Will they want to, carrying such news to their masters?" said Åsa. Survivors of battles were suspected cowards and never welcome. These men were more likely to make for parts unknown than return to Denmark. Åsa shrugged. Their fate was with the gods.

Olaf's fleet beached among the captured ships. Åsa fought the urge to run, forcing herself to stay and greet him as courtesy demanded. She waited on the shore while he disembarked, Stormrider clutching her shoulder, staring at the shrieking gulls as they wheeled over the bay, snatching at corpses. She did not turn her head, but from the corner of her eye, she watched him approach, tall and fair, hers no longer.

"Thank you for responding to my signal fire," she said, still watching the gulls.

"I wish I could have arrived sooner."

"I know you came with all haste."

Olaf said awkwardly, "Your people fought well."

Åsa nodded, watching her weary recruits as they dragged the dead from the waves and bore the wounded to higher ground. They were farmers no more.

"Make camp and rest your men," she said. "Tomorrow we will burn the dead."

Olaf nodded. Åsa turned and followed her warriors up the trail to the hall.

Ragnhild stood over Behrt's inert body, sword dangling from her hand. Her head was bowed, her shoulders slumped.

Åsa approached her and looked down on the Christian. He lay still, his face pale as skim milk. Blood stained his chain mail and glistened on the trampled grass around him.

Heid made her way over and looked down at him. She shook her head. "He was a good man, for a Christian."

"I wish I knew how they handle their dead," said Åsa. "I'd like to give him a fitting burial."

"He was Norse-born, a great warrior," said Ragnhild. "He was one of us. He should be honored as one of our own in death."

Heid knelt in the bloody grass. "I think it's a moot point," she said. "This one's alive."

# CHAPTER 26

The survivors gathered the wounded and carried them to the barracks, where Heid and her apprentices tended to them. The women set a great cauldron of leek and herb soup to boil over a fire in the yard, and they fed this strong-smelling broth to the wounded. If the wounds smelled of leeks, then vital organs had been penetrated and the patient would die.

Behrt was conscious enough to swallow the spoonfuls Ragnhild ladled into his mouth, and the shield-maiden sniffed anxiously at the stab-wound in his gut.

There was no scent of leek or herb. Her hands shook just a little as she packed his wounds with cobwebs, smeared honey over them, and bound them up with linen strips. She eased Behrt down on the cushions, covered him with a comforter, and departed to help tend to the dead.

Olaf's men helped the folk of Tromøy to lay the bodies side by side atop a great stack of wood. After Freyja claimed her share for Folkvang, her warriors' field, Odin would take the rest to Valhöll. There they would feast and fight with the gods, awaiting the final battle of Ragnarok.

The enemy corpses, including King Rorik's body, were stripped of weapons and armor, then beheaded so they could not rise again. Their bodies were piled on their own great pyre, for they had died in battle too and earned their place in the halls of the gods.

As great clouds of smoke carried the spirits of the dead to Asgaard, Heid and her followers gave thanks to Freyja and Odin for victory.

The war booty had been piled in the great hall by the high seat, waiting for Åsa to share it among her warriors before the feast.

Tromøy's folk began to gather on the benches. Åsa watched Olaf climb the hill, and the sweetness of her victory took on a bitter taste. She whirled and took the high seat, where Storm-rider waited, perched on the carved chair back. The falcon roused, fretful as Åsa sat twisting her wool shawl between her fingers.

It seemed to take forever for Olvir to lead his men up the trail. Åsa forced herself to remain in her seat though she wanted desperately to run back to the door and watch them.

When at last the door creaked open and men's voices sounded in the entry, she had nearly shredded the fine weaving of her shawl. She stilled her hands and soothed Stormrider while Olvir ushered Vestfold's men into the hall, where they took their places on the benches among Tromøy's warriors.

As custom required, Olvir escorted Olaf to the place beside Åsa on the high seat. She nodded to him but could not meet his eyes. When Brenna brought in the horn, Åsa had to still the tremble in her hands before taking it.

"Welcome, King Olaf," she said, drinking without meeting his gaze. She offered him the horn, her eyes fixed on the silver-chased rim.

"Thank you, Queen Åsa," he said gravely, accepting the horn

and drinking. He returned it to Brenna, who carried it round to the warriors on the benches.

"I thank you for responding to my signal fire," Åsa choked out. "Your alliance is of great value to Tromøy."

The húskarlar cheered at her words.

"King Olaf, I offer you half the Danish ships."

The warriors beat their weapons on their shields in approbation, raising a din that shook the rafters.

"I accept your generous gift," Olaf replied formally.

Åsa turned to the warriors and called them up, one by one. She and Olaf took turns distributing the war booty captured from the Danes: helmets, ring-sewn leather armor, spears, axes, and swords, as well as arm rings and cloak pins of silver and bronze. Åsa watched with pleasure as the newfound spoils transformed Tromøy's ragtag fighters into a well-outfitted hird.

Another cheer greeted Toki and his crew as they staggered in under the weight of a roast pig on a huge platter, followed by steaming bowls of turnips and cabbage and stacks of fresh-baked flat bread.

Silence fell over the hall as the warriors ate. As soon as the food was cleared, the ale began to flow again and their voices rose in happy boasts, each more outrageous than the last. Soon warriors were wrestling, cheered on by their hearth mates.

Åsa watched from her high seat, her mouth trained in a smile, her heart a sodden lump weighing down her chest. She was glad the attention was on the antics taking place on the hall floor and not on her. She felt Olaf's gaze each time it flicked toward her, but she kept her eyes focused on the húskarlar.

As the longfire burned low, the warriors began to falter, empty cups slack in their hands. Åsa's sideways glance at Olaf told her he was dozing in his chair. She risked a full-on look, lingering over his finely sculpted features, his lashes casting shadows on his cheeks, his soft lips relaxed in sleep.

She rose and Stormrider stepped silently onto her shoulder. She climbed down from the high seat carefully, then slipped into the bed chamber and out the side door.

The night air was cool, refreshing after the stuffy hall. The moon lit the clear night sky bright as day. Stormrider lofted into the air. Åsa's feet took her across the fields to the tree that hung over the water's edge where she had always taken refuge as a girl. She climbed into the welcoming branches and sat in her favorite spot, hidden from view, and stared out to sea.

Movement caught her eye. Her heart leaped when she recognized Olaf's tall figure coming across the field. She shrank back into the foliage and held her breath, but he stopped beneath the tree and looked up at her. He stood there in silence while Åsa choked back a sob. Her throat constricted, and she could barely breathe as she forced herself to look down at him.

He looked up, his eyes gleaming with unshed tears. Åsa felt a drop escape her own eye and burn a trail down her cheek.

They did not speak. After a while, Olaf bowed his head and walked away.

Åsa remained in the tree while the moon set. Then, in a flurry of wings, Stormrider landed in the branches. Åsa smiled and let her mind enter the falcon. Together they soared out over the Skagerrak.

As the sun rose over the harbor, the falcon watched Olaf's fleet depart.

Tromøy's folk set to their fall work. The cattle were brought down from the summer pastures, along with the cheeses made in the dairy. The shaggy sheep and goats with their heavy, waterproof coats lived outside through the winter, feeding on wild grass and seaweed. The strongest cattle and hogs were selected to shelter in byres, while the rest were slaughtered, their meat preserved by smoking and salting.

The folk spent the last of the warm autumn days roaming the island, gathering berries, apples, mushrooms, and wild onions. Cabbages and turnips were brought in from the gardens. All the produce they couldn't eat immediately was dried or pickled for winter storage. They festooned the hall and bower rafters with fragrant herbs.

Tromøy's barracks was still filled with the wounded, Behrt the Christian among them. Ragnhild tended him and the two could be seen talking together.

When the work was complete, Åsa held the traditional ale feast. The warriors competed in footraces and wrestling matches. Åsa rewarded the winners with arm rings and cloak pins from Solvi's treasure.

The kitchen staff dragged the long trestle tables and benches into the yard for the last time that year, and they cooked meat in huge cauldrons over outdoor fires, along with fresh vegetables and greens. The ale and mead flowed like a river in spring.

Behrt had mended well enough to attend the feast, though he had to be propped up in his seat. Ragnhild sat beside him and kept his mead cup full.

After everyone was exhausted from their games and sated with food and drink, they drank to the memory of those no longer among the living.

Helga's sisters rose together and offered a tearful toast. "Our sister, the bravest of us all."

As the fire burned low, the folk of Tromøy took turns telling the stories they all remembered so well. When the great log was no more than embers, they wandered off to their beds.

~

IT WAS time to sail north to trade in Skiringssal before the winter storms set in. Word had come that Björn had returned from the East with spices, gemstones, silks, and more wootz steel ingots. Ulf had given up trying to duplicate the steel after his weapons had failed in the battle against Solvi. Åsa was loath to go, but if she wanted the wootz, she had no choice.

She had three ships loaded with soapstone and bog iron that had come in from the hinterlands. Ulf contributed a surplus of axes, knives, and fine bronze riding tack from the smithy.

With Stormrider perched on her shoulder and Halfdan nestled in her lap, Åsa rode in her father's splendidly restored flagship, *Wave King*. The carvings gleamed with new paint, the strakes black with a fresh coat of pitch. Ragnhild followed in her dowry ship, *Raider Bride*, rowed by her shield-maidens. Heid and her apprentices brought up the rear in the völva's grand vessel, *Freyja*. Behrt, not well enough to travel, stayed behind with Thorgeir, Svein, and Jarl Borg. Tromøy would be well defended in Åsa's absence, should any be foolish enough to launch an attack.

The three ships glided easily on the calm sea, but Åsa's stomach heaved. Soon she would see Olaf--and his wife. Word had come that Sonja carried Olaf's child.

But Åsa would have to make her peace with them eventually. Olaf was her most important ally, and she had to get the wootz ingots for Ulf. Truthfully, she was as eager as the rest to see what other wonders Björn had brought back this time. And most importantly, she had to secure Halfdan's inheritance.

As the ships entered Skiringssal's harbor, she spotted Olaf's blond head gleaming above the others crowding the wharf. While they landed, Åsa calmed herself and smiled in his direction, unable to quite meet his eyes. Olaf reached out to hand her up. She placed Halfdan in his arms, then scrambled unaided onto the wharf.

Olaf held his son in his arms and stared at the little boy, his expression a mixture of joy and regret. Then he set off up the boardwalk.

The ship's company followed Olaf. Åsa was relieved when he directed their attention to the merchant's booths and their exotic wares.

"The market has grown," said Åsa.

"Yes," said Olaf, pride evident in his voice. "Skiringssal is becoming known, and many new craftsmen have come. Some now make their homes here year round."

Among the usual comb makers, ivory carvers, and fur traders from the north, Olaf showed them to a booth where a Frankish family displayed fine glassware. Another merchant offered silks from the East in colors Åsa had only seen in her dreams. She was glad that she had brought plenty of trade goods. Her ships would return as fully laden as they had arrived.

Having seen the full offerings of the boardwalk, Olaf turned toward the trail that led to the hall. As they began the climb, Åsa's stomach roiled again. Halfdan squirmed out of Olaf's arms, and she took the boy's hand, distracting herself by pointing sights out to her son, who trotted along with the adults on his sturdy little legs.

Olaf walked close beside her.

"Halfdan will not suffer with the birth of my child," he said in a low voice. "He will have Borre when he comes of age, as I have promised."

Åsa looked up at him and nodded. "And Sonja need never know the truth."

As they neared the hall, a woman emerged from the doorway. Sonja. Åsa's gaze swept her ripe body, just beginning to show signs of pregnancy. She wore a skillfully embroidered gown of sky-blue wool over a pleated linen shift. Beads of carnelian, silver, and amber hung between her silver tortoiseshell brooches. Her hair, fair as Olaf's, shimmered down her back from an elaborate knot.

"Welcome to our hall," she said. Her smile seemed sincere. Did she realize that she greeted her husband's former lover?

Åsa let out her breath as Sonja conducted her to the seat of honor, then brought the welcoming ale horn with obvious pride.

Åsa signaled Olvir to bring her chest. She opened the brass-bound lid and pulled out a length of linen embroidered in a geometric pattern, and another of finely woven wool dyed a shade of blue that suited her hostess's eyes. Sonja seated herself beside Åsa and exclaimed over the gifts. "You have a fine hand with embroidery," Sonja said.

Åsa looked at Ragnhild, who was choking on her ale. "I am blessed to have many skillful embroiderers in my bower, but I am not one of them. My talents lie elsewhere."

Ragnhild let out a guffaw, echoed by Tromøy's other women. At a loss for words, Sonja turned her attention to Halfdan, taking him on her knee with a practiced hand.

"You have a strong son," she said.

"Yes," Åsa replied, trying to keep her voice neutral.

Sonja stroked Halfdan's glossy black hair. "Does he take after his father?"

Åsa stopped her gaze from going to Olaf. "No, he favors my mother. She was dark-haired."

"Well, he is most handsome. I am sure he will grow up to be a famous king."

"Thank you. You will soon be blessed with a child of your own."

"Yes." Sonja laid a hand on her stomach. "We will see ours after Jól."

"My congratulations."

Just as the conversation strained to the breaking point, the scent of meat wafted into the hall and servants came in bearing platters. Sonja rose and took her place beside Olaf.

After the meal, Olaf and Sonja stood before the fire and entertained their guests with a poem. It was the story of the star-crossed lovers Brunhild and Sigurd. Sonja took the part of the Valkyrie maiden, while Olaf played the hero.

As she spoke her lines of undying love for Sigurd, Sonja's voice echoed with passion. When Olaf swore his own fidelity, he gazed into his wife's blue eyes with devotion.

Åsa realized Olaf looked truly happy.

"Are you all right?" asked Heid, beside her.

"Yes, I'm fine." But Åsa could not stop the quaver in her voice.

"Remember," the sorceress whispered, "you are a queen. You need not be alone, married or not."

A painful smile scraped across Åsa's mouth. Who would she want? One of the other warlords from the Ting? She shuddered as she thought of their crude leers. For them she only had a sword. One of her own warriors? That would sow dissension and jealousy among her hird.

The evening passed at last, and Åsa retired gratefully to the guest house with her women and Halfdan. She snuggled in next to her son, who slept in the furs where he'd fallen, his toddler's energy completely used up by the day. She envied him, but as she listened to his breath, she fell into a deep sleep of her own.

In the morning she led her entourage down the path to the bustling port. Surrounded by traders from all parts offering exotic goods, Åsa threw herself into bargaining with enthusiasm. The Frankish merchants gave her news of the Danes, who were once again consumed by their struggles over the throne.

With one brother less.

Having traded all their goods, the Tromøy ships were loaded with their new acquisitions. Åsa was looking forward to seeing Ulf's face when she presented him with half a dozen wootz ingots. She was happy with the imported spices and dyes for their weavings, and the piece of silk brocade. That evening the feast went more easily for her, and she slept well.

In the morning, Sonja and Olaf stood at the door, waiting to say goodbye. Åsa thanked her hosts and headed down the trail.

The favorable wind promised a brisk passage home. They made sail and settled back for the trip.

As they passed the headland, Åsa saw a familiar horseman on the hilltop, watching them go. Olaf. The wind whipped his hair, glinting in the sun. Åsa raised her hand and waved.

# AFTERWORD

Next book in the series: *The Raider Bride*

King Solvi is dead--at the hands of the Irish king. To claim her inheritance, Ragnhild must sail to Ireland with her brother and avenge her father's death. But things don't turn out quite the way she planned...

~

Thank you for reading! If you enjoyed this book a review would be appreciated. Reviews on Amazon and Goodreads help other readers find books they love.

For updates of forthcoming titles in the Norsewomen Series, as well as blog posts on research into Viking history, visit www. JohannaWittenberg.com or join my mailing list.

# GLOSSARY

- **Álf**—elf, male, often considered ancestors (plural álfar)
- **Berserker**—warriors said to have superhuman powers. Translates either as "bear shirt" or "bare shirt" (also berserk)
- **Bindrune**—three or more runes drawn one over the other
- **Blót**—sacrifice. i.e., Álfablót is sacrifice in honor of the elves, Dísablót is in honor of the dís
- **Bower**—women's quarters, usually a separate building
- **Breeks**—breeches
- **Brynja**—chain mail shirt
- **Dís**—spirits of female ancestors (plural: dísir)
- **Distaff**—a staff for holding unspun wool or linen fibers during the spinning process. About a meter long, usually made of wood or iron, with a bail to hold the wool. Historically associated with witchcraft.
- **Draugr**—animated corpse
- **Fylgja**—a guardian spirit, animal or female
- **Fóstra**—a child's nurse (foster mother)
- **Fylfot**—magical symbol

- **Flyting**—a contest of insults
- **Galdr**—spells spoken and sung
- **Gammelost**—literally "old cheese"
- **Glima**—a specific form of wrestling dating back before the Viking Age, still practiced today in Iceland
- **Godi**—a priest
- **Gungnir**—Odin's spear
- **Hamr**—"skin"; the body
- **Haugbui**—mound-dwelling ghost
- **Haugr**—mound
- **Hird**—the warrior retinue of a noble – húskarlar
- **Holmgang**—"island-going"; a duel within boundaries
- **Hudfat**—sleeping bags made of sheepskin
- **Hugr**—the soul, the mind
- **Húskarl**—the elite household warriors of a nobleman (plural: húskarlar)
- **Jarl**—earl, one step below a king
- **Jól**—Yule midwinter feast honoring all the gods, but especially Odin
- **Karl**—a free man
- **Karvi**—a small Viking ship
- **Kattegat**—"cat's throat"—a sea between Denmark and Sweden, connecting to the Skagerrak Sea and the Baltic
- **Kenning**—a metaphorical expression in Old Norse poetry
- **Knarr**—a merchant ship
- **Lawspeaker**—a learned man who knew the laws of the district by heart
- **Longfire**—a long, narrow firepit that ran down the center of a hall
- **Mjölnir**—Thor's hammer, a symbol of fertility
- **Norn**—the supernatural sisters who weave fate named Skuld, Verdandi, and Urd

- **Odal land**—inherited land
- **Ørlög**—personal fate
- **Primstave**—a flat piece of wood used as a calendar. The days of summer are carved on one side, winter on the reverse.
- **Ragnarök**—the final battle of the gods—the end of the world
- **Runes**—the Viking alphabet, said to have magical powers, also used in divination
- **Saeter**—a summer dairy hut, usually in the mountains (a shieling)
- **Seidr**—a trance to work magic
- **Serkland**—the middle east
- **Skáld**—poet
- **Skagerrak Sea**—a body of water between Southeast Norway, Southwest Sweden, and Northern Denmark
- **Skerry**—a small rocky islet
- **Skutching**—scraping the flax stalk from the inner fibers
- **Skyr**—a dairy product similar to yogurt
- **Small beer**—a beer with a low alcohol content, a common drink
- **Stook**—a group of sheaves stood on end in a field
- **Sverige, Svea**—Sweden and Swedes
- **Swine horn**—a v-shaped battle formation
- **Tafl**—also Hnetafl, a chess-like board game found in Viking graves
- **Thrall**—slave
- **Tiercel**—a male falcon, usually smaller than the female
- **Ting, All-ting**—assembly at which legal matters are settled
- **Ulfhed**—"wolf head"; another warrior like a berserker (plural ulfhednar)

- **Urdr**—(Anglo-Saxon *wyrd*) the web of fate, the name of one of the Norns
- **Valhöll**—"corpse hall," Odin's hall
- **Valknut**—"corpse knot," a symbol of Odin
- **Valkyrie**—"choosers of the slain," or corpse maidens. Magical women who take warriors from the battlefield to Valhöll, or Freyja's hall Folkvang
- **Vardlokkur**—a song to draw the spirits
- **Völva**—a sorceress. Literally, "wand-bearer"
- **Weregild**—the value of a person's life, to be paid in wrongful death
- **Wights**—spirits of land and water
- **Wootz**—crucible steel manufactured in ancient India

# CHARACTERS

Tromøy—an island off the east coast of Agder, Norway

- Åsa, age 17, Queen of Tromøy, daughter of the murdered King Harald Redbeard
- Halfdan the Black, Åsa's two-year-old son
- Brenna, Halfdan's nurse (fóstra)
- Toki, Brenna's husband, steward of Tromøy
- Olvir, head of Åsa's household guards
- Jarl Borg of Iveland, Åsa's military advisor
- Ulf, blacksmith of Tromøy
- Bram, Ulf's apprentice
- Heid, a famous völva (sorceress), Åsa's mentor
- Sigrid, Heid's slave
- Harald Redbeard, King of East Agder, Norway Åsa and Gyrd's father (deceased)
- Gunnhild, his queen, Åsa and Gyrd's mother, a noblewoman of Lista (deceased)
- Gyrd, their son, Åsa's brother (deceased)

## Vestfold

- Skiringssal, the Shining Hall of Vestfold, Norway
- Borre, another stronghold of Vestfold, north of Skiringssal
- Olaf, age 18, king of Vestfold, son of king Gudrød
- Kalv, captain of Olaf's guard
- Gudrød, deceased king of Vestfold, Olaf's father, formerly Åsa's husband
- Alfhild, Gudrød's first wife, Olaf's mother (deceased)
- Halfdan the Mild, Gudrød's deceased father—Olaf's grandfather

## Ringerike

- Astrid, daughter of the King of Grenland, foster sister to Åsa, wife of Sigurd
- Sigurd Brodison, son of Ringerike's king, Brodi
- Gorm Halvorson, foster brother to Sigurd Brodison

## Solbakk, Rogaland

- Solvi—king
- Ragnhild—Solvi's daughter
- Harald Goldbeard—Solvi's eldest son
- Orlyg—Solvi's younger son
- Katla—Ragnhild's foster mother
- Einar, Thorgeir, Svein—warriors of Solbakk

## Oppland (Uppland)

- Eystein, King of Oppland
- Sonja, his daughter, age 16

Daneland

- King Rorik, one of five brothers who rule Denmark
- Gorm, his representative
- Harald Klak, uncle of the brothers and contender to the throne, exiled in Francia

Others

- Knut, a famous traveling skáld (poet and historian)
- Hrolf, Gudrød's natural son, age 19, Olaf's half-brother and rival, a berserker
- Hrafn, an outlawed berserker and sorcerer, Hrolf's mentor
- Helga, eldest of five sisters from a farm in Agder's hinterlands
- Behrt, a displaced Christian warrior
- King Orm of Telemark
- King Alfgeir of Vingulmark
- Jarl Arn of West Agder
- Björn, a Svea trader
- King Horik of Denmark, brother of Rorik

The Gods

- Odin—lord of the Aesir gods, of many names
- Valhöll--Odin's hall—literally, "corpse hall"
- Einherjar—heroes slain in battle who come to Valhöll
- Gungnir—Odin's spear that marks an army as his
- Sleipnir—Odin's horse
- Thor—Odin's son, god of thunder, preserver of mankind
- Mjölnir—Thor's hammer

- Freyja—originally of the Vanir gods. Goddess of love and magic. She gets first pick of the slain heroes for her hall her hall is Folkvang—"People's Field"
- Frey—Freyja's twin brother, fertility god of peace and plenty
- Loki—originally a giant, a trickster god
- Hel—Loki's daughter, mistress of the dead who don't fall in battle
- Nifleheim—cold and misty land of the dead, ruled by Hel
- Ran—goddess of the sea
- Yggdrasil—"Odin's steed", the world tree, that holds the nine worlds
- Norns—three sisters who spin the lives of men and gods

# AUTHOR'S NOTE

*The Falcon Queen,* like *The Norse Queen,* is based on the story of the semi-legendary Queen Åsa. Sources state that she avenged her father's murder and regained control of his kingdom. The sparse written record was created 400 years after the fact, by Icelandic men whose culture was very different than Åsa's.

Åsa ruled for 20 years in the early 9th century, the height of the Viking age, but nothing has been recorded of her reign. The sources skip on to her son, Halfdan the Black, and her grandson, the famous Harald Fairhair. I took it upon myself to fill in those missing 20 years, starting with the second book, *The Falcon Queen.* I tried to imagine the first years of her reign. She was starting over with very little after the devastation of her kingdom. Who were her enemies, and her allies? A woman ruling alone must have had to fend off attacks and marriage proposals from powerful men. How did she develop the power to withstand them?

Like Åsa, Olaf and Halfdan the Black are based on semi-legendary characters, as is Harald Klak. The Danish King Rorik is a fictitious representation of one of the sons of King Godfried whose name and fate is lost to history. It is very possible that he tried to bully Åsa into marriage, but there is no record of it. Ragnhild, her father, and brothers are completely fictitious, and their kingdom in Rogaland is based on petty kingdoms in the area at the time, but the historical records are silent as to their identities. All the other characters are also from my imagination.

So much of history was written from men's points of view, but in reality women were a strong force. Many of their stories have been lost, but in writing this series I am able to bring back some long-forgotten voices.

# ACKNOWLEDGMENTS

I have so many people to thank in bringing this novel into being: My beloved mother who first introduced me to Åsa and the Viking world; my wonderful fellow writers at Kitsap Writers, each of whom contributed so very much and kept me going; and to critique partners DV Berkom, Chris Karlsen, and Jennifer Conner. Thanks to my dear husband Brian who is always on my side and eager to read more, and beta readers Colleen Hogan-Taylor, Paula, and Linda S., each of whom gave me priceless insights. I owe many thanks to editors Ruth Ross Saucier and Jessica Cale. Any errors that exist in this book are entirely my own.

# ABOUT THE AUTHOR

Like her Viking forebears, Johanna Wittenberg has sailed to the far reaches of the world. She lives on a fjord in the Pacific Northwest with her husband, whom she met on a ship bound for Antarctica.

Thank you for reading! If you enjoyed this book a review would be appreciated.

For updates of forthcoming titles in the Norsewomen Series, as well as blog posts on research into Viking history, visit www.JohannaWittenberg.com

Subscribe to my newsletter and receive a free short story, *Mistress of Magic*, the sorceress Heid's origin story.

**Join fellow author, K.S. Barton, and I on our podcast, Shieldmaidens: Women of the Norse World. Available on most platforms:** https://linktr.ee/womenofthenorseworld

**Follow me on Facebook:**

 facebook.com/TheNorseQueen